WYN

The Battle of Beardly

MW01134765

JOE STEARNS

outskirts
press

Outskirts Press, Inc.
http://www.outskirtspress.com

Paperback ISBN: 978-1-9772-4176-4

Outskirts Press and the "OP" logo are trademarks belonging to Outskirts Press, Inc.

PRINTED IN THE UNITED STATES OF AMERICA

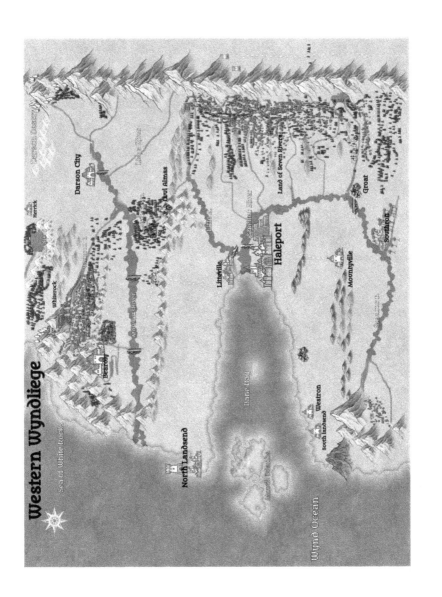

PROLOGUE

The Final Task (Now It Could Begin)

The old midwife was an ancient Human lady with jet-black wrinkled skin and grayed hair pulled back into an always-tight ponytail. A long, flowing dress always covered her ultra slim frame, and no one had ever seen her wearing shoes. Her wrinkled hands had rapidly become famous as the best midwife in the city of North Landsend. She had attended many births in North Landsend since she had come to this town.

The old hag had wandered the wilds for many years and had been harassed by the Mounties for not having proper papers. She had no desire to follow the ways of the pompous little people in their self-proclaimed Republic. She snorted derision at the thought of the Mounties and their labeling her a criminal. All involved were thrilled when she made her way to North Landsend some years earlier.

She had midwifed in many various places before, and it allowed her enough money to feed and shelter herself in the city. Her shock had been complete when the voice spoke to her. She had left the city proper and was walking along the shore of the great bay just south of the city when she heard it. It seemed to come from the waves, but she knew the voice and where it really came from. Her people had been keepers of the secret of the First for years and generations beyond count. She was honored that the voice had found her.

"Do you carry it?" asked the voice.

Looking around and seeing no one nearby, she answered, "Yes, I am the carrier."

"The time has come, and you are to put it into the next baby you see born. You must place it in the baby before it breathes its first breath. I foresee you will have that opportunity with the next one. Are you prepared to do this despite what it will cost you?"

"Yes, I am here to serve you as we have always done. I will complete the task with a smile on my face," replied the old hag.

"I am humbled by your service."

The old lady happily returned to her small apartment and wrote a long note. Then she went outside and started feeding the pigeons that always gathered in the small square near her apartment. Soon, she found a certain pigeon amongst the gathering of birds and whispered a magic word. The pigeon immediately walked over to a dark corner, and the old lady followed with a quickness that belied her advanced age. The pigeon held out a leg, and in the darkest corner of the small square in North Landsend, the old lady expertly attached the carrier with the note and sent the bird soaring into the air.

Two days later, the runner came, calling for the midwife. She headed out to the moderately upscale home in central North Landsend. A pair of eyes watched her leave in a hurry and followed at a safe distance. Excitement and dread filled the person as they watched the old lady.

A woman was having her third baby and was doing well. The mother's attendants were well prepared, and the family had called the midwife as extra insurance to make sure all went well.

As the birth approached, the old midwife instructed the attendants, and all was going well. As foretold, as the baby's head came out, the attendants happened to do this and that. The slippery baby boy entered the world into the waiting hands of the old midwife, who quickly set the precious thing on the ground. Moving quicker than you can imagine, the old lady pulled a blue, glowing object out of her right ear and placed it by the right ear of the newborn. As the baby took its first breath and let out a healthy scream, the glowing thing wiggled into the tiny ear, and the old woman fell backward with a big smile plastered across her aged, and now, dead, face.

Eighteen years later . . .

Chapter 1

VONN

Vonn was ready. As Magi, he was dressed in a black, multilayered satin robe, a shiny, black satin beret, a heavy leather shirt, and black pants with black boots mostly hidden by the satin robe. The robe was without decoration except for a small insignia on the left breast featuring a large raven in even blacker-colored embroidery circling above a light gray-stitched army marching in formation. For twenty-five of Vonn's nearly sixty years, he has donned the black robe that signifies his position of "Magi," the leader of the Magicians of the Mounties. This Magi was always ready to meet with the Congress and president of the Republic of the Mounties.

Standing not more than four feet tall, Vonn had a narrow face defined by dark, narrow-set eyes that peered down over an angular face and rather pointed nose. A full mustache and trimmed beard surrounded his mouth and framed thin lips over straight, white teeth. His dark complexion complemented thinning, graying hair that had once been jet black and was oiled back in a style common amongst the leaders of his people. He had the muscular upper arms and bull neck that is, along with diminutive height, the most identifying characteristics of his race, the Mounties. The Magi was by no means a physically powerful or strong Mounty, but his manner and bearing signified him as powerful and important. He was a confidant of, and advisor to, several past and the current president of the Republic of the Mounties.

Vonn was deep in thought and did not hear the footsteps behind him; however, the mirror in front of him clearly showed the intruder. "Tell me again what General Arsestrong was thinking," said Vonn.

His loyal aide, Jules Junin, was sneaking up behind her great friend and boss, Vonn the Magi. Jules was about the same height as Vonn, with a lighter complexion. She was a typical middle-aged warrior of the Mounties. Her rather pretty face showed some battle scars. Her hair was cut short in a military style, and her body, while thin and physically fit, showed the wear and tear of a veteran of many campaigns. She had been an aide, personal protector in battle, confidante, and friend to the Magi for many years.

"Arsestrong is a complete idiot," spat Jules in the clipped, short voice used by military people everywhere.

"The two Dwarf princes made him look the fool he really is. A simple flanking maneuver, lack of a reasonable scouting plan, a little bad luck, and we lose a lot of territory near Beardly."

Vonn remained silent.

Jules dared to add, "And now, they will be trying to blame the Magicians who were there."

Vonn smiled a tight-lipped smile and turned to face and give a quick hug to his loyal aide and longtime partner. "Well, there is plenty of blame to go around. Speaker Rinson and General Arsestrong could not have picked a weaker group of Magicians to accompany the troops. Four White Robe trainees and only two light Gray Robe First Levels were all that was sent. The Magicians were unable to heal as the magic was very weak. I even felt a weakness in the magic on the day they needed it the most."

"You felt it here?"

"Yes, every now and then, I feel a disturbance in the magic. It concerns me for what might happen in the long run, but it is so little now."

"What can you do about it?"

"The disturbances in the magic of the land . . . nothing," said

Vonn with another tight smile. "But, today, I will go in front of the politicians, play their games, answer their questions, and get a sense, a feeling of how scared they are. All of them have powerful Magicians advising them, and those Magicians are feeling the same disturbances I am feeling. These guys and gals know what is going on, and they are being told something is changing. Mostly, I hope to get a feel for how scared they really are."

Jules was about to respond to this disturbing news when they were interrupted. Into Vonn's chambers walked the current president of the Mounty Republic, Taver Wrigger.

President Wrigger was a very large Mounty standing just two inches short of five feet, with massive arms, a rather flat, broad face, and almost no neck because of the muscle structure of his shoulders. He maintained a large, unruly, black beard, and many often thought that he looked as much Dwarf as Mounty. However, none would live to say that to his face.

He was in his fourth year as president, despite only being in his late twenties, simply by being the mightiest warrior in the ever-on-going battles against the feisty Dwarves and the Orcs, Goblins, and Trolls on their borders. Amongst Mounties, those who won elections were always the best, or most clever, warriors.

"Magi, Jules, glad I caught you before you headed out," said the boisterous and at times overbearing president. "I want to know what your answers will be before you say them in front of that pack of morons called the Congress. You have told me several times you feel changes and fluctuations in the magic. Will you be bringing that up?"

Vonn waved Jules out of the room, and she was more than happy to scamper out and close the door behind her. "I think I will be careful about bringing that up. The land is tough on magic up near Beardly, and the Magicians selected could not have been a weaker group."

President Wrigger glared at the Magi. His temper always seemed to be right below the surface as his expression led one to believe an explosion was coming. With Vonn, it never happened, but Vonn was never entirely sure. The president's temper was legendary.

"Look, Vonn, I want you to try not to bring up any fluctuations or changes. The Elves have been our slaves for hundreds of years, and any change in that status could cause panic. The magic holds them prisoner in their minds, and we don't want people to think that might change."

"You sound concerned, Mr. President."

"Dammit, Magi, just be careful!" And with that, Taver Wrigger turned on his heel and headed out the door Jules had just closed.

Vonn listened to his footsteps as he walked rapidly down the marble hallways to the Presidential Hall of the fabulous Presidential Palace in the capital city of Haleport.

The huge and utterly beautiful Presidential Palace had been built several hundred years ago by the Elves, Dwarves, Humans, and Mounties during the Golden Era of Wyndliege. The Golden Era was a time of peace between the four races that preceded the Mounties taking control of the lands. It was a magnificent building with a large central portion called Hillcenter and separate halls going the four points of the compass. Each hall ended in a beautiful soaring tower many stories high and topped by a spire with a beautiful statue on the peak. A Human statue topped the West Spire, a Dwarf statue topped the North Spire, an Elf statue topped the East Spire, and a statue of a Mounty topped the South Spire. The Hillcenter was simply gigantic in scale. The Golden Era saw unprecedented cooperation between the different peoples: Mounties with their structuring and scheduling talents, Humans with an ample supply of physical labor, Dwarves with industriousness and underground work, and Elves with graceful architecture and talent to finish it with grace and beauty. They had created a wonder of a building. Ten pyramidal levels were built aboveground, and the Dwarves carved ten levels belowground. The Hillcenter was centered on a small rise near the midpoint of Haleport. The rise was only about two hundred feet high, but the effect of being slightly elevated made such a large structure a dazzling sight.

The Hillcenter is divided into four triangular sections on the oversized first floor with a grand entrance on either side of the great halls leading to the towers with the spires. The eight grand entrances were each a spectacular architectural achievement. Each was slightly different as they represented the distinct characteristics of each of the four races. To the north were the strong, well made, stone arch entrances of the Dwarves, and this strength best survived the reign of the Mounties. To the east and the west, the areas of Human and Elven influence were not maintained by the Republic and fell into disrepair. The Elven entrances were once spectacular achievements, with many inlaid gemstones and beautiful, polished marble. The Human entrance had been flaked with pure gold. Both entrances had been defaced by the Mounties, who considered them too flashy. To the south, the Mounties were occupying the halls that were designed for their use. Their entrances were very functional but not as spectacular as the rest. Artwork and clever uses of architecture were lost on the ever-practical Halflings.

The upper floors of the Hillcenter were mostly office spaces used for the workings of the government. At the top were the office and living quarters of the president, which afforded spectacular views in all directions. The main office was intimidating for all visitors going there for the first time. Belowground, the ten floors were all the inner workings to support the beautiful halls above. The clever Dwarves had created living space with running water from natural springs; kitchens and forges were cleverly ventilated. The smoke was moved out far away from Hillcenter. A small city existed beneath the ground to serve those in the government. Most of the menial workers were Elven slaves.

The Mounties were one of the four civilized peoples that inhabited the world they called Wyndliege. For as long as anyone could remember, the Mounties had been a part of the western half of Wyndliege. The earliest known histories discussed this Halfling race right along with, and beside, all the other races.

The Mounties took political leadership over most of the Western

Lands of Wyndliege about two hundred years ago. The great wars of that age were bloody affairs fought by Elves, Dwarves, and Humans against the Mounties. The Mounties discovered powerful magic that allowed their Magicians to heal battle wounds that were not instantly fatal. The Mounty Magicians quickly became the most powerful force in the land of Wyndliege. Whenever a conflict broke out, the Magicians could make a seriously wounded soldier healthy and rested in a matter of two to three hours. The Mounties went from a small, insignificant Halfling people to a powerful, armed force with amazing speed. The Mounty armies conquered much of Western Wyndliege, but the stubborn Dwarves continued to battle from the north. The Human race known as the Wyndswept maintained two independent city-states, and the rest of the Humans had pleaded for peace and been given a northern land called Darson. The Elves were utterly defeated by the strange healing magic and were unaware of who they were. They were strangely docile and slaves to the Mounties.

The current president of the Republic of the Mounties, Taver Wrigger, was an ill-tempered bully of a man who threatened and oppressed almost everything and everyone. President Wrigger fought with a fierceness few could withstand. He was utterly ruthless, and his dark eyes shone brightly in great anger as he fought while screaming like a madman. Fear was widespread amongst his opponents when Taver Wrigger took the field of battle. Few could stand before him in battle. Most of his opponents threw down their weapons and ran away when he came at them. He wielded a short but enormously powerful sword called "Chopper." His powerful arms could remove a Dwarf's head in a single fell stroke. Chopper and President Wrigger had a fearsome reputation throughout the land of Wyndliege.

The president fought with a wildness that caused him many wounds in every foray. The injuries were painful, but he always gave much more than he received, and toughness was the source of his considerable pride. The faithful Magicians, often the Magi himself, would follow President Wrigger and heal him almost as fast as he received the wounds. By the following day, the magic healing powers would refresh him, and he could continue fighting.

All the great fighters of the Republic relied on the Magicians to heal them fast enough as to appear indestructible to the enemy. This appearance of indestructibility was as crucial to the continued success of the Mounties as anything. These great fighters were not only the leaders, called generals, of the factions of the armies, but they were also the leading politicians in the Republic. Any failings of their retinue of Magicians would cost them politically—and possibly cost them their lives. Vonn the Magi sometimes wondered which was more important to those vain leaders.

The always vain Vonn checked his appearance one last time before leaving his quarters to head to the public meeting before Congress and the president. He thought he still looked very dignified, despite his advanced age, in his black robes. Many Mounties held great respect for the Magi, and Vonn had done nothing but improve the public opinion for his exalted position. However, many younger Magicians were continuously looking for signs of weakness in the aging Magi. Sixty was an advanced age for the shorter-lived Halflings, and many were looking to the day that the position would become available.

This meeting was a first for Vonn. The Magi would have to defend his Magicians' failures in a public forum. Healings of wounded soldiers had not gone well in the most recent battles. This had caused a significant defeat in a rather sizeable offensive put forward by the Dwarves. The Dwarves, led by the two oldest sons of the king of the Dwarves, had pulled an old but effective battle technique and had routed the Mounty troops near the northern city of Beardly. As this happened, the magic of the land had weakened for a few hours, and the Magicians were unable to heal troops as effectively as usual. Vonn debriefed the Magicians present at the battles, and he thought he had a good understanding of what happened. However, on a deeper level, the Magi knew a truth about the magic of the land out there that must remain hidden. He wondered if the president and Congress were aware of, and as scared of, possible changes in the magic. He knew he was, and the recent conversation with the president confirmed that Taver Wrigger was!

Vonn and his retainers, Jules, three assistant Magicians in their brown robes, and six apprentice Magicians—two per assistant—in tan robes swept into the Presidential Hall. The darker the color of the robes signified the experience and power of the Mounty Magicians. The Presidential Hall was the largest room in the Presidential Palace in Haleport, the largest city in the land. Furthermore, the Presidential Palace was the centerpiece structure in the great city.

The Presidential Hall that Vonn entered was a magnificent room with marble floors and stark-white, fluted columns. With the hall facing north, the columns were arranged in three rows running east and west. The hall was over three hundred feet from the two huge entries in the north to the open balcony curving gently from east to west on the south end. The open balcony allowed public access to the meetings held by the president and Congress. The Mounties were not a delicate or artistic people, and they even managed to bring drabness to this magnificent room. No flowers were set out to complement the beautiful stonework. No wonderful tapestries were hung from the ceiling to celebrate significant events of the past. Nothing a person would consider artistic or attractive was in sight. In the center of the room sat a row of thirteen very practical, comfortable-looking chairs facing the open balconies to the south.

Vonn noted that all thirteen of the seats were full as he and his group swept into the hall. The entire Congress was present for this session. Six congresspersons were aligned on each side of the slightly raised chair of President Wrigger. To the right of the president sat the leader of Congress, the Speaker, Bagatur Rinson of Litteville. Litteville was the other great city of the Republic. It was north of Halespot, just across the mouth of the Smelter River. Vonn was very wary of Speaker Rinson, as the Speaker had designs on placing his lead Magician, Polli, as Magi.

Amongst Magicians, Speaker Rinson was generally thought to be clever and conniving but not especially brave. The Magicians took note of how the leaders fought in battle. None of the leaders were cowards, but some fought bravely like President Wrigger. Others, like Speaker Rinson, planned carefully to *look* good, with minimum risk to them, even though troop carnage might be significant. The Magicians did not like the damage that these leaders, like Rinson, would create so they could be the hero.

Vonn and his party entered through the northwest entry and walked, as was the custom, along the west side of the hall to the farthest southern point of the great room. Commoners, at times, were allowed to take grievances and complaints before the Congress and the president, but they would walk along the east wall. Only the most important guests came before Congress and the president by walking along the west wall. This custom of the Mounties spoke to the deep dislike they maintained for the Elves, which were represented on the east side of the building.

Magi Vonn showed no emotions as he walked the long walk, but inside, he was furiously thinking about what to say. Here in the public forum, he would have to be extremely careful; too much information could panic the ordinary people; however, too little would not satisfy the fierce but intelligent leaders he would face. The president was bound to be furious at the losses to the Dwarves, and his temper always needed to be accounted for. Vonn's competitors for the position as the Magi would always be looking for ways to use his supposed failings against him. Vonn took a deep breath as he neared the end of the long walk. Competition is a good thing, he reminded himself, and it keeps the mind sharp and him doing the best job possible.

At the far southern point, the small party stopped and stood quietly, not facing the president and Congress. The congressional page, a pompous Mounty named Geminol, loudly called the names of those appearing before the assembled politicians. As each was named, they turned to face the politicians. As the last named, Magi

Vonn turned, and as always, the sight dazzled him. A large portion of the great city was visible, as was the magnificent North Tower. President Wrigger and the stern-looking congressional members looked like the magnificent kings of old as they sat in their appointed chairs. The effect was dazzling. That was how the ancients had designed it, and the modern Mounties used it.

President Wrigger spoke. "Most courteous greeting, Magi Vonn. Welcome and thank you for coming."

Vonn replied, "As you command, Mr. President, and honored representatives. We are pleased to be here. How may we serve?" This was the traditional greeting, and Vonn was surprised to get no telling vibe from the greeting. Generally, the rough-and-tumble warrior politicians hated the formalities and wanted to get right to business. Today, Vonn noted, he sensed no impatience. They were scared, he realized, and his next thought, *They should be*, had to be quickly put aside. He could betray no emotion.

"Magi Vonn," boomed the great voice of the president, "we are here today to discuss the recent battles against the hated enemies to the north. The battles went well, and we continue to pound against the stubborn enemy. They continue to hide away in their little caves in the cold, Far North."

Vonn knew this was mainly for the people listening in from the balconies. The Dwarves were safe in their city of Whiterock, in the land they called Ngarzzorr. Whiterock was built deep into the mountain in a great cave where the Whiterock River rose. The river protected the entrance, and the clever Dwarves had created a safe and defensible city in which to live. Invading the Dwarven stronghold was preposterous, and all those great fighters in front of him knew that. However, Vonn knew that keeping the Dwarves contained was a never-ending battle. With an inspired thought, he wondered if that had to be the case forever.

The president continued angrily and even louder. "However, during the battle, several of our brave warriors were injured, but the Magicians—*your* Magicians, Magi Vonn—took several days to heal them. This should have only taken a few hours. *Why did this happen?*" Vonn had expected this and waited to see how far the president would go. *"What do you have to say, Magi?"*

Vonn was stunned. So many more things had gone wrong that remained unsaid. He realized just how fearful the president and Congress were. They did not want too much said here in a public venue.

Vonn replied, "Great and honored President, the Magicians sent to those battles were far from the most powerful in our great society. Those there did not have the needed experience or knowledge to heal as fast as they should have. I was also informed that the ground where this battle was fought is dry of magic. It would have been difficult even for more experienced Magicians to heal. After an extensive debrief, the Magicians present at the battle convinced the other Magician leaders and me that the Dwarves were *not* employing any of *their magic.*" Vonn ended his statement with a loud, commanding voice. The people in the back balconies murmured amongst themselves, but about what Vonn could not tell. The president seemed content, if that were possible.

The Speaker then quietly asked, "Magi, what are your plans to counteract the magic the Dwarves used to cause the slow healings by our Magicians?" Again, Vonn could hear murmurings in the back, louder this time, but he paid them no mind.

"Honored Speaker," Vonn began, much calmer than earlier, "after extensive consultation, we are certain the Dwarves used no magic against us. It was simply a combination of lesser Magicians and an area of our great land in which feeling the magic was most difficult." Vonn continued. "Remember, our magic comes from the land. We feel the magic and can shape it to serve us. In some areas, the magic is easier to feel and seems stronger. At other times, it is harder to feel and does not serve us as well. This is the way with all magic in Wyndliege and our Great Republic."

Speaker Rinson turned red in the face. His anger was plain for all to see. Vonn just gave him a lecture that every eight-year-old in the land could recite. To do so here was dangerous, but Vonn knew he had to refute the Speaker's comment to end any rumors of Dwarven counter magic. The great advantage of the Mounties for the past two centuries was the discovery of healing magic. No other people could match the healing magic, and no others had a counter to this magic. The morale and confidence of the Mounties were dependent upon this fact.

The president, seeing the discomfort of the Speaker, grinned and quickly went on to other business. "Magi, we are planning a large, northern offensive to push the enemy out of their small holdings north of the River Mowkries. They call this place Beardly. Will you be sending more experienced Magicians to this great battle, as we do not want a repeat of the last battle?"

This was a question Vonn was prepared to answer, and he outlined who he was sending and why. "I will be asking the very best of the Magicians to attend this next battle. I will personally consider going if the planned offensive will include our brave president."

The president smirked at this comment and said, "We will decide that very soon. Thank you for your help, Magi." With that, he dismissed Vonn.

As he made the long walk from the Presidential Hall to his quarters in the South Spire, Vonn thought, *This is not the end of discussions regarding the magic failure.* He expected to be summoned to a private meeting with several of those he just met with in public. Again, the question, how much should he say? As he reached the door to his quarters, he turned to Jules. "Send the others away; I want a word with you."

After the others left, Vonn reflected on all the years that Jules had been by his side. From the early days when he was a fast-rising apprentice, and Jules was a private in the army. Vonn remembered healing a badly wounded Jules when others had said she had a heart wound—where beheadings and heart wounds were considered not healable. Later on, Jules and her troops rescued Vonn when a former president was beheaded, and his private guard and Magicians were overrun. Jules and her troops fought furiously to save what remained of the presidential entourage, including Vonn.

They formed a friendship from these experiences, and over thirty years ago, Vonn made Jules his assistant. In all that time, Jules remained loyal and trustworthy. Vonn knew he must soon trust her with information that would be critical to their relationship—and their lives. Vonn hoped he was right to trust her with so much.

"Jules, I have long trusted you, have I not?" asked Vonn.

"Yes, Vonn, you have trusted me with much, but of late, you have been very quiet. Something is not right, and I can tell it is quite serious. Both you and the Congress did your best to say nothing today," she replied.

Vonn started to laugh. He laughed in that very Mounty way of completely giving into a deep, hearty laugh. Jules stood quietly but was puzzled by his behavior.

Vonn replied as his laughter quickly ended, "Thank you, dear friend. I thought I did such a good job of hiding my concerns, and you show me I am being a fool. Yes, we have a few challenges with these fluctuations in the magic of the land. We are all scared of the effect on the Elves. It is nothing we cannot overcome with some knowledge and a little luck."

"Vonn, have you considered whether the continued care we must give to the Elves is worth the slave work they do for us. They are almost useless unless they are the Elves originally enslaved. All the offspring for the last two hundred years are practically worthless. They seem to be almost asleep as they go about their duties. Many in the military have thought about using them as an army, but it would be genocide."

Vonn considered these words carefully, as he always did when Jules spoke. "I know what you are saying about the Elves. Maybe we should look into that, along with this errand I have for you now. I want you to go to the Magician's library and get me certain books. I will make you a list." Vonn made the list, constructed a note for the grumpy old librarian to help Jules, and sent his loyal assistant to receive the information he wanted.

Vonn was convinced that many things were happening, and the war near Beardly was just the beginning . . . Or maybe it could be the end. He recalled his thoughts during the meeting with Congress and the president. Maybe, just maybe, it was time to consider if the everlasting battles against the Dwarves needed to end. It was treason to say it out loud, but perhaps it was time to start planning for it in secret.

Chapter 2

WAR PLANS

As Jules left his quarters, Vonn walked quickly through his outer rooms and into his private study. He went to his personal bookcase and pulled out that special book he was looking for. As he removed the book from the shelf, a section of bookcase spun around to reveal an opening into a different room. The clever Dwarves had designed this secret chamber during the Golden Era when the Presidential Palace was built. As far as Vonn knew, he was the only one who knew of its existence. Vonn had been here often, especially recently, and he knew he must report today's activities.

The room that Vonn entered was obviously a Wizard's room. Many objects were scattered around the room that the Magi would use to learn things that could, or would, help Vonn maintain his position as Magi. The Magi was the leader of all the Magicians of the Mounties and a top advisor to the president and Congress. Vonn planned to use every advantage he could find to stay Magi for as long as possible. He knew changes were coming, and he planned to stay ahead of the game for as long as possible.

In the center of the room was a strange circle of small, round rocks. Inside the circle was a black spot on the floor where a fire had recently burned. The marble floor seemed otherwise unharmed, proving the magical nature of the fire.

Vonn moved immediately to the circle and sat down cross-legged. He whispered a command, and instantly, a small, magical fire flared in front of him. He carefully pulled a little yellow rock from his robe, and, holding it comfortably in his left hand, he reached his hand holding the yellow stone into the fire. Vonn showed no sign of pain. The rock began to glow and created a yellow globe that spread up his arm and continued to grow and spread until he was sitting inside the golden glowing orb of yellow light. It grew until it filled the entire area inside the circle of rocks. There it stopped until Vonn was finished, and then the globe disappeared as quickly as it came until Vonn was back in the room holding a small, yellow rock in a fire.

Vonn had done this many times, and he was always surprised when the globe overtook him, and he was transported to the different level of existence where his master lived. Lojzue La Yellow was the name that every Magi had used for him since the first Magi, Zigfurn. Lojzue had taught Zigfurn how to use the small rock and had instructed him in many things. This teaching had led to the ascension of the Mounties in general and the position of Magi directly. Vonn did not know how much the use of the rock had helped Zigfurn and the Mounties hundreds of years ago. He just wanted the help and advice from Lojzue that had helped him so many times in the past.

Lojzue La Yellow was clearly a Human Wizard. He was very old, gaunt, and always wore a beautiful, yellow robe. The old man had a commanding presence, and Vonn's innate sense of magical power told him that Lojzue's wizardly power was beyond anything he had ever experienced. Vonn knew that Lojzue's power was why every Magi since Zigfurn the Great had been subservient to this odd Wizard.

Vonn was always surprised at the amount of yellow in this strange world. The sky was yellow, the ground was yellow, and the few plants he could see were different shades of yellow. The odd man who was almost always there when Vonn arrived was dressed in yellow and even had yellow-colored skin. It was also very hot, and Vonn had been taught by Lojzue a magical word to repeat in his mind over and over again to protect himself from the heat. Vonn did this, and the heat was bearable.

Lojzue listened carefully as Vonn relayed the information from the meeting, and as usual, gave very concise, simple instructions to Vonn.

"Vonn, my loyal Magi," began the odd-colored man with a high-pitched voice, "the next great event is about to begin. The magic of the land is weakening, and you must change to survive. Have you done the studies as I have directed?"

"Yes, Master," whispered Vonn.

"Good. You will need to practice every word I have taught you. Practice only in the room, inside the rocks to contain the effect," warned Lojzue. "You will accompany the president to the next battle. The defeat earlier this spring will need to be avenged. Force the president to take this threat seriously, and you will achieve much. The world is about to change. Contact me after the battle and tell me how it goes. Also, tell me everything that happens between now and then. Do not be surprised at defeats as they may be the road to long-term victory."

Vonn knew it was his time to return to his world, and he began to fade. As he did so, he overheard another voice. This was the first time Vonn had ever heard a second voice, and he was very surprised. Vonn clearly heard, "Lojzue," said the other voice, "we will be sending . . ."

With that, Vonn was sitting back in his magic room, holding his precious rock. He quickly pocketed the rock, extinguished the fire, and then voiced the six magic words Lojzue had talked about. Vonn could not believe the disruption of magic within the circle that he could feel as he said the words. If he had a slight mispronunciation, the magic flow was not affected. When he said them correctly, he felt the magic. In this way, he practiced over and over till he could recite them accurately. Today, he was perfect on all six words the first time through.

Pleased, Vonn quickly moved through the secret door and replaced the book that activated the hidden door. He was waiting for Jules to return when he received a visitor. A page from the president arrived, ordering Vonn to a meeting in the president's office in one hour. Jules was also invited. Vonn knew this would be the real meeting today.

Once again, Vonn checked his appearance carefully before he and Jules were to attend to the president once more. This time, he knew the questions would be more pointed, and much more would get done.

President Taver Wrigger was an intelligent Mounty and a great warrior. Tact and patience, however, were his weak spots. He was very tired of the constant complaining of three of the most powerful congresspersons. Bagatur Rinson, the Speaker of the House, was the leader of these three. He, Ormarr Caapo of Seven Rivers, and Cadon Arsestrong of north of Great Bay were the three whiners that Taver would have to deal with if he were to consolidate his power and defeat the Dwarf uprising.

President Wrigger knew that this could be when the Mounties finally lost ground to the Dwarves if he could not get these three to work with him. Arsestrong represented the district that the Dwarves had invaded, but he would not call for the considerable effort that was probably needed to push back the Dwarves. Congressperson Caapo was not the warrior the others were, and he did not like leading his people to war. How he had won the election was a mystery to Taver. Usually, one had to be a hero to win an election. Bagatur Rinson was the president's biggest problem. The Mounty Speaker was a conniving sneak who had found ways to win in battle that were shady, at best. He always had huge troop losses and then showed up uninjured and was proclaimed a hero by his followers—but only after his troops were severely massacred.

Bagatur was, however, a consummate politician. He worked the back rooms to consolidate his power to hide his deficiencies. Taver knew that to defeat the Dwarves, he would need to pull together all his leaders. He had to convince all in the meeting that all-out war was needed and needed immediately. Taver knew that Donaghy Kinched of Westron and old Willey Swordsinger of Groat would be on board with him. They both truly loved to fight, and both were undeniably brave. Vonn would probably be the tipping point, and the president did not know how the esteemed Magi felt about the situation.

President Wrigger did not want to have the discussion return to the past battle problems. He wanted to look forward to what was needed to reverse the fortunes of the recent Dwarf offensive. To this president, only a massive effort involving a total commitment of all the Mounty leaders would regain the lost land. The Dwarves would be challenging, and Taver Wrigger knew it.

The meeting was held in the president's office of the Presidential Palace. The room was at the top of the enormous building and had great outdoor balconies on all sides. Tonight, the meeting was outdoors on the north side. The north spire with the Warrior Dwarf Statue was only slightly below the president's high office. Looking at the statue was a reminder to the president of how capable the other little folks could be.

Donaghy and Willey arrived first, and the two men and the female, Donaghy, reminisced about past battles. All three knew that another chance for glory was upon them. Vonn arrived next, and he was calm and much more relaxed than earlier today. Taver noted that this grouping seemed to be comfortable to the Magi. That gave him hope that the Magi would be on his side.

Bagatur arrived with the other two in tow. The group was now all present, and the fact that seven chairs were set around a rectangular table told the others that that would be all. Each had brought a second, and they were invited to stand near their liege as the meeting took place. This was a tradition among the Mounties. Nothing was done in private as the representatives were responsible to the people, and the seconds could and would tell everyone when a representative was out of line.

President Taver Wrigger opened the meeting in an unusual manner. He asked Cadon Arsestrong to give a report on the battle with the Dwarves occurring in his constituents' area. This was unusual as all there knew the status, so it was not necessary to rehash. President Wrigger's request put Cadon in the unusual position of describing how the Dwarves had overtaken a large portion of land in his area. This would make him seem foolish if he did not want a large war to push the Dwarves out.

Bagatur Rinson had to listen to his ally's attempt not to make the lost portion seem too bad. Donaghy and Vonn both asked pointed questions about the areas lost, and Bagatur's attempts to interrupt were weak and in vain. Cadon was not the smooth politician, and his frustration was plain for all to see. Taver loved the uncomfortable position he had put his rivals in on this issue and the fact that Vonn seemed to be supporting him.

The president was about to make a long prepared announcement that an all-out war was needed when the ever crafty Bagatur moved first.

"Mr. President, Magi, and fellow Congresspersons," announced Bagatur Rinson as he suddenly stood up. "We must stop the evil Dwarves and push them back to the mountains near Beardly." There was a general murmur of agreement that the Speaker ignored and continued. "I propose that we battle with a small force led by Cadon and myself. We will wear down the Dwarves over the summer, and by fall, we can begin to push them back. By then, they will be tired of supplying troops so far from their home in Whiterock."

Ormarr Caapo of Seven Rivers, seizing her opportunity, immediately called for a vote on the proposal. Cadon and Ormarr both had smiles cross their faces as they thought this ploy was going to work. They wound up looking like the idiots they were as Vonn slowly rose to his feet. The smiles left their faces, and even President Wrigger was unsure what would happen next.

Vonn looked at each of the assembled politicians in turn. None save the president and the Speaker could stare into the eyes of the Magi. Vonn had spent years of his life waiting for this moment. He knew the vote on the results of this meeting would be decided by him. He also knew that none of them would expect what he was going to say. Surprise was on his side, and the president would owe him much for this . . . Maybe his life!

"Fellow citizens and great representatives of our Republic," began Vonn, "we enter into the next great period of Wyndliege. The magic of the land is changing. What this means, none of us know. We are faced with changes that may or may not alter this Republic. I don't know, and you don't know. The healing magic is still powerful with many of us Magicians. This makes us invincible in warfare. The Dwarves won a battle. That is all.

"Let me review what happened in the north. Near the city of Beardly, the Dwarves completed their clever tunneling under the Ngarzzorr Mountains. This tunnel was a remarkable feat for the Dwarves. We believe they planned to connect up with the trading port of Rocky Point to expand their trade. We responded twelve years ago with a great offensive to trap the Dwarves in their tunnel. That had held until the last two years. First, last year, the Dwarves, led by the two sons of the king of the Dwarves, led a small offensive against Cadon here. They were able to establish a small area north of the East Reservoir. We allowed this last summer and did not respond. This spring, we have paid for that inaction. Princes Ragnar and Ronjit proved to be very capable leaders, and they attacked us very effectively. Troops of the Republic led by Cadon were essentially routed, and we may have had a real disaster without troops of General Swordsinger moving north from the Lower River Bridge, who stopped the Dwarf offensive. We have now held the line north of the bridge and at the Beardly River flowing south through this area.

"Our founders lost battles and responded by winning the next one, and the one after that. Now, we must respond. This time, we must not trust Cadon. We must call all our resources and go to war. All of us must do our part to defeat the Dwarves and make them sue for a workable peace. We must finish this war and make a sensible peace with the Dwarves at long last. Spending a long summer doing very little will allow the Dwarves to establish trade contacts with the Wyndswept, and then they will be dug in, and north of the Mowkers will be lost! If this happens, peace will come at the terms of the Dwarves, and we cannot allow them to have that opportunity.

We all know what great friends the Elves and the Dwarves are, and the peace must not include terms involving the Elves."

All the politicians were stunned to silence. Seldom, if ever, did a Magi call for war—let alone call for an all-out war. This was something that the others did not expect and was not something the others could refuse. The Magi and his Magicians were the real strength of the Republic, and they knew it. Also stunning to the politicians was the mention of peace with the Dwarves. Most of them knew that it needed to happen, but never would they mention it in a formal meeting.

Vonn continued, "Mr. President, I offer my services to you as a personal healing Magician as you lead our country to war. I also offer to each of you my very best Magicians as we conquer and make peace on *our* terms with the Dwarves—finally, and for all time!"

The silence ended as the six politicians all stood and cheered the Magi. This was an amazing thing, and all the seconds joined in cheering Vonn. Jules was amazed at what she had heard. Her boss and friend had just trumped the powerful politicians. She had always loved the man, and now he had just proven himself yet again.

The president rapidly accepted Vonn's offer, and plans were initiated to go to war. The Mounties were united in that they would defeat the Dwarves and consolidate their power in Western Wyndliege.

All the politicians had left later that night with instructions of their part in the upcoming war. They all had a lot to accomplish. Finally, Vonn and Jules were left alone with the president. Taver Wrigger had not missed one part of Vonn's speech that the others had not picked up on.

"Vonn, you said the magic was changing," said the president. "What does that mean to the Elves?"

"For the time being, nothing," responded Vonn. "I feel that we will not see anything significant on that in our lifetimes. However, there will come a day that the magic on the Elves will fail. My concern is if the Elves get outside help, how we should respond. If we respond too strongly, it will alert others that maybe help would work. If we respond too weakly, someone or something could succeed changing the Elves' situation."

"Well, I will respond strongly," announced the president.

All Vonn could say was a very quiet, "We will see, if it happens."

Vonn returned to his quarters and invited Jules in for a late-night glass of wine. After the Magi's staff had seen to his and Jules's needs with a cold bottle of wine and some snacks, the two longtime close friends sat down for a lengthy talk.

Jules started the conversation. "Why are you and the president so worried about the magic and the fate of the Elves? They really don't add that much to our economy, nothing to our defenses, and they have a huge population explosion that we are forced to feed. It seems to me that freedom for the Elves would be less of a burden to the Republic."

"Ah, that is a complicated issue," replied Vonn. "We are not as afraid of the Elves finding themselves as we are afraid of the magic failing. The wonderful magic of the land has given us the healing magic, and it is also what traps the Elves. None of us really understands what happened centuries ago, but the magic we use to heal affected the Elves. We need the magic to keep the evil creatures at bay. The ill fate of the Elves was an unfortunate turn that was not expected."

Vonn continued. "The bravery of the Mounty fighters and the healing of the Magicians allowed us to form this Republic. We established our borders and have aggressively defended them. It has been so long since the average citizen of this Republic has seen an Orc, Goblin, or Troll that many think we have nothing to fear. We fight on our borders constantly to keep them at bay. Way down south, the roving troops and supporting Magicians battle to keep the Southland Orcs at bay. Goblins are still in the highlands of the Great Divide above the Land of the Sevens Rivers and in the high mountains around the great southern volcano of Mt. Geisel.

"We know that, slowly, the power of the land magic is weakening.

Will this help the evil creatures, will it help the Dwarves, will it free the Elves, or what other changes will occur because we don't know?"

Vonn finished this statement, and Jules sat quietly, absorbing what she had just heard. Finally, she framed a question with great care. "Why mention peace with the Dwarves? Do you think the magic changes will create more problems with the evil creatures?"

"Yes, I do. We may need better weapons and better magic to maintain our power. We may need to reach a lasting peace with our current enemies to battle what may come as the magic weakens."

"What can we do?" asked Jules.

"Learn. We must learn what other choices we could make," replied Vonn. "The answers will come, but we do not know what form those answers will take. I constantly wonder if it changes faster than expected, will we need the Humans, the Wyndswept, and the Dwarves to survive as a civilized society? Will we find the wisdom to do what is needed? Will the Dwarves find the wisdom to do what is needed? What is King Hjalmarr Zopfarn thinking about in his great city of Whiterock?"

Chapter 3

CLAN ZOPFARN

The king of the Dwarves, Hjalmarr Zopfarn, sat on his oversized chair in the middle of the great Blancfrought in the center of the city of Whiterock in the country of Ngarzzorr. Blancfrought, which meant "White Palace" in the old Dwarf language, was the largest open area in Whiterock. Whiterock was, like most Dwarf cities, built under a great range of mountains. As was customary for the Dwarves, they would find a natural entrance into an underground cave. Over the years, they would fortify and safeguard the entrance and then create a wonderful, well lit, underground city by mining and carving the rocks, creating what they considered a beautiful home. Blancfrought was the enormous open cave where the king held court every day when he was in his city.

The Blancfrought looked out over the great underground lake that was the true headwaters of the Whiterock River. This beautiful underground cavern holding a large lake was what so attracted the Dwarves to this place. Hjalmarr Zopfarn was the perfect king for this group of Dwarves. He was not tall, even for his short-statured people, but he was stoutly built with a large barrel chest, powerful arms, a full, dark beard that hung down at least two feet, and mischievous, sparkly eyes that seemed always to be telling a funny joke, something the good-looking, intelligent king was often doing. Hjalmarr had grown to love his city, and his yearnings for the Luul Almas of his childhood had diminished but were always still there.

Zopfarn was facing a problem that no Dwarf king had faced for two centuries, and he was deep in thought about what he should do.

The leader of the Dwarf clerics, Zebrok Hardvenner, had just brought him news that he both loved to hear and feared to hear. The part he loved was to know that one existed, which could lead to hope for his people. The part he feared was that he knew he had no choice but to do what he must do to the young Dwarf they had just been discussing. As he pondered this, the king reflected on the past.

Luul Almas was the great underground home of Clan Zopfarn since the beginning of recorded time. Luul Almas has been the largest and most spectacular underground cave and mine in Western Wyndliege. The whole of Wyndliege, west and east, had benefited from the work of Clan Zopfarn in Luul Almas as the largest producer of gold, silver, and many gems in Wyndliege. Most coinage was struck in the deep underground forges, and the Dwarves grew wealthy. Many peoples desired more from the Dwarves for less. The Dwarves did not like that one bit.

Then came the great discovery, the secret of Luul Almas: diamonds! Deep in the mine was discovered the most beautiful gem. It all went wrong from there. Petty arguments, small wars, and even a few large wars were fought over the millenniums as the stubborn Dwarves wanted top dollar for their superior goods. Luul Almas was a fantastic wealthproducing mine, and while the Dwarves loved the place, it was a constant source of friction between the races. As a young prince, Hjalmarr saw his father, King Ragjit, negotiate with the other races and watched the bitterness overflow. Finally, a few hundred years ago, the little Mounties went to war against the Dwarves. They wanted more say in how much the Dwarves could charge for the diamonds they so desired. The female Mounties had developed a lifestyle that required diamonds, and correspondingly, they developed an insatiable desire for them. The females forced their people to go to war. The Dwarves prevailed, and a tenuous peace accord was reached through the work of the Elven queen, Gavriel. Even this was suspicious to King Ragjit as the Elves had been at war with the Dwarves only a few decades before.

The Mounties broke this peace in a spectacular fashion. They launched an all-out attack on the Elven forest home near the Jarven River. Using their new healing magic, the Mounties proved unbeatable in long, drawn-out warfare, and, worse yet, they somehow imprisoned the minds of all the Elves. The Elves were soon nothing more than willing slaves to the Mounties, and the attack turned to nearby Luul Almas.

Many untold tales occurred during the long, underground battles in Luul Almas. Neither Dwarves nor Mounties tell of what terrible things happened during this long battle. Years of underground warfare led to more carnage than either side would admit to. King Ragjit fell, protecting his throne, and the Dwarves were defeated. The battles were so terrible and the Mounty losses so horrible, diamonds quickly fell out of favor with the Mounty women and were soon forgotten by most of the Mounties.

A small contingent of Dwarves led by Hjalmarr and his mother, Queen Aiella, escaped to the surface and moved northward. The maddened, war-hungry Mounties wildly pursued the escaped Dwarves. The exhausted Dwarves would have been destroyed had not Queen Aiella let it be known that she was moving west. She sent Hjalmarr and the remaining Dwarves east. Hjalmarr never saw his mother again as she faked the Mounties into following her, and that bought time for the large contingent with Hjalmarr. Queen Aiella and her loyal servants were caught after a wild three-day race to the west, and the Mounties killed them all. Her sacrifice allowed Hjalmarr to collect stragglers from the underground battle, and eventually, Hjalmarr had nearly eight hundred Dwarves heading into exile. The remaining Humans at Darson City held off the Mounties for a while, but the healing magic was too strong, and the Mounties eventually crushed the Humans and took over Darson City. At this point, the Humans sued for peace with the Mounties and were allowed to gather in and around the Darson Desert.

Whiterock had been a slightly desperate choice of a home for the Clan Zopfarn as they had been driven ever northward by the armed *might of the Mounties. After the Humans had pleaded for peace, the Dwarves of Clan Zopfarn were isolated against the terrible little people and their magicians. The Whiterock River had been a river to follow away from the great Human settlement of Darson City. Retreating upstream, the desperate Dwarves sent scouts to explore the large mountains to the west. The scouts were gone for some time before returning to tell what they found. With great excitement, they told of discovering the start of the Whiterock River. An enormous underground cavern with a large lake was the headwaters of the Whiterock River. From the lake, the river flowed through a very narrow canyon and then down a thirtyfoot-high waterfall as the river plunged spectacularly into the outside world. The scouts were very eager to tell of how easy it would be for Clan Zopfarn to secure the entrance to the cavern and how they could make a secure home that was defensible against anyone, even the Mounties. With that news, Hjalmarr led his people to the place the scouts had found and set to work making Whiterock. The Mounties had not followed that far north as winter was setting in. The Mounties were a southern people and were not prepared for the harsh winter season of snow. They rapidly retreated to the south to prepare for future battles against the Dwarves.*

That was a harsh winter for Clan Zopfarn. Food was scarce, and the cave that would soon be Whiterock was completely undeveloped. But the Dwarves are a hardy race, and they put up with the hardships and began to settle in. The wars against the Mounties had been brutal and deadly, and both the Mounties and the Dwarves were ready for a break. Both sides ignored the other for many years. By the time the Mounties planned for another invasion against the Dwarves, Whiterock was fully secure from any attack by the little people. In fact, the rapidly multiplying Dwarves began to have battle successes in the north and carved out the land they called Ngarzzorr, or "Courage," in their ancient Dwarf language. The battleground for the adversaries became the land around the Ngarzzorr Mountains as they dwindled out west of Darson City. The Dwarves then tunneled under the mountains near the ancient city of Beardly. They needed to control all the way to the mouth of the Mowkries at the port city of Rocky Point to obtain desired trade with the Wyndswept. For decades, the battles ebbed and flowed between the two races.

King Hjalmarr Zopfarn broke out of his reflections with a start. Many of the Dwarves attending him in Blancfrought were getting impatient at the king's lack of action. Finally, King Hjalmarr called for the young Dwarf cleric to come before him. Led by Zebrok Hardvenner, the young Dwarf came before the king. Hjalmarr had not met the young Dwarf before, and as she came before him, Hjalmarr took one look at the youngster and knew it was true. The current leader of the clerics, Zebrok, was not of the time before the fall of the Elves. He would not know what he had. The king, however, was a young prince in Luul Almas, and he remembered seeing many of this type of Dwarf.

"Step forward, young Dwarf. Let me look at you closely," commanded the king. The king rose from his throne and walked to stand directly in front of her. "Tell me about her schooling in the art of magic," the king commanded Zebrok.

Zebrok replied, "This young Dwarf is Greentea Gravelt, Your Majesty. She is perhaps the best candidate for cleric-hood that we have had in over one hundred years. She has the best feel for magic I have ever seen, but her strengths are not the usual ones for our kind. Usually, Dwarf clerics' magic is centered on mining, tunneling, making weapons, or creating clever traps. So far, the only thing we have found with Greentea is that she can make incredible magical flower arrangements. Many of her best are what so beautifies our great city." The leader of the clerics continued. "I do not understand why Your Majesty would have such an interest in our young trainee."

The Dwarf king continued to walk in front of and around the young Dwarf, looking her up and down, causing her much embarrassment. Finally, the king addressed all who were in the Blancfrought at that time, probably over fifty Dwarves, assorted scribes, attendants, a few cleric friends of Zebrok, and the king's security guard. It was enough, the king hoped, that the word of what he was going to say would spread rapidly. It was a sign of hope for his people, and he wanted them to know all. He felt a great deal of guilt toward putting the young cleric through this, but there was no other way.

The king began, "Over two hundred years ago when I was a young prince in our great home of Luul Almas, the Elves were not as they are now. They lived in unbelievable tree cities in the great forests north of Luul Almas, and they had fantastic cities built into the sides of the river canyon above the Jarvein River. These cities were under the great roots of the fantastic trees of that region. These Elven cities were almost invisible to the eyes of Humans and Mounties. They blended into the trees and cliffs and overhanging root systems of the river valley. Nature blended perfectly with the needs of the Elves and others who lived there. Much of the magic this required was supplied by Dwarves. The Elves were, mostly, our friends. They sent help to us, and we sent help to them. This was accomplished by the birth of Stone Elves in Elven society and by the birth of Druid Dwarves in our society.

"How these births happened was never understood, but both sides benefited from the others. Stone Elves came into Luul Almas and were responsible for many of the fabulous creations in our homes. They were the ones that perfected the art of cutting diamonds. No Dwarf could combine the natural grace and beauty with the stone- and rock-working magic the Stone Elf possessed. We reciprocated by sending out a very special Dwarf who was more comfortable in the great forests. These Dwarves could communicate with trees and animals. They were the inspiration and master builders of the great forest homes of the Elves. Dwarf Druids supplied a special type of magic to make these cities the most beautiful places in the world. Both races learned so much from these exchanges.

"When the Mounties attacked the Elves, all of the Druid Dwarves died protecting their Elven friends. The Mounties were and are no lovers of nature. They knew that to capture command of the Elven country, they had to destroy everything that made an Elf an Elf, and they tried to do the same to us. The Elves had no magic against the evil Halflings and were enslaved, and the brave Druid Dwarves died trying to save them. Our valor and magic were sufficient, and so we survived."

The king paused for a moment or two as many cheered this last remark. Then he continued. "As my mother left to go west and lead the Mounties away from the bulk of our survivors, sacrificing her closest advisors and herself so we could live, she told me that she had a vision that our people could not rise again until we had more Druid Dwarves. She prophesized that a Druid Dwarf would one day come again and was needed to free the Elves from their ensnarement by the Mounties. I tell you all this today because I believe, nay, I know, that in front of me today stands the first Druid Dwarf born in several hundred years. It is our responsibility to take this young Dwarf out into the world and allow her to find her true callings in the woods south of the Whiterock River. If my mother's vision is true, the Elves may rise again. We must help this young Dwarf learn the correct skills for her magic. There is maybe one who can help her. I will take her to my old friend, Knolt."

At this, all those present began to speak at once. The king turned on his heel and strode out of the Blancfrought into his private chambers located behind his throne. As he went, no one noticed the sly smile cross his face as he led all his staff and retainers out of the Blancfrought.

In the Blancfrought, everyone excitingly weighed in on what they had heard. Most who knew of Knolt considered him a crazy old Dwarf who had left the relative safety of Whiterock and had taken up a lonely residence in a small cave way up high in the mountains above the southern exit of the underground city. Most thought him crazy to leave Whiterock, and many thought he was mad at or jealous of the king. None knew that Knolt and the king were old friends. Others weighed in with the opinion that Greentea was a fake or fraud and just wanted out of the extreme studies required of a cleric in training. They were unconvinced that a Dwarf could be anything other than what they felt a Dwarf was.

Zebrok Hardvenner was very deep in thought at all that he had heard as he stroked his long beard. He, of course, knew that the Druid sect had existed and was very powerful. It had crossed his mind that Greentea might be one, and that was why he called the king's attention to her, but it was, he thought, impossible. However, the king had simply looked once at Greentea and proclaimed her a Druid. Was it that obvious to the king, or was he playing some game that Zebrok and Greentea were caught up in? Also, the cleric leader did not wish to leave Whiterock. He was recently gifted with twins from his wife and wanted to stay and teach. He wanted nothing to do with the things he had heard about Knolt.

Greentea listened to the king's story with great wonder. She intuitively knew that she was what King Hjalmarr was talking about, and she wondered what it meant to her. Then the king dropped the bombshell that she was journeying out of the safety of Whiterock, something she had never done and that she was going to see her great-great-uncle on her father's side, Knolt. The family had often talked about the crazy relative who was older than any living member of the Clan Zopfarn. Many family stories were told about the strange magic he seemed to have and how he seemed impervious to the harsh conditions where he made his home. He was admired and feared, and to learn he was a friend of King Hjalmarr made him even more mysterious.

As Zebrok and Greentea made their way back to the large quarters set aside for the cleric's training, the rumors and stories out of the Blancfrought actually beat them back to the main living hall for the trainees into the cleric-hood. As they entered, they were both the centers of attention. It seemed that everyone had something to say or had a question to ask. Greentea tried to answer what she could. She repeated everything that happened so many times that she was no longer sure what had really happened. Her story got turned and twisted, and soon, the other trainees just started making up stuff to go along with the bits and pieces Greentea could remember correctly. The main result of all this was the other train-ees who were friends to Greentea had her as the next hero to de-feat the Mounties and retake Luul Almas. Those not so friendly to Greentea proclaimed her a fraud.

Zebrok stormed through the mob in the living hall and slammed the door to his office. He immediately called for a council of the cleric-hood leaders. Before going to his meeting, he reviewed ev-erything that had gone on in the Blancfrought and, once again, shook his head. What was the game being played with his young trainee?

The cleric leaders were a group of five old and wise Dwarves. Zebrok and three of the others were born after the great retreat to Whiterock. Only old Hludowig was old enough to remember the Druids. Zebrok and the others looked to Hludowig for his input in this matter. The old cleric had never before mentioned his opinion on Greentea. Now, with the news spilled by the king, the old Dwarf spoke on the matter for the first time.

"Yes," he began, "I have known from the very first day that Greentea was a Druid. There is a certain aura about the Druid Dwarf. One can almost feel the strong influences of nature and nat-ural things in the Druid. Other visible signs are Greentea's some-what smoother skin and lighter complexion compared to average Dwarves. She even is often dressed in shades of green in her cloth-ing tastes. All things have always added up to her being a Druid. That being said, I am very fearful for this young Dwarf. I was there when Queen Aiella proclaimed her prophecy, and it was an unusual proclamation at an unusual time. I have lived with the fear of what our people might expect out of the next Druid. I stayed silent so she could remain here and have some youth. I feared that once this news got out, her life would irrevocably change. We are but young once. I was protecting her for as long as I could. Now that the news is out, we must help her all we can. None of us can train her in what she needs to know. We have few books that even mention the phenomenon of what she is, let alone how to train one such as her. All we can do for Greentea is let her go to the woods and let her examine her magic as she will."

Zebrok and the others were both thrilled and scared for the young Druid. Recognizing what she was made the wise leaders realize that to help Greentea, they would have to let her go.

Greentea was shocked that night with the realization of what she really was. She had always been a little different, and now, she knew why. She was wondering what this meant to her and her training as a Dwarf cleric. Just before her bedtime, Zebrok and Hludowig came to her small quarters, and over a few glasses of the best mead in the kingdom, discussed her situation. Gravely stroking their long beards, jet black in Zebrok's case and mostly gray in Hludowig's case, they explained as much as they knew about the miracle of the Druid sect.

Hludowig explained that Druids were very much in tune with the natural world of animals and trees and were often able to perform a powerful type of magic. The two older Dwarves told what stories they knew that put the Druids in a very good light. Hludowig recalled a couple of the Druid Dwarves that he remembered from the Golden Era and told tales of things they accomplished with their great friends, the Elves. Zebrok promised that the Dwarf clerics would find out as much as possible about Greentea's magic from the library of the Zopfarn Clan. Both pledged to give Greentea as much as they could before she went out into the world with the king and his entourage. With that came a small measure of peace for Greentea, and after they left, she went to bed but slept very little. Her life had rapidly changed from everything she had previously known.

King Hjalmarr spent the evening giving orders pertaining to the errand he had assigned to himself. He felt it essential to protect the young Dwarf Druid until he could get her into better hands. Was Knolt better hands? The king did not know, but nonetheless, he was taking her to Knolt.

Knolt had long been a thorn in the side of Hjalmarr. The old Dwarf had always been odd. Knolt had been a pain in the side of

Hjalmarr's father as he was always thinking ahead and predicting what would happen. Many back then had said that Knolt could see into the future. Unfortunately for Knolt, he predicted many of the problems with the Mounties. He early on had pushed to stop the little people, and some of the early battles were at his urging. The Dwarves won all those battles with ease, and Knolt was discredited for fearing the Halflings. Once the Mounties returned to the battle-fields and were unbeatable, Knolt disappeared and only showed up a few times in certain places and did certain things. He was a real mystery, and many forgot about him.

Many decades after Clan Zopfarn had settled in Whiterock, the old Dwarf showed up one day and lived with relatives in the safe city for many years. The king called for him to come and take up a leadership position in the clan, as was his right. The stubborn Knolt always refused, saying he had a different purpose for being there. About thirty years ago, Knolt once again left Whiterock and made it known that he had settled high on the mountains above the city.

Two weeks after meeting Greentea in the Blancfrought, the king's traveling party was ready to set out. Hjalmarr traveled with a small army of three hundred fifty King's Guard troops and about another two hundred Dwarves who provided for the king and his attendants. It was an impressive display, and thousands of Dwarves came out to see the king leaving his city. As for Greentea, she was just glad to be finally moving. The last two weeks had been a crazy time of preparing for what was ahead of her. The clerics had come up with some information and tried very hard to help Greentea. The truth was, the druid magic was so different from the Dwarves' regular magic that they were not a lot of help.

The first day was spent traveling the narrow pathway along the south bank of the underground river as it left the lake and plunged into the protecting canyon. A five-foot path had been carved into the canyon walls both north and south of the river. The northern route had no exit around the waterfall, so a tunnel had been cut through the mountain that came out about halfway down the falls.

Then a ten-foot-wide path had been carved down to plains below in the shape of the letter S. On the south side of the river, the canyon path opened to a large stairway for the first twenty feet down and then gently sloped down to the wide plain below. At the bottom of the stairs to the left began the great bridge of stone that the Dwarves had fashioned to connect the two exits. From a point high on the mountain arcing down to the bridge supports at the river's edge ran a ten-foot-high, four-foot-wide wall. Each wall had a massive wooden gate that led out to the plains below. When the gates were shut, an army would have to defeat the gates, fight uphill, through stairs on one side or a tunnel on the other, and then through a narrow canyon. The clever Dwarves had set many traps, both physical and magical, on the way into Whiterock. They were very safe in their mountain cave, and everyone in Wyndliege knew it.

The king's traveling party did not make it more than two miles beyond the gates before setting up camp for the night. Zebrok Hardvenner had gotten his wish; he did not accompany his young student out of the city. Surprisingly, Hludowig had volunteered to go along with Greentea. Greentea had spent very little time beyond that one evening with the old cleric and found him a strange travel partner. Hludowig spent most of his time riding in a carriage, saying nothing and appearing to be napping.

Greentea had rapidly made friends with a horse named Whiteleg and would ride along feeling everything about the animal. She could not yet directly communicate with Whiteleg, but she could pick up on the horse's feelings and emotions, so much so that after the first day, Greentea would generally walk alongside the horse feeling and touching the horse's mind. She was slowly beginning to understand Whiteleg. Riding it seemed wrong to her until she learned that the horse did not seem to mind. Greentea felt that this was part of her, to understand these sorts of things. What little she had learned had told her communication with animals was part of her magic. She was determined to learn what that meant. The openness of the outside scared her a little. Greentea had never before been out of the caves of Whiterock. The night was very frightening, and Hludowig had come to her the first night, anticipating this, and comforted Greentea by explaining what the stars and the moons were.

After three days of mainly traveling south alongside the Whiterock River, the river curved to the east, and the king's party continued south. The slow-moving traveling party was in no hurry. Hjalmarr intentionally set a very slow pace to allow Greentea time to figure out as many things as possible before meeting Knolt. The king knew that getting to Knolt would take a very small party, leaving the host and hiking up a great mountain called Mt. Konch. It would be a two- or three-day hike to reach Knolt's cave.

For Greentea, these first days in the wildlands of Ngarzzorr would always be memorable. She was discovering things about her magic and what she really was. She could touch trees and feel their very souls. She could hear birds sing, and if she drew magic from the land like she had been taught, she could understand their meanings. She found that the whole natural world was very understandable to her. She understood why the falcon hunted the little animals that lived in the ground. She understood that the caterpillar would turn to the butterfly. She did not know how she knew; she just did. Also, she found that the magic was always there for her from the land. Hludowig explained that he had to work to feel the magic out here, whereas in the caves, he could always feel it. For her, it was exactly the opposite. To Greentea, this was the revelation that never would she go back to living underground, away from her magic. The thought was both thrilling and frightening to her. She knew not how to survive out here, but she knew she had to learn.

Chapter 4

JACKROL

T he twenty-eight young men in armed combat class had been working very hard. Sweat poured off the glistening bodies as they, students at North Landsend Finishing School, went about their work in all phases of combat practice. Two young men in the center of the large dirt patch battled back and forth with the sword and shield. The blunted blades slashed back and forth as they each tried to score hits on the other. The two were by far the best in the senior class at the school. Johnsen Windward and Jackrol Tiller had been beating up on the rest of the class for the entire school year, and now that it was spring and the year was winding down, the instructors had finally allowed the two best to square off. The other boys slowed and eventually stopped practicing to watch this battle. The instructors did not try too hard to force the youngsters to practice as they were interested in seeing what would happen between Jackrol and Johnsen.

Jackrol was working hard parrying Johnsen's best, but not too hard. Jackrol was anticipating his opponent's moves with ease, confirming what Jackrol had felt . . . He was the best in the school. After one flurry from Johnsen, Jackrol made his first real concentrated move up under the thrust and down quickly, then a quick wrist flip to backhand, and the first hit was scored for Jackrol. The onlookers gasped with the quickness and control of Jackrol's move.

The battle continued, and a few minutes later, another smooth, quick, and balanced move had another score for Jackrol. Sweat poured off the combatants, and with a measure of desperation, Johnsen plunged in again even harder. This time, Jackrol retreated, staying just out of reach until Johnsen got slightly off balance and began to show fatigue. Then Jackrol struck back. With a quick slashing move forward and a flick of the wrist, Johnsen was disarmed as his sword was sent flying out of his hand and through the sky, only to land with a loud clang on the hard dirt. The contest ended suddenly, and Jackrol as a clear winner. Immediately, Jackrol put down his sword and shield, reached out, and shook the hand of his good friend, Johnsen. Jackrol Tiller was never one who wanted to show up anyone, especially his best friend.

The crowd of boys all whooped and hollered in appreciation for the fine swordsmanship. They all knew just how good both Jackrol and Johnsen were at swordplay. The head instructor ordered everyone back to work, and all the students went back to practicing the craft they had just watched being performed at a very high level.

Jackrol and Johnsen were talking amicably about the just-occurred battle. They were true friends, and they discussed every move, as this was what they both loved to do. The head instructor looked over the two young men who had just battled. Both young Wyndswept boys were eighteen years old and had long, flowing, blond hair matted with sweat. Their strong yet slender bodies were nicely proportioned for the six-foot-five inches or so as they both stood. Johnsen might have had an inch on Jackrol, but Jackrol was slightly thicker through the shoulders. *Perfect examples of the young men that will lead our peoples in the future*, thought the head instructor. Johnsen was of a lessor line of the Royal Family and was bound to be an advisor to the crown prince eventually. Jackrol's family was not quite up as high, but with his obvious skills, Jackrol was destined for a high position in the military leadership of the Wyndswept.

It made the arms instructor quite proud of his people and his school. All Wyndswept boys from age fourteen attended the North Landsend Men's Finishing School to age eighteen. The youngsters spent four years in this school to finish their education and determine their futures in the Wyndswept society. For several hundred years, the Wyndswept had taken all the young men in North Landsend and provided an education and training in a vocation in this school.

The young girls in North Landsend had a similar school called the Women's Finishing School. The two schools taught a very similar curriculum, and almost everyone in Wyndswept society was educated and prepared for their place in society. Contact between students of the two schools was monitored and frowned upon until they entered their final year. From this system, the tall Humans called the Wyndswept maintained an educated society that competed effectively in a world controlled by the Republic of the Mounties.

Two hundred years ago, when the Mounties had defeated the Elves, ran the Dwarves out of Luul Almas, and were about to overrun all the Humans in Western Wyndliege, the Wyndswept bargained for peace with the only power they had left. The Wyndswept were the sailors of Wyndliege. No other peoples could build and handle boats with the skill the Wyndswept possessed. The Mounties were no lovers of the water, and they knew they needed the assistance of the Wyndswept. Using this small amount of power, the Wyndswept kept control of their two cities, North Landsend and South Landsend, which were the only major seaports around Bane Bay. They also negotiated lands north of Darson City for the other Humans who had taken up arms for the Elves and Dwarves.

Physically, the Wyndswept were much larger than all the other races and generally very fair-skinned with blond hair and green eyes. Humans who were not Wyndswept (often called native Humans) tended to stay separated from the Wyndswept as the Wyndswept seldom left their coastal homes. Few native Humans were effective sailors, and none sailed the great oceans. Native Humans, Elves, Mounties, and Dwarves were very curious about the Wyndswept. A few of the wise in the past had tried to research the story of the

Wyndswept, but the Wyndswept kept their story secret.

The Wyndswept had built a beautiful city on the spit of land where the Bane Bay met the Sea of White Rocks. The land curved to form a huge, natural harbor to the north and had a small harbor in Bane Bay. This was perfect land for this nation of sailors as the entrance to the spit of land was narrow and had been fortified in the early years of their landing. To the south, a smaller community of Wyndswept built the city of South Landsend. Very close to the Mounty settlement of Westron, this city had an excellent harbor on Bane Bay, and the Wyndswept mostly used this city for trade around the bay. A great friendship between the Mounty leadership in Westron and the Wyndswept leaders in South Landsend led to profitable trade all around the Bane Bay.

The sailors of South Landsend had provided trade and ease of movement for all the races of Wyndliege, and it was their influence on their brethren in the north and friendship with Westron that had led to the peace between Humans and Mounties. The Wyndswept had prospered under the Mounties, and the Mounties were ever uneasy about the sailor folks' success.

Jackrol was the hero of all the other students that night in the mess hall, yet he deferred all his success to luck and spoke highly of Johnsen's skills. Johnsen Windward was no fool; he knew that Jackrol had beaten him fair and square. Johnsen was amazed and gratified at everything Jackrol did for him after his defeat. He just hoped they would not meet in combat again. Once was enough to prove to Johnsen about the difference in skill level. Jackrol appreciated all the attention, but he was not one to have a big ego, and he deferred as much as he could and used his success to teach the younger students that they needed to work extra hard to get to his and Johnsen's level. He did, however, feel a real sense of pride at how much he had accomplished. After mess, Jackrol received a note to meet with the president of the school and the head of the arms instruction class.

Jackrol had never been a troublemaker, so he had not been

to the president's office before, and he was quite nervous as he wondered what he had done. The president of the school was a large man, even by Wyndswept standards. Thomas Canvas stood over seven feet tall and was heavily overweight. He wore a large-brimmed hat to look even larger and more intimidating. He dominated his office and could put the fear of a sea monster into a young miscreant. Jackrol was an exemplary, attentive student and a good student citizen. Mr. Canvas was well aware of what students thought of his appearance and the big man moved quickly to put the young student at ease.

"Relax and take a chair, Mr. Tiller. You are not in any trouble, and I have heard many good things about your work," spoke the school president. "As you can see, Jackrol, if I may call you that, Mr. Plank, the head instructor of your armed combat class, is here, and he has an offer for you. I think you will be very interested in what he has to say," finished the large man.

Kenneth Plank, the instructor of the armed combat class, was darker than most Wyndswept. He was slightly smaller and not shaven, as he sported a full beard. Rare was a beard among the Wyndswept, and Mr. Plank wore it trimmed noticeably short. He had the menacing manner that all good arms instructors needed to get the best from their young students. Jackrol had always liked the stern instructor and was thrilled to hear what would be offered. Mr. Plank smiled, like it was something he was not used to doing, and began, "Jackrol, you have been given a chance to take on an army or navy swordsman in next week's Trials."

Jackrol was stricken silent. The Trials were a contest in which the best swords in the kingdom would meet and compete. The military leaders and the Royal Family would drift through the matches and look for the best swordsmen. Many promotions and other advantages came this way in Wyndswept society, where lives were changed for the better even to have a contest in the Trials. It was a mark to carry you for a lifetime.

Mr. Plank misinterpreted Jackrol's silence. "You will be fine in the contest, young man. I have watched you for some time now.

You will be capable of competing."

"Sorry, sir," sputtered Jackrol. "I am not worried about competing. I'm just amazed and honored to be chosen. I will do my best to make the school proud, sir," finished the stunned young man in a nervous voice somewhat higher-pitched than usual from nerves.

Both the president and Mr. Plank laughed at the young man's outburst. "Good. It is settled then. You both have great amounts of work to do in the next week to prepare," spoke the large school president. "Make me proud," he finished as he ushered the instructor and Jackrol out of his office. The president of the school wondered if putting the young man in this position was a good thing or not. "Well," he sighed, "it's done."

Kenneth Plank and Jackrol Tiller retired to the small office that was the armed combat instructor's and spent several hours forming a schedule to get the young man as ready as possible for the Trials.

The week flashed by with lightning speed for Jackrol. If he was a hero to the other students for beating his rival Johnsen, it was worship now that they knew he was in the Trials. Hours of training against the other instructors and Mr. Plank followed. Jackrol found that other than Mr. Plank, he could easily handle the other instructors. Mr. Plank had competed in the Trials when he was younger and in the army, but he was the only one of the instructors that had. Mr. Plank constantly was in the ear of young Jackrol, telling him he had to get better if he did not want to get embarrassed.

As the week progressed, it began to click for Jackrol, and he evened up with Mr. Plank, and, Jackrol thought, maybe exceeded him in skill. Kenneth Plank knew how difficult the trials could be as he had only won one time in three Trials matches. He continued to push Jackrol, and two days before the Trials, put him through the most punishing workout Jackrol had ever experienced. A day of rest and a review of rules took up the last day.

Mr. Plank went over the rules with Jackrol, and they were all simple to Jackrol . . . until he got to the part about magic. "Jackrol, as you know, all Wyndswept can use the magic of the land. As a student, you have not been trained in magic use yet. Magic use is the last two months of instruction before you graduate. That is good because the use of magic is strictly forbidden, and any usage is punishable by law. Members of the Wizard Guild will be present, looking for magic use, and should they find it, they will disqualify and shame any fighter breaking the rules."

Jackrol, Mr. Plank, and Johnsen (as Jackrol's chosen second) arrived early and learned that Jackrol's match was listed in the main arena as a warm-up to the main matches. This was a position of honor and guaranteed that many influential people would see his battle. Jackrol went from confident to a jumble of nerves upon learning this news. Rarely was a first-timer in the main arena. Mr. Plank went to find out what was going on and quickly discovered that the crown prince wanted his buddies, Jackrol and Johnsen, to be in this position. True enough, they did know Prince Junney Crowsnest, but not well, and they were not "buddies." He was the class ahead of them. Apparently, the rather vain young prince was playing up his slight relationship with the student chosen for the famed Trials.

Mr. Plank chose to withhold this information from the nervous young fighter and returned to the two youngsters and told them when to start warm-ups. The wait was on. The two youngsters had the morning to drift among the outer fight rings and watch some of the warriors. Johnsen was in awe of the excellent swordplay they watched and was bubbling over with excitement. Jackrol was also amazed, but he saw things he could exploit among many of the fights they watched. Jackrol saw things he would have missed just a few days before . . . a slight misstep here, a little balance problem there, things he would be able to counter that a lesser fighter would not see. Jackrol's confidence began to grow that he could compete with most of the fighters he saw.

As instructed, they began warm-ups at the appointed time and with Mr. Plank arriving shortly after warm-ups were completed.

They were ushered into a small room where they would await the call to Jackrol's contest. In the room, Mr. Plank breathlessly told Jackrol that he must be cautious against his opponent because he was a three-time Trialer. He was very good with both hands and considered an up-and-comer. That was all he knew.

The call to the arena, the fighter introductions, the large crowd already gathered, the full king's box, including King Robinson Crowsnest and the crown prince, all spun by Jackrol as a blur. He would later try to fill in the details, but he could not take it all in fast enough for now. His opponent was about his size, although heavier muscled and several years older, and Jackrol could see the nervousness in his eyes, and somehow, that made his own nerves worse.

The official called the fighters to the middle and told them the fight would go to seven touches or that a disarming would end the fight. Both already knew this, but it was tradition to announce it and summarize the rules before the fight. With that, the battle was underway. Jackrol immediately knew that the fight was going to be easy. The heavily muscled army man had an awkward style, and he was often off balance, and Jackrol quickly scored the first touch. The awkward style fooled Jackrol, and the man got the second touch. Then Jackrol took over. He rapidly scored four additional touches as the crowd roared in admiration at his evident skill. At five to one, the confidence Jackrol was feeling was destroyed as the army man, showing his skills, scored a solid hit on a careless move by Jackrol. At five to two, Jackrol regained control, and after a pleasing flourish, he scored to the roar of the crowd.

The final battle began with the man advancing desperately. Jackrol knew this move and how to counter it. The rush forward tired, and Jackrol countered, opening the apparent mistake from his opponent he needed to finish the match. Suddenly, Jackrol felt magic creep over his sword hand and slow it down. The desperate soldier was resorting to magic in defiance of the rules. Most of the crowd felt the usage as it was not masked at all, and the head of the Wizards, Eudeyrn Mastmaker, was personally in attendance. He immediately called foul and awarded Jackrol the match, but no one noticed. While all this was going on, the young Jackrol felt the magic, and without thinking, he threw the magic off his arm and finished the touch. The official immediately gave the signal for the final touch and the win for Jackrol, but no one noticed this. What everyone *did* notice was in the process of throwing off the magic on his arm, Jackrol, for the first time, used the wondrous magic of the land.

Jackrol did not really know about the magic of the land. He just wanted to finish his match and win in front of the king and the crown prince, and all the other fans. But once he broke the spell, everything seemed to happen quickly. When any spell is broken, all the power used to break it is redirected, along with the power originally used to cast the spell. The result, on this day, was disasterous.

First, the cast-off spell reverberates to everyone in the area. In this case, it was a spell to freeze his position to stop the strike, so when Jackrol broke the spell, everyone in the area was momentarily frozen in place. The magical strength of the person breaking the spell would determine how wide of an area would be affected. In this way, Jackrol revealed the power of his touch to the magic of the land. Everyone was frozen—not just the contestants, as would be expected—but everyone in the whole arena, everyone in North Landsend, and for many miles around the port city. Second, the power of breaking the spell is violently sent back through the original spell caster. In this case, the army swordsman was the unfortunate person in the direct use of magic. The army man was tossed over forty feet in the air, and when he landed, he was already dead. The force of the Jackrol spell was more than the poor man's heart could take, and it blew up inside his chest.

Lastly, the magic is released, causing a small ripple or wave in the magic of the land. Usually, only an experienced magician on sight would feel the magical wave. With Jackrol Tiller, however, the wave was larger—much larger. All the fans in the arena, many of the people in North Landsend and South Landsend, magicians in Halespot, including Vonn, a very young Druid Dwarf way up north, her great-great-uncle, and a certain few others felt the ripple or wave that Jackrol Tiller's touch to the magic of the land caused. For a split second, the magic touched Jackrol, and Jackrol touched the magic. The combination caused a wave of magical energy to go across the land of Wyndliege. All who felt it, from a distance, were Wizards of great power, and none of them would ever forget it. This single event would prove to change the course of Wyndliege forever. A great power was back in Western Wyndliege!

Chapter 5

FALLOUT

Vonn, the Magi, stood in his private quarters in the south spire of the Presidential Palace in the Great City of Haleport. The wave felt very strong to him. He had always had a very personal attachment to the magic of the land. The Magi drew from it greedily, and he knew what it was telling him. The wave spoke to him like a conference speaker who was competent on his or her subject. The message from the wave concerned Vonn. In fact, it chilled the Magi to the bone. A new and incredibly powerful player had entered into his magical world, and he knew nothing about whom, what, or where. He knew he must act quickly, and he was prepared to do just that.

Vonn immediately dismissed his servants and headed back to his private room. He quickly headed for the circle of rocks and was soon in front of his master. Lojzue was not happy with what he had felt (of course, he had felt the wave), but he told Vonn it was just part of the changes coming and that presently, there was nothing Vonn could do. Vonn was sent back to his room, feeling that this had been the least helpful his master had ever been. Vonn knew this was important, but his master was right . . . He could do nothing . . . for now.

Vonn decided not to show fear or any other emotion. Those who would know what it meant and had felt the magical wave would try to use it against him as the Magi. He knew that much of what he had long dreaded was about to begin. He felt that what was to happen would happen while he was alive and in the position of the Magi. The blame many would put on him was a heavy burden to the loyal Magi, but he planned to accept the responsibility as it came. He also planned to fight. He was more determined than ever to figure out how his people could have the advantage when the magic changed—or even if it failed.

Lojzue was one who truly feared that this event would change his life. He was considering his retirement from all the games he had played with the little peoples west of the divide. Vonn and his predecessors were the pieces he had used to alter events in Western Wyndliege. He really did not care for the Mounties, but he used them to end the Golden Era effectively. He was from Eastern Wyndliege, and the rapid advancement of the West made him angry, and he did what he could to slow it down. Now . . . This wave and all that it might portend . . . He was amazed the First had moved, and he suspected that he would be discovered if the wave were caused by what he knew it was. He hated the sailor peoples, and he laughed at them for the fools they were, but he knew that the truth would cause them all to come after him.

Maybe it was time to leave and go where none would ever find him. He would try to stop the others, and if that failed, he would plan his exit carefully. No one could ever know all he had done. That brought an evil smile to his yellow-shaded countenance.

In Ngarzzorr, Greentea felt the wave with no comprehension of what it portended. She was trying to communicate with some trees in a pine forest at the base of the Whiterock Mountains. As the wave passed, the tallest and oldest Black Pine seemed to call to the Druid Dwarf. She rapidly went to it, put her hands on the tree, and pressed her beard against the rough tree trunk. Suddenly, the tree began to communicate with Greentea. The vibrations of the tree's bark rang against the hands placed against the tree. A level of comprehension came to Greentea through those vibrations. All she could make out from the tree was the following: *"He comes."* This strange message was a mystery to Greentea, but she felt that it must have something to do with the magical wave. Upon reporting to King Hjalmarr and Hludowig what had happened, she was advised to keep it secret until they got to Knolt. Hludowig had felt the wave, but he did not know what it meant and did not consider it important.

Knolt felt the wave also. He was surprised, and that was very unusual for the ancient Dwarf Wizard. He had his way of learning things, and he knew that significant events were about to happen in his world, but this amount of power was surprising to him. He was one of the very few that knew the great secret of Wyndliege, and he wondered if the deed were actually done. He knew the people to ask, and he knew where to find them. But, dammit, he needed *her* to have the reason to go there. Many, many times, he wished they would hurry up! This time, he may be forced to act. He decided he would give the fools one month before he would return and take her. He began to plan how to do that.

In the Far North, near the land of Darson, a group of pious Monks felt the wave with great interest. The leader of the group suggested that they send for a scribe. The others agreed. It was time for the next chapter of history to be written. They would be there to record it as always. Also, in that same building, a guest of the Monks felt the wave. She knew it was soon to be time to move. Just a bit more patience and it would begin to change . . . again!

Those in the grand home of the Wizards, east of the Great Divide Mountains, felt the wave with great wonder. It was very weak across the great mountains, but its importance to those who study magic was not missed. Many began to call for the Wizards to look to the West again after centuries of neglect. There was one there who would carefully try to keep the Wizards away from the West. Two of the three met in private and made some decisions that the third would just have to go along with. The Wizards of Stachieze would look to the West for the first time in centuries. In Western Wyndliege, another group of Wizards felt the wave, and, as usual, they patiently waited.

Far north of Darson, near the ice-covered northern ocean, a large contingent of the evilest creatures ever gathered together. They were led by two who felt the wave. The two female Dragons looked at each other and smiled. Canga looked at Mounga. *That was our magic*, she said in thought.

Mounga replied in the same way. *Yes, what was ours is back in the world, and we must recover it. We must destroy all that Aauga "the Cursed" has created. Our armies must now march south and destroy all. We are too limited to do much till we get our magic back.*

Canga cautioned her sister. *We do not have to destroy all. I have my Elves down there, and even though they are but slaves, I must help them recover.*

Mounga did not reply. In her heart, all must be destroyed, and then she would start over and succeed where the others had failed. She would let none stand in her way, including her sister. She planned to destroy every work that her weak brothers and sisters had done. The little peoples had to be destroyed. If she could get the magic back that belonged to her and her siblings, she planned to do just that. She sent out a message to a group of her troops to immediately move south with a mere thought.

To Jackrol, the match was a success. He had been declared, by the referee, as the winner. His thoughts were on celebrating his win. Arms rose in victory. He turned toward Johnsen and Mr. Plank to share his victory. Only when he saw the stricken look on Kenneth Plank's face did he even think of his opponent. Jackrol had no training in magic; therefore, he had no idea what he had done. Johnsen saw the army man pitched through the air, and he was perplexed. Jackrol's moment of jubilation was short-lived and was the last happy moment he would have for some time. He quickly realized that a tremendous commotion was breaking out. The King's Guard attended the match because of the monarch's presence, and they immediately moved to protect the royals in attendance. This included springing into action and surrounding Jackrol.

Eudeyrn Mastmaker, as head of the Wizards Guild, knew he must move quickly. He was amazed at what he had seen and felt, and he was afraid for the young man. From Eudeyrn's seat, he had watched with amazement the fine young fighter from the school. He had attended many, many Trials, and never had he seen so young a fighter be so accomplished. Then he felt the magic used by the army soldier. He immediately called out the foul and saw the official of the match do the same. Eudeyrn knew this breech of the rules was going to have to be punished. What happened next so amazed the experienced Wizard that he still could not believe it. The youngster used a level of magic that was unmatched in all of Eudeyrn's long life. The raw touch to the magic of the land was unlike anything he had ever experienced. He also knew that every experienced user of magic in Western Wyndliege was going to feel that touch.

He knew that the touch was wild. No one with any training in magic would have done what the youngster had done. He also knew that convincing the army leaders that this was an accident would not be easy. He quickly foresaw the problems that would follow, and he moved to mitigate before any others could react.

Eudeyrn moved quickly to the Royal Box and found the king looking on, shocked, asking what happened. Eudeyrn moved to King Crowsnest and quickly whispered what he had felt and surmised in the king's ear. He told the king that the young army soldier had died instantly and that this would be a problem with the military bosses. But most of all, he emphasized that the young man must be brought to the Tower of the Wizards for the safety of all involved.

Robinsen Crowsnest had been king for over fifteen years, and he understood the problems as he heard Eudeyrn's words. The loyal Wizard leader had served him well, and he knew he had to trust the Wizards. The king yelled out over the rising din of the crowd for the young man to be taken to the Wizards Tower. His loyal guards reacted swiftly, and Jackrol was seized and forcefully hauled away. The king was pained to see the young man look so confused and scared. It was evident that Jackrol was still comprehending what had just happened. Jackrol had killed a fellow Wyndswept.

Jackrol was suffering through that incredibly devastating realization as he was grabbed, and he heard the words of His Majesty for him to be taken to the Wizards Tower. Probably no combination of things could have scared Jackrol more than those words. The Wizards Tower was the most mysterious place in North Landsend. Students whispered dark things about the tall tower at the very westernmost point of land on the peninsula. The Wizards Tower had existed before the Wyndswept had landed here. Who had built it and why was a mystery to the Wyndswept. The tower was sinister-looking, and most members of the Wizard's Guild of the Wyndswept had, for many generations back, maintained a separate and somewhat secretive residence in the tower. Most children's stories designed to terrify the youngster into good behavior used the threat of sending the wayward child to the Wizards Tower.

The king had commanded his guard to take Jackrol to the Wizards, and the guards would follow the king's commands to the death. The military leaders had reacted slowly, and they let the King's Guard take Jackrol first. The anger from the military leaders was extreme. They had a murdered soldier on their hands, and that dead man was being accused of cheating by using magic in a Trial's fight. None of the military leaders were very accepting of this story. None of the military leaders had attended this match, and although they felt the magic, they did not believe that the young student could have possibly killed their soldier all alone.

What had happened was rapidly turning into the sensational news of the Trials. The rest of the Trials were postponed, and King Crowsnest and the military leaders retreated to the castle to argue what should happen next. All involved knew that this was going to be a long process of sorting things out. Most were trying to figure out how to gain as much as possible in the eyes of the king.

Eudeyrn Mastmaker was not going to let these leaders involve the Wizards Tower in all these affairs of state. His concern was that the powerful magical touch of Jackrol had to be trained and brought under control.

The King's Guard brought Jackrol to the entrance to the tower. Jackrol was ushered into a small room attached to the huge gate that crossed the narrow spit of land that held the tower. The small room contained two young Wizards who seemed to be expecting Jackrol. They rapidly and efficiently thanked the King's Guardsmen and asked them to leave. They appeared to be glad to get away from the intimidating place. Then in a quiet but commanding voice, one of the Wizards said, "Say nothing and follow."

The route they took would take Jackrol many months to learn. The Wizard guards led Jackrol down some steps behind the only wall in the small room. At the bottom of the steps was a door that led into a room that looked almost like the first. Two Wizard guards there took over for the first Wizards and walked around the only wall and down more steps. It seemed to Jackrol that this second room and steps went at different angles than the first. These Wizard guards led Jackrol into a much larger room this time, and many more Wizards were here. Many were relaxing or sleeping, as this was obviously a central room for the guards. There seemed to be several walls at different angles (Jackrol assumed behind each was a stairway).

Two new guards replaced those that had brought him here, and they waved him toward the longest wall in the room. Behind that wall were a few steps up and then a long, flat tunnel that ended up coming out into an open area between the gate behind them and the tower in front of them. The sun was about to set over the ocean behind, and the tower was blocking the sunlight. The Wizard guards visibly relaxed, and then one spoke. "Pity you will miss the sunset from the tower. There is probably no sight as beautiful in all the land."

Jackrol was amazed. The middle-aged Wizard was very relaxed in talking about the tower. He spoke fondly of the beauty of the place and how much he loved living here. All the childhood stories Jackrol had heard were just that . . . stories. The best Wizards of the Wyndswept lived here and liked it very much. As he got closer, Jackrol realized the massive size of the tower.

The defenses of the Wizards Tower were both physical and magical. Jackrol was amazed at what it took to finally enter the tower through a lower side entrance and be taken to a subterranean room that was well appointed and not at all the jail room that he was expecting. The guards were very friendly, and they only asked for Jackrol to stay in his room until the head of the Wizards called for him. Jackrol was assured that anything he wanted would be provided. The guards were genuinely puzzled when Jackrol asked if he were in prison. They laughed and replied that they were told to make him comfortable until Head Wizard Mastmaker arrived.

The long night that Jackrol spent in the room in the Wizards Tower was one of the longest nights of his life. Jackrol went through all the events that had happened. He was most amazed at the feeling of strength and power that flowed through his limbs when he escaped the magic of the soldier. Jackrol knew in his heart that the man had been killed, but he did not understand how just escaping a magic spell could cause such a catastrophe. In just a few seconds, he had shown the power that made him a marked man amongst every purveyor of magic in Wyndliege. Little did he know that he was now the most talked about—and probably the most famous— person in all the city of North Landsend!

Chapter 6

CHARGES AND CHANGES

Several days of confinement left Jackrol feeling very lost, confused, and abandoned. Eudeyrn Mastmaker, the headmaster of the Wizards, had come to his room after that first night and informed him that he would stay in the Wizards Tower until the king and the Tribunal heard his case. The killing of a fellow Wyndswept was very serious under any circumstances, and this was undoubtedly an odd circumstance. The fear felt by Jackrol was only exceeded by his confusion about what had happened. His knowledge of the power to throw off a spell was unknown to him. Jackrol knew that somehow this terrible thing had happened, and he had caused the death of a fellow Wyndswept.

The biggest disappointment to Jackrol was that he could not go back to school and see his friends, especially Johnsen Windward. Jackrol had received his parents as visitors, and his mom was weepy. His stoic dad was very quiet about his situation. Both parents told him very little as they were terrified for their son. Jackrol was of that age that he had formed a very nice separate life from his parents, and their visit confirmed to him that he needed to go live his life. He would always love them as parents, but something told him that his future would be much different from anything they could offer.

Jackrol had no guards, but he was limited in the places he could reasonably go by the size and complexity of the Wizards Tower. He had all that he needed to be comfortable and was even shown access to the exercise and armed play areas. The exercise and swordplay gave him at least one outlet for his pent-up energies.

For three weeks and one day, Jackrol had no idea what was to happen to him. This period ended in an extraordinary way.

King Crowsnest and Headmaster Mastmaker walked into the small room that Jackrol had been living in. The messy state of the room was exactly what one would expect of a school-age youngster. The king and headmaster surprised the young man as he was changing sweaty, smelly clothes from a tough workout. The sweaty young man was preparing to bathe just as the two most powerful persons in the kingdom walked into his room.

The king quickly took control of the situation. "Jackrol Tiller, I am Robinsen Crowsnest. I believe you know Head Wizard Mastmaker. We are here today to discuss the situation you are in and the proposed solution we have found. Eudeyrn and I have been in long discussions with the leaders of our fine military over the death of Private Midas Mast, your opponent at the Trials. Several leaders of the military have used this unfortunate event to try to advance their positions."

Jackrol, stunned and amazed, could only manage a weak, "Yes, milord."

The king continued. "You have accidentally, and unfortunately, killed a fellow citizen and have created quite a stir amongst our people. Now, Eudeyrn and I know that this was an accident, but convincing others, including public opinion, has proved impossible."

Jackrol suddenly found that he was barely able to breathe. For the first time, he was truly scared. The king, his king, was standing in front of him and had just told him that people believed he had killed a fellow Wyndswept. His thoughts raced about how they would put him to death. Public hanging was the only method he had ever heard of his people using. It sounded terrible. He did not even know what he had done to cause the death.

Eudeyrn now spoke. "Jackrol, do you have any idea what happened during your match?"

"No, sir, I don't understand."

"As you thought!" exclaimed the seemingly always animated King Crowsnest.

"Let me explain this to you," said the Wizard. "The young soldier tried to put a spell on you that would limit and slow the movement of your arms. You reacted, not unreasonably, to try to free your arms. You broke his spell as he cast it. When that happens, the magic reacts back on the spell weaver with tremendous power. The magic then measures the power of the spell caster and the power of the spell breaker. The strength of the breaker, if more, can turn all the strength of both back onto the caster. That is what happened here. The magic strength of Midas was fairly weak, and the strength shown by you was the most powerful ever seen."

To Jackrol, these words did not immediately sink in. He asked, "So what killed Midas? All I did was free my arms to finish the winning stroke."

The king interrupted again. "You did, and your powerful magical strength destroyed Midas immediately as you broke his spell. Your magical strength was the most powerful anyone had ever seen."

"Mine? I don't even know how to do a spell," protested Jackrol. "How do you know it was just me?"

"I don't," exclaimed the king, "but he does!" pointing a finger at Eudeyrn.

Eudeyrn raised his hand in a strange gesture of resignation and continued. "Look, none of the best Wizards of the Wyndswept understand what happened. We all study the magic we use to learn all we can. We want to learn to get better at using magic so we can create spells to do certain things for us and the people of North Landsend. We try to feel the magic as it reacts to the magic of the land. In your case, you broke the weak spell that Midas was using by using your magical strength. This is what has us all so amazed. Your magical strength was so unbelievably powerful that we do not know how to control the power of your magic. You must start learning magic, and you must learn to control that magic. Obviously, to the Wizard community, you are a great Wizard. One of the most powerful we have ever felt. Your first touch to the magic tells us that you are untrained. We all feel the wildness in your magic. That scares all of us."

The room remained silent as both the king and Jackrol took this all in.

Eudeyrn continued. "Many of my colleagues do not want you to use magic. They feel that you may not be trainable. You may just destroy your teachers in error. Therefore, I have volunteered to train you in the art of being a Wyndswept Wizard."

The king had now caught up to the line of reasoning Eudeyrn was taking, and he jumped into the conversation. "Jackrol, to limit the outcry over the killing, we have confined you to the tower and will have you train like a Wizard. You will be confined to live here for one year while you complete your training. By then, the public will have forgotten the unfortunate accident at the Trials. There will always be some who will call you a kin slayer, and that is unfortunate. We all feel you should stay here and complete your training as a Wizard."

Jackrol's head was spinning. So much of his future had been decided while he had been confined for three short weeks. He began to realize that he would not complete school and that alone made him less of a citizen in the world of the Wyndswept. His disappointment was profound, but he could not find a voice of protest with the king and the headmaster standing in front of him. The news was just too new . . . and too painful.

Several days later, Jackrol was still feeling the pain of his punishment. He thought that what the leaders had done to him was unfair, and he planned to somehow clear his name. He did not want to be a wizard; he wanted to be a fighter. He had been given the lesser robes of a Plebe Wizard and had started a training regimen that he thought strange and stupid. He went to classes that taught him to concentrate his mind. They called it meditation. He felt it dumb. He had to focus his mind so much when in battle that these classes were easy and somewhat pointless.

Eudeyrn came by often and talked to Jackrol about feeling the magic of the land. Jackrol felt nothing. Eudeyrn tried to teach Jackrol simple spells that everyday Wyndswept individuals without Wizard level skills could do. Jackrol could do none of them. He seemed barren of magical skills.

One day, Eudeyrn was flustered about what to do with his trainee and stormed out of the training session early, leaving a confused Jackrol fuming. Jackrol was in a courtyard facing the ocean, trying to light a fire in an outdoor fire pit. He could not feel this magic that Eudeyrn said, "every Wyndswept person could feel." He looked toward the ocean in anger, picked up a rock, and threw it toward the waves. Several of the young trainees and their trainers witnessed what happened next, or else none would have believed it. Jackrol did not even watch the small hand-size rock after he let it fly.

Eudeyrn and most of the other experienced Wizards felt the disturbance to the magic. Somehow, Jackrol had touched the magic by his anger when he threw the rock. The Wizards and their trainees who were watching saw the rock sail toward the ocean. An average guy with a strong arm could have hit the sea with a good throw. Jackrol's rock went farther than anyone could believe. It sailed about a quarter of a mile, *and* it grew in size as it flew. When the stone finally hit the water, it was the size of a small ship. The wave created by the huge rock's tremendous splash rolled toward the small courtyard, and as Jackrol slammed shut the door to the tower, the wave drenched all those in the courtyard and rushed water right up to the door. Jackrol was utterly unaware of all this as he stormed through the tower to his small room and found solace in the quiet of his room.

Eudeyrn felt this magical touch of Jackrol Tiller with several of his most experienced Wizards standing around him. They immediately started discussing what they had felt. They all agreed on one thing: Jackrol was not using the magic the way they all did. He was using air magic to use the land magic. None of them could do anything like this as they had only heard of old rumors of air magic. The tales spoke of the magic of the air that only Dragons could use.

They had no idea how to get the magical wildness out of the young man.

These were not Wizards without resources. The Wyndswept Wizards had brought many books when they came to settle in Western Wyndliege. They had not researched a problem like this before, but given this challenge, several of them headed to the basement library of the great tower and began to study.

Eudeyrn waited an appropriate amount of time and then went to find his young student. Jackrol was still in his room, trying to calm down. He, in his anger, had felt something more magical than ever before. What that was, he had no idea. Eudeyrn knocked quietly and heard a very quiet invite to enter.

Going into the small room he had last entered with King Crowsnest gave Eudeyrn an idea. "Jackrol," he began, "the last time I walked in here, the king was with me. Until I just walked in here, it had not occurred to me what an experience that might have been for you. I have long been a confidant of the king and am used to his presence. Certainly, you felt it was terrifying for him to appear in front of you in such a way."

"I was wondering if I would be put to death," was Jackrol's only comment, made in a sad small voice with his eyes staring at his feet.

Eudeyrn, hearing that simple statement, realized what was probably wrong with the young man. He started down a different trail. "You had everything you knew taken from you and had really never got any answers." Jackrol could only nod at the statement from Eudeyrn. He continued. "Before we talk about what is going on here, the training in magic, why I am training you, and those things, let's talk about you and what you are missing the most."

The dam burst for Jackrol. All the hidden emotions of what had happened to him poured out, and for the first time in his life, tears streamed down the young man's face. The emotion in his voice was raw and painful for Eudeyrn to hear. "I am a prisoner in this awful place. I am being trained to do something I do not want to do. I will be an outcast with my own people because I did not finish school and graduate. I do not get to see my best friend Johnsen, and I did not intentionally hurt anybody!!"

Eudeyrn was an old man by Wizard standards among the Wyndswept. An average Wyndswept would live a long life compared to other humans. Approaching two hundred years was not uncommon for the Wyndswept. For the Wizards, almost double that was average, and among Wizards, Eudeyrn was especially old. He was three hundred seventy-two years old this upcoming fall season. He had forgotten how important things like friends and completing school were to the young. He had forgotten how intimidating this building that he loved could be to others. The sad young man in front of him had awakened memories that he had long suppressed.

However, Eudeyrn had not risen to be the headmaster without learning a few things along the way. Among things he knew was what he could and could not do for Jackrol.

"Young man, listen to me and listen well," started the wise Wizard in a firm but friendly voice. "You will have the opportunity to finish your studies. We have probably the ability to teach you from here, and whatever it takes, so you will complete your schooling. As far as seeing your friends, they are welcome here anytime. We can show them how they can come and go as they please and teach them that this is not a scary, bad place. This building is not scary to any of us who live here; we love the place. Those on the outside tell tall tales about this place, but once your friends come, they will understand what a wonderful place it really is. However, you cannot leave this building for the time decreed by the king unless it is to go to sea."

Jackrol immediately understood what Eudeyrn was saying. A tour at sea was always allowed by any Wyndswept citizen at any time. These seafaring peoples were constantly in need of sailors who could help defend their ships against the many pirates that raided up and down the coast. Certainly, Jackrol was a fine swordsman, and some time at sea would calm the public's interest in him.

With this slight change in the possibilities for his future, Jackrol became his old self again. He plunged into the training by Eudeyrn and began to have more understanding. The ever-resourceful Wizards found things to help Jackrol and Eudeyrn in training. A couple of strange spoken words in the old Dragonspeak language helped Jackrol attach to the land's magic easier. Once Jackrol had mastered the strange words and connect to the magic of the land, from there, Eudeyrn could properly train him. Eudeyrn was able to help Jackrol control his power as long as Jackrol stayed calm and under control.

Johnsen Windward came and visited, as did several of the teachers at the finishing school. Removing the magic training that took the last few months of classes made it very simple for Jackrol to take the finals tests. Thomas Canvas, the school president, even came by and personally presented Jackrol with his fairly earned diploma. Mr. Plank and a few others did not come and visit Jackrol, but Jackrol attributed that to the fear of the Wizards Tower. He did not begrudge them that as he once felt that way.

Jackrol and Johnsen were welcomed in small arms training, and the swordplay and combat simulations rose in prestige. Many of the military's best began to come to the tower to compete with the rapidly growing reputations of the two young men. Many of the military's fighters rapidly forgave Jackrol, and he was encouraged by the relationships he developed with these men. They were friendly combatants working daily to improve their skills. Many of them were of the opinion that Jackrol's Wizard training was a waste of a great fighter.

Conversely, many Wizard leaders began to wish the young man would quit the fighting and concentrate on his studies as he was obviously one of the greatest Wizards they had ever seen. Eudeyrn and King Crowsnest watched the growth of the young man carefully and knew he was something extraordinary. They met regularly, and often, the discussion would turn to Jackrol Tiller and his unique skills. They decided to sit back and watch Jackrol and attempt to do what was best for the youngster. They were wise enough to both know, without directly saying it, Jackrol Tiller's future was to do something way beyond what either of them had done.

Chapter 7

JOURNEY IN THE MOUNTAINS

Greentea Gravelt was enjoying the slow pace the king and his guard were taking through the wild lands of Ngarzzorr. The assembly of King Hjalmarr Zopfarn was moving south and west at a leisurely pace toward the tall peaks of the Whiterock Mountains. They had entered into the heavy pine forests of the land at the foot of the most towering peaks in the range. King Hjalmarr had led his large contingent into a deep valley surrounded by steep mountains. The narrow trail through the thick forest had really spread out the King's Guard. There looked to be no outlet except for the way they had come. Many of the Dwarves were mumbling about the route the king had insisted on taking. They knew the narrow canyon could contain many unfriendly creatures that would love to trap a group of Dwarves. Those responsible for the king's protection were always nervous, and many were very ready for this adventure to end.

For Greentea, every hour was a learning experience as she continued to learn more about her magic. She somehow knew that she was only just touching the surface of her magical powers; yet, she did not know what to do to increase her ability to use her magic. She would stand for hours just listening to the animals and birds make sounds. She could almost understand what the sounds meant, and she could definitely understand the feelings behind the sounds that she heard. Some things were beginning to become very clear to her. She knew that she would eventually be able to communicate with most animals and that trees could communicate on a very limited basis, and she would have ways of listening to them as she had done with the old Black Pine. She could also feel that her magic could affect animals and plants to do things for her if she could use the magic correctly.

Greentea talked that evening, and every evening, with the old cleric, Hludowig. He listened to the young Dwarf's excited talk about what she was discovering, and he could only feel frustration as he had nothing to add that could help her. She needed someone who could teach her to be a Druid, and all of those Dwarves had been dead for several hundred years. Hludowig would make a small suggestion now and then, but he had no idea if he was helping or not. As Hludowig, from frustration, was about to cut off Greentea, in walked the king of the Dwarves.

King Hjalmarr came very quietly without the usual fanfare of his movements. He wanted to talk with the clerics he had brought along on this journey. He quickly put both Greentea and Hludowig at ease and told them that this was an informal discussion of what came next.

Hjalmarr started, "We are nearing the end of the easy part of our journey to find Knolt. The old Dwarf lives up in the tall mountains to the left of our current direction. That would be mostly to the south. Tomorrow, we shall break out into a wider valley with fewer trees, and the camp can close up around us. Once this happens, we will need to head up the mountain. The trail up the mountain is too narrow for the size of our current group. I will be taking a very small, loyal contingent up the mountain. I, of course, am going, and Greentea will go to meet Knolt. The question I must ask, are you going with us, Hludowig?"

The older Dwarf looked up at his liege and said, "No, Your Highness. I can go no further. I would only slow you down if I could even make it all the way. My years of going up steep mountain trails ended long ago."

The king smiled. "As I thought, but I would not deny you if you wished to go. We will leave at daybreak and take twenty-three of my best troops, and with Greentea and I, we will number twenty-five. That should be enough to protect us from the dangers that are always present in these mountains."

Greentea had a few questions, but they all stuck in her throat in front of the king. King Hjalmarr hurriedly told her what she needed to bring. "I expect a three-to-five-day trek up the mountain and about the same back down. Spring storms are always a possibility, so bring your warmest coats and boots as we will have several pack animals to carry what we must bring. Dangers are always a possibility as lots of Goblin tracks are around these parts. But my troops will protect you from any harm." With that, Hjalmarr spun on his heel and headed out into the dark night.

Hludowig laughed quietly when the king had departed. "I wager that no creatures will dare attack a group of Dwarves that large. I think you shall have many difficulties following Knolt's trail up the mountain, but an attack will not be one."

Greentea had a thought. "Master Cleric, if there are Goblin tracks about, is it not possible that Knolt is in danger or perhaps already dead?"

Hludowig laughed even harder. "No, young Dwarf. Knolt will not be bothered by any marauding creatures, or bad weather, or anything else these high mountains could possibly do to him. Let me tell you some more about Knolt."

With this, Hludowig sat back and thought deeply for a few minutes, and then he broke the silence with this story. "When I was but a young Dwarf in the city of Luul Almas, Knolt was already old. As a young trainee in the cleric-hood, our leader was Knolt. It was said that he possessed more power as a cleric than any who had ever lived. He would travel outside the caves of Luul Almas as much as he was home. He was an advisor to Elf kings and queens, Human lords and ladies, and Mounty leaders of all types and kinds. He was always able to appear at the right time to advise those most in need. He, it was said, could communicate outside our world with creatures and beings that lived beyond our levels of thought. This allowed him to know much about the current, the past, and even the future that no one else could know. I have no idea if that is true, but he was definitely the most powerful cleric I ever witnessed. Later on, he claimed the title of Wizard, not cleric, but I have never heard why. The king knows much of this, and that is why he wants to take you to him. Hjalmarr hopes that Knolt could provide some additional training in finding your true calling."

Greentea was very restless all that long night as she got mentally ready to leave with the small party that would find her uncle, the most powerful cleric who ever lived. The thoughts tumbled through her mind: communication outside our world, advisor to kings, most powerful cleric but now, mysteriously, called a Wizard, and former trainer of Hludowig were all titles that were applied to her lost relative. What was Knolt like? She imagined a somber, wise old Dwarf issuing sage advice with a long, white beard hanging below his belt. Greentea could not have been farther from the truth.

Morning dawned gray with heavy snow-laden clouds hanging low over the tall mountains. The valley had opened up into a beautiful and rather large meadow, as the king had said, and the large contingent had moved in and realized that they would be there several days. Runners were sent back to Whiterock, and many more supplies were ordered from the vast underground city as bad weather was threatening.

The king had selected his twenty-three troops, and Greentea was glad to see several females amongst the busy troops. Female Dwarves were very similar physically to males. The Elves and Humans could never tell them apart, but for some reason, Mounties had no trouble separating the sexes of the Dwarves. Greentea felt more comfortable knowing that she would not be the only female, although it is doubtful that Hjalmarr selected any but the most dependable and loyal, regardless of sex.

The always-industrious Dwarves had completed packing up, and the smaller group had separated from the main host before lunch. Traveling on foot, the first part of the journey continued on the same path the main host had been following. Moving quickly, the smaller party soon turned on to a very narrow footpath that turned left, due south, and rapidly began a steady but not too severe slope upward. The forest was very thick, and the path went winding up the mountain, crossing back on itself several times. At dark, the troop scouted out a suitable camping site in a fairly flat hollow, and in no time, they set up tents, and dinner was served. After dinner, the camp settled down rapidly as all were tired from the fast-paced march. A watch was set, and the camp rested. The night passed quietly, and after an early breakfast, camp broke, the pack mules were loaded, and they were back following the path. Midmorning, they passed over the first summit, only to realize that the higher peaks were now closer but still high above. The trail followed through a beautiful high country meadow where no trees grew. Wild grasses had begun to grow as winter was leaving the mountains down this low. The meadow was a wonder to Greentea as she could feel the rebirth of the land as the snow was gone. She found the feeling of the small animals scurrying around was one of positive optimism. It buoyed her spirits tremendously to sense these feelings of the small animals after the long winter.

In this fine mood, Greentea missed the warnings. She would later learn that when the animals went silent, the danger was near. For now, Greentea was just puzzled by all of the wild sounds stopping. Her puzzlement was rapidly erased as she was barreled into from behind and knocked facedown to the ground. The king and one other soldier had shoved her down and were signaling for silence. As Greentea regained some of her composure from being hit from behind, she noticed the experienced troops were all crouched in the long grass. A group of Goblins was marching right through the meadow toward the now-hidden Dwarves. The hideous Goblins walked right into the middle of the Dwarves. The Dwarves attacked the poor creatures. The gangly arms and legs of the Goblin creatures and their poorly made weapons were no match for the experienced fighters and high-quality, forged weapons of the stout Dwarves. The king did not even make it into the fight before the slobbery Goblins were either killed off or scattered off, running for their lives. Not one Dwarf was even scratched by the encounter.

Several Dwarves chased the scared Goblins and butchered all that they caught. However, a few got away, fleeing high into the mountains. This was concerning to some of the Dwarves, but the king thought it a good thing as he suspected that the now-warned Goblins would stay far away from the Dwarven soldiers.

Greentea surveyed the fight scene differently than any Dwarf alive. She was mainly appalled at all the damage to the wild grasses the fight had caused. The evil Goblins had affected her Druid sense with an extreme sadness—sad that such a creature could exist. The Goblin deaths were nothing that affected her one way or the other, but the trampled grasses were suffocating, and Greentea could feel the extreme loss to the natural feel of the mountain meadow. This saddened her much more than she had expected. She was nearly in tears as her magic was more and more teaching her to appreciate the beauty of nature and natural surroundings.

The Dwarves gathered up the dead Goblins and burned the awful creatures on the edge of the meadow. The fire was a natural thing in the meadow, and Greentea, to her great surprise, was not bothered by it at all.

The Dwarves continued their journey, and once they reached where the trail left the meadow and started to go back into the heavy forest, the trail suddenly ended! Hjalmarr had, up to this point, stayed well back in the traveling party. Now, for the first time, he moved to the front. It was evident to many in the group that the king was expecting this. King Hjalmarr stopped right where the trail ended, turned, and said directly to Greentea, "This is where you must be able to lead us. You must use your magic to uncover the block that Knolt has put on the trail."

Greentea felt panic rising in her as she slowly walked toward the front of the group. She saw anticipation on her fellow traveling companions' faces, which made her even more nervous. She had no idea how she was going to find the now-vanished trail. Her insides were rapidly becoming a jumble of nerves. Her mind raced with what Hludowig had told her about Knolt being the most pow-erful cleric ever. If Knolt wanted to hide his trail, how would a poor-ly trained apprentice such as her ever find it?

Her apprehension, however, was unfounded as she reached out her mind to the magic of the land, and her slowly developing Druid sense felt the damage to the ground where the trail went. She looked up, and her magical powers felt the trail as much as she could really "see" the trail. With confidence that belied her nervous state, she marched past the king and sharply followed the "trail" to the right. Her magic was true, and the Dwarves fol-lowed Greentea as she led them on into the forest on a path only she could see.

After a short distance, one of the trailing Dwarves looked back down the trail they were on and noticed that looking backward, the trail was very visible. He pointed this out to some of the oth-ers, and soon, everyone knew that Greentea was leading them on the correct path. Eventually, Greentea heard the others talking about the trail being visible in the other direction and stopped to see this for herself. Once she confirmed that the other direction was visible, she asked the king what he thought of this. Hjalmarr laughed and said that Knolt probably made several different por-tions of the trail hidden in different directions to keep creatures such as the Goblins away from his front door.

The journey continued up the mountain, and after a couple of hours, the group forded a small stream, and the trail became visible again. The weather turned snowy, windy, and much colder and the hardy Dwarves bundled up against the suddenly harsh conditions. After a good march, the king called a halt for the night, and camp was quickly set up in a heavily forested area. The forest canopy provided little protection against the storm, but it was better than nothing. It stormed all night, and the Dwarves woke up to several inches of new snow. The king told everyone who would listen that he thought that they would reach Knolt by nightfall. The grumbling Dwarves went about their duties, but at-titudes were sinking on what many felt was a fool's errand. The average soldier did not understand the purpose of this journey and just wanted to get it over with.

Shortly after breakfast, the Dwarves were packing the animals in a small clearing and preparing to move out when they were attacked. The attack came from all sides and was led by four giant Snow Yetis. A Snow Yeti is the most enormous creature in the high mountains. Mostly covered from head to toe in snow and ice, the creatures were really fur-covered animals that fought violently and were difficult to kill because they used ice as armor. Usually, Snow Yetis were over seven feet tall and very slow moving. Three of the ones that attacked the Dwarves were about this size. Over seven feet tall, with massive, furry arms and a mostly fur-covered face that might have looked humanoid if shaved, the three Yetis wielded large tree branches as weapons. They would swing the branches, attempting to take several Dwarves off their feet with each swing. Truthfully, they had little success overall, but individually getting hit was very bad for the Dwarves.

The fourth Snow Yeti was a giant. It probably stood over eight and a half feet tall, and it carried a tree trunk over two feet in diameter and about six feet long. The creature was ponderously slow and moved in long, slow strides. It would swing the huge log toward any who let him get close. A large contingent of Goblins accompanied the Yetis.

The Dwarves were surrounded and attacked by four giant Yeti monsters and probably seventy or so evil Goblins. The morale of the troops immediately went up. These soldiers trained extremely hard for moments just like this one. The battle was very intense, and the Dwarves were hard-pressed for a while, but the swinging tree branches caused the Goblins more problems than the Dwarves. The stupid Goblins could not stay away from their giant allies, so they kept getting hit. Also, the Goblins were the only ones hit by the giant Yeti with the large log. The maddened Yetis screamed and shouted and killed many Goblins. However, a few Dwarven soldiers were hit by swinging branches and suffered wounds when hit.

The pack animals had scattered when the attack first started, and Greentea had paid attention to them as they left. She used her magic to calm them as they ran away. None of them ran very far. After that, she had moved to the middle of the melee and tried to stay out of the way. Greentea reached out with her Druid magic and touched the Yetis. The result surprised her. Previously, the Goblins had filled her senses with sadness, but now, the Yetis filled her senses with their extreme evilness. Greentea immediately knew that the Yetis had to be destroyed.

The first Snow Yeti to go down was cleverly stabbed in the back of the leg where the ice was not as thick. A clever Dwarf warrior had circled behind the beast with a large burning stick from the morning fires and got the stick very close to the back of the leg. The fire had burned some of the visible fur on the back of the Yeti's leg and had thinned out the ice. On the next turn, a different Dwarf warrior had implanted his blade just above the back of the knee. The now-hamstrung Yeti lurched around and caused even more confusion as many Dwarves and Goblins got hit by the stumbling creature.

The next Yeti was stabbed by a courageous female soldier who took a vicious blow from the tree branch as she plunged her sword into the unprotected throat of the Yeti. The young female soldier landed right next to Greentea. Greentea handed the brave young soldier the sword that she had been given to use. All the Dwarves gave a yell as the Yeti stumbled and fell for the last time.

The third Yeti was very wild. Two Dwarves were able to get a rope around its feet, and when they tightened the rope, the Yeti fell flat on its face. A Dwarven soldier who used a war hammer as his weapon of choice slammed the hammer into the back of the prone beast, busting most of the protecting ice. Then several Dwarves plunged swords into the prone creature, killing it instantly.

With two of his fellow Snow Yeti down and out, the hamstrung Yeti threw down his branch and ran. The Dwarven soldiers pursued, and the rout was on. The Goblins saw the flight of the Yeti as a chance to get out of the fight and also ran away. The soldiers were not about to let any escape and were in hot pursuit.

While all of this was going on, King Hjalmarr and some of his closest personal guards fought in the direction of the giant Yeti. With tremendous care, this elite fighting group separated, fought, and killed all the Goblins left standing in that quadrant of the fight and avoided the awkward efforts by the giant to swing his log. The now-surrounded giant seemed impervious to the blades of the soldiers. He was so encased in ice that no blade could penetrate his ice armor. The rather slow, giant Snow Yeti took a few minutes to realize that he was the only one of the attacking party left in the fight. When he realized this, he tried to run away.

As the fight turned rapidly in the Dwarves' favor, Greentea ran to the trees surrounding the open area the Dwarves were in when the ambush occurred. Using her Druid magic, she communicated to the trees what she needed. Greentea was wondering if her plan would work when the giant monster turned and ran toward the trees. As luck would have it, the giant Snow Yeti ran just a few feet away from where Greentea stood, leaning against a huge pine. The Druid magic worked on the surrounding trees, and as the lumbering Snow Yeti ran between the trees, a few huge branches reached down and picked up the log-bearing monster and tossed it high into the air. This was exactly what Greentea had been asking the trees to do.

Fortunately, all the pursuing Dwarves, including the king, were missed by the now-flying Snow Yeti. The giant landed with a tremendous explosion as the ice broke away from the doomed creature and fell into a million smaller pieces. Ice flew everywhere, and all the dwarves were showered with it. Again, fortune was with the Dwarves as none of them were seriously injured. If the fall did not kill the Snow Yeti, the angered King's Guard, led by Hjalmarr, ran to the giant and stabbed the now-very-vulnerable monster.

With this done, the battle was over. The king and his personal guard suddenly looked with great wonder at Greentea. None of them had ever seen such a thing, and all were impressed. A few of them even questioned what they had seen. The magic of the

Druid Dwarf was unknown to them, but they were happy to have help in destroying such a monster.

The rest of the Dwarves returned shortly to tell of the fall of the fourth Yeti, and an accounting of all of the Goblins was done. None escaped the angry Dwarves this time. Once all was finished, Greentea led the pack animals back to the clearing, much to the amazement of the rest. They could not believe their luck that the pack animals had not scattered. All the soldiers were happy that the animals were still nearby. Greentea said nothing about her role in that; however, Hjalmarr stood off to one side with a knowing look on his face. He too said nothing.

The king ordered a halt to the journey to take care of the wounded and destroy the creatures by fire. The storm had slowed up considerably, and the Dwarves made camp in the same place as the night before and posted a double guard. The mood of the soldiers was much improved, and even the wounded seemed pleased with the battle. Two seriously wounded were going to have to be taken down the mountain to Hludowig for medical care. Greentea was not yet trained in the skills used by Dwarf clerics to heal the wounded, and this caused much grumbling among the soldiers. However, Greentea's heroics with the giant Snow Yeti kept the complaining to a minimum.

The party was lessened by eight members the next morning as the wounded were to be taken down the mountain by a group of that size. With those eight gone, the party now numbered only seventeen.

The remaining Dwarves continued up the mountain, and the weather now became a problem. The trail was harder to follow, and the going was much steeper. Greentea was often in the lead, using her powers to feel the trail under the snow. The snow was piling up, and the walking was challenging. Two of the strongest Dwarves would lead Greentea, carefully following her yelled instructions as the wind had started to blow harder. All the Dwarves followed in single file, trying to all step in the same footprints.

The difficulties of the trek cannot be overstated. The tough Dwarves were cold and tired and had no idea if they were on the right trail, and the route kept going up and up and up. Greentea followed a trail that only her magic could see, and she had no idea that magic could even do that. The king placed his faith in the powers of the young Druid, but he also was figuring out when he had to turn around and give up on this idea. He would not risk his life in this venture. The loyal soldiers were grumbling as all Dwarves would, but they trusted in their king.

As the day wore on, the snow decreased somewhat, but the wind picked up, and drifts became a problem. It took several minutes in one place to get through an especially large drift. Greentea was insistent that they go straight through and not to either side of the drift. This caused more complaining until they got to the other side and realized a drop-off was to one side. They traversed this ledge for about one hundred feet and then came over a small pass. The pass was somewhat protected from the wind, and the party rested for a bit.

The king held a small meeting and told the soldiers and Greentea that the group would only go on a bit more before returning to this area to spend another night, and then go back down the mountain. One of the soldiers suggested that only a small party go on and the rest could set up a camp. Many of the soldiers seemed to agree with this idea, but the king did not.

The loyal soldiers packed up after the meager meal and started beyond the sheltered pass. At the end of the pass, Greentea felt the trail split into two directions. The trail went around a very large boulder and between two large trees into a flat valley area to the left. To the right, the trail continued up the mountain, and the heavy snows that had not yet melted from winter were covering the trail in that direction. To Greentea, the left path felt more correct, and she told the king this. He said that going up any more was folly and to take the left path.

The weary troops lined up behind the young Druid Dwarf and followed Greentea around the boulder and between the trees.

The newly fallen snow was piled high through the narrow but generally flat valley. As the group neared the end of the valley, the trail had to go between two huge rocks taller than any of the Dwarves. As Greentea passed between the rocks, she was startled by an amazing sight.

Chapter 8

KNOLT

The small but hardy group of Dwarves followed Greentea between the two rocks, and they too were shocked by what they saw. The small area in front of them was completely clear of snow. The temperature was in the mid-70s, and a small garden off to the left was growing very nicely. An apple tree and a pear tree off to the right were heavy with ripe fruit as if it were early autumn. The area was about forty feet wide and twice that in length and extended to a small cave cut into a towering rock facing the mountain at the back.

Standing in front of the cave was a very old, extremely short Dwarf with a brilliant red beard reaching almost down to his toes. The diminutive Dwarf looked very energetic and active despite his apparent age. He was staring at the incoming group with his hands on his hips, and his eyes were shooting daggers through each of them as he sized up all of the incoming Dwarves. The old Dwarf was obviously angry, and none of the weary, rapidly overheating Dwarves understood why. Knolt (of course, this is who it was) began to yell at the Dwarves.

"What has taken you fools so long? I have been waiting for you to bring her to me for many years," he yelled. "Hjalmarr, what are you thinking? Did you believe that the fools you have in your group of clerics could train her? Why has it taken so long for you to bring her here? What kind of fool king are you anyway? This is the *one* hope we have of ending this terrible situation that the West is in. She could be—no—she *is* the answer to many of our prayers!" The old Dwarf was obviously winding down his initial rage after this part of his tirade. Greentea noticed, much to her delight, that the brilliant red beard began to fade as Knolt's temper cooled. Greentea had immediately been drawn to the magical nature of the beard, and it was very entertaining to her.

Hjalmarr was initially taken aback by Knolt's anger, but he quickly responded, "I did not meet the young Druid until just a few days ago, and I immediately set out to find you!"

"Oh, blah," responded Knolt. "You moved very slowly and probably have all kinds of excuses about why it took you so long to get here!"

The soldier Dwarves, sworn to protect the king, were getting very upset at hearing their liege being yelled at by this grumpy old Dwarf. A couple of braver soldiers jumped in front of the king in a protective stance. Hjalmarr began to laugh. At first, he was chuckling; then his mirth grew until he was barely able to cough out commands for the soldiers to step down because he was laughing so hard. He soon gained control of his mirth and began to speak to his troops.

"Soldiers of Ngarzzorr, let me introduce to you one of the most honored members of Clan Zopfarn, my old friend and Wizard Supreme, Knolt! We come in peace to ask for Knolt to help us train the young cleric Druid Dwarf, Greentea Gravelt. I warn you, soldiers, that your weapons are useless against the powers of Knolt!"

Knolt began to bristle about full of pride with this short speech, and his beard began to change to a blue color. Greentea mentally noted that, while she loved the magic beard, she had best not say anything. The old Dwarf was really very vain, and he liked to be complimented.

Knolt then added, much appeased, "Thank you, King Hjalmarr Zopfarn, and members of my clan, welcome to my mountain home. Please set aside your weariness from travel. We will eat heartily and rest comfortably. Please, come in, and we will get you properly quartered."

This statement was seemingly ridiculous as the cave appeared very small, and the soldiers began to set up a very tight camp in the clearing. Now, it was Knolt's turn to chuckle. He removed the illusion of the small cave, and the traveling party could suddenly see back into the beautiful cave that extended deep into the mountain. Now, with some energy and excitement, the Dwarves made their way into the very comfortable-looking Dwarven home. Several Dwarves appeared that lived with Knolt as servants and helpers for the old Dwarf. Greentea excitedly recognized the servants as aunts, uncles, and cousins of hers. Her relatives knew her, of course, and greeted her in friendship. Many hugs and inquiries about the health of the family were made.

A number of the servant Dwarves was known to Hjalmarr as relatives of Knolt's. Upon seeing the reception Greentea received from these Dwarves and overhearing bits and pieces of their conversations, the king began to understand.

"Knolt!" shouted the king, "You have made a fool of me! This girl is a relative of yours, and you had to know something of her before today! Some of that anger you directed at me was in part anger because you have let things be for all this time!"

"No, no, my King. I would never make a fool of you. I did what I thought was best for the young girl," responded a suddenly solemn Knolt. Greentea had heard this before, and it did not make her too happy. The two powerful Dwarves began to argue about who knew what and when. It became apparent to those listening that Knolt had left Whiterock after observing the birth of Greentea. Knolt went out to look for an appropriate place to train a Druid Dwarf. He expected one of the remaining old-timers from the Golden Era to recognize what Greentea was and alert the king. Then, Knolt knew the king would seek him out. Hjalmarr responded by saying that the old-timers, just like Hludowig and Knolt, tried to give the young Dwarf a more or less normal childhood, so they did not talk of her calling. The two old Dwarves were arguing back and forth about what happened, what should have happened, and whose fault it was that she had not been trained.

Greentea had been listening closely and now interrupted her king and her great-great-uncle and spoke with some force. "All right, you two. Stop bickering like two old maid Dwarves! I now understand much more than I did before, and it seems everyone has been trying to do what is best for me. But the past is the past, and I am here now, and maybe everybody ought to let me have a say in what is best for me! Apparently, everyone has tried to do what is right for me, and it seems to have caused problems in whatever I am supposed to have received. I know I am different. My magic is different, my wants and desires are different, and I know I belong outside, not in a cave somewhere like most of my kin. Let's stop talking about what went wrong in the past, and let's talk about the future! I have experienced some of my magic, and I want further training!"

The two powerful Dwarves stopped talking and stared at the young Dwarf. "Well, she is growing nicely," stated Knolt, somewhat sarcastically, as his beard shaded toward green.

"Yes, she is looking forward, while we two old fools discuss our failures," laughed Hjalmarr. Both the wise old Dwarves realized that Greentea was a very special young Dwarf, which extended beyond her strange magic.

Knolt took command of the plans. He gave instructions for the weary troops regarding the layout of his home and how to find rooms to settle in. He asked his servants to help prepare an appropriate feast for the evening. The industrious Dwarves then began to do all that he had asked, and good cheer went up as some casks of mead were brought out. The Dwarves began to celebrate the success of finally uniting Knolt and Greentea.

After a fine evening meal, Knolt and the others sat in the very spacious dining hall, and conversation flowed, as did much mead. After several stories of the day's news, Knolt asked if they were aware of the great wave that went through the magic of the land. Greentea and Hjalmarr answered that they knew about it and that Greentea had felt it. Knolt knew more about the magical wave than probably anyone in the land. He explained to Hjalmarr and Greentea that it came from the human settlement of North Landsend, and it was very powerful. He knew that the magic was wild magic. By that, he meant that the person using the magic was untrained and probably touching the magic for the first time. He thought it essential that they gather as much information about this as possible. That was why he felt it was vital to be on the move out of the mountains as soon as possible.

Greentea then told Knolt the story of the old Black Pine tree reaching out to her right after the wave. The strange message from the tree, "*he comes,*" caused a very odd reaction from the old Wizard Dwarf. He signaled for the others to be silent, and he sat very still for a while. He was mumbling something as he sat there, not moving a muscle. The others also sat quietly, and the firelight seemed to go very dim.

After a few minutes, Knolt suddenly stirred as if waking up, and he spoke. "What you are telling me is very surprising to me. There are forces in this world that we do not understand completely. One of those forces used that pine tree to talk to you. I think I need to go to that spot and try to see what else could be learned. My guess is that the force wanted to talk with you and found that you were not trained enough to communicate back.

"Yes," Knolt concluded after another pause. "We must make for that tree with all haste so that I can find out what I can find out. We leave in the morning!"

The next morning, the rested, well fed Dwarves, a few with splitting headaches from the mead, headed back down the mountain to rejoin the main group. The journey went very quickly as Knolt knew the paths very well, and several of his servants who traveled supplies up the mountain went along as guides and scouts. Knolt proclaimed two days down the mountain as soon as he heard where the main host was located.

Knolt laughed at the stories of the king's troop's trip up the mountain and the battles with the Goblins and Snow Yetis. He told

Greentea that he would teach her much about her magic and how much of what happened could have been avoided. He told her that some simple magic and the dumb Goblins would have never been able to find them. Knolt instructed her on the use of her magic, and she learned more in just a few hours with Knolt than in her whole time with the clerics. Her magic was based on nature, and anything in nature could be under her control if properly done. For example, she could easily alter the trail through the mountains with her magic. Just move plants and grasses aside, and a new path appears. This easily fools the Goblins, and they will follow her new path wherever it takes them. She literally can make them walk off the side of a mountain. Trees will gladly help her with evil creatures, as will bushes with thorns and poison plants. Old tree branches will fall on the heads of ice-encased Snow Yetis and on and on with other evil creatures.

For Greentea, the trip down the mountain went extremely fast. She was constantly practicing things that Knolt was teaching her. She thought she was learning quickly, but Knolt was scant with praise and harsh with errors. His beard changed color often, and from Greentea's view, there was much more red (anger) and black (disgust) than silver or gold, which signified happiness. However, when Greentea accomplished magic that was Druid in nature, the beard turned a deep green color that stirred great joy in her heart. Hjalmarr and the troops stayed to themselves and were very on guard despite Knolt's assurances that nothing could happen with him there.

On the afternoon of the second day, the small group was marching down the mountain, sure to reach the main group by nightfall. Spirits were very high when suddenly, Knolt called for a halt. The weary troops were grumbling about this stoppage when Knolt did a very unusual thing. He suddenly sat down cross-legged in the middle of the trail, and in front of him appeared a magical fire. All the others rapidly backed off, including Hjalmarr and Greentea. After less than a minute, the fire extinguished, and Knolt stood up with a very black beard. His face was furious and disgusted.

Knolt called to the others to surround him and close in very tight. "There is a problem down in the valley below," he started. "Our friends are under attack by a large contingent of Goblins, Orcs, and maybe some other evil creatures."

The experienced troops allowed only a small murmur to be heard at this pronouncement. King Hjalmarr immediately began to arrange for his best scouts to sneak ahead and bring back reports. Knolt suggested that some of his helpers go with the scouts as they were most familiar with the area. Soon, three groups of three were organized to head out in three directions: down the trail (mostly north), to the left of the trail (northwest), and to the right of the trail (northeast). Surprising them all, Knolt expressed a desire to go with the scouts heading to the left of the trail. King Hjalmarr, of course, agreed with this, and the scouts set out.

The others, as was agreed, retreated up the trail to a small clearing in the heavily forested area to make a base camp and prepare to spend the night, if needed. Knolt estimated that they were less than an hour's walk to the bottom of the valley. If there were no problem, the rest of the trek in would be very easy. If there were a problem, they would have to have a place to work out a plan to help the main force.

With ten group members out scouting, the remaining group and the pack animals quickly retreated to the small clearing and set up a small camp and set a very heavy guard. Greentea was using her unique magical abilities, and she realized she knew something. She went to find Hjalmarr.

The king was standing off to one side of the small area, looking down the trail. It was as if he were willing the scouts to return to give him information about what, if anything, was happening to his most loyal subjects. The King's Guard was a carefully chosen elite group that pledged their lives to protect their king. He had left General Rocky Coalfinder in charge. General Coalfinder was a competent leader, and Hjalmarr trusted his decision-making. The only thing the general lacked was experience on the battlefield. Hjalmarr had hoped to send General Coalfinder off to the wars near

Beardly to gain additional experience.

Greentea stood quietly near the king for several seconds before gathering herself to talk to him. Obviously nervous, she began, "Your Majesty, I think I need to tell you something."

King Hjalmarr started out of his thoughts and spun toward the young cleric. "Yes, Greentea, speak your mind."

Startled, it took Greentea a minute, and then she began, "Your Majesty, I have been reaching out with my magic, and I feel something. It is dark and evil, and it lies northwest of us. I sense darkness coming from the closed end of the valley below. To the east, I sense light. I also feel it getting darker in that direction." She pointed northwest.

The king looked at his subject carefully. "Yes, Greentea, I think we are involved in a battle at the bottom of this trail. Knolt would never have stopped us with a false alarm. But you are holding back. What is it that you sense that you don't want to tell."

"I am sorry, Your Majesty, but they did not make it back!" The young Druid clearly had tears in her eyes.

The wise king did not need to ask who. He suddenly knew what Greentea had sensed. It saddened him greatly, but he also knew that she was correct. The troops that had taken the injured back down the mountain had stumbled into the enemy and had been slaughtered. For the first time, Hjalmarr knew what a powerful young Druid she really was. "Thank you, Greentea. I believe your magical sense is correct. The time for tears for them will be later. First, we must avenge them. I wish that you call me Hjalmarr. I also wish for you to speak freely to me anytime you know something in your special way."

"Thank you, Your Mag . . . Hjalmarr," stumbled Greentea.

The young Druid left more amazed than she could believe. The king had asked her to call him by his real name.

Hjalmarr continued his waiting for the scouts, but now, his face was set in the fierce, determined look of the leader of the Zopfarn Clan ready for a war of revenge!

Chapter 9

BATTLE OF DEVIL'S VALLEY

The scouts returned to the small campsite just as night settled over the mountain. King Hjalmarr had said very little while the scouts were out. Now they were back, and it was time to form a plan. A weary-looking Knolt had been the last to get back. He had insisted on going further west than the others, and he had insisted on going alone.

The scouts were all telling the same story. The King's Guard was under heavy attack by an army of Goblins, Orcs, Snow Yetis, Trolls, and ugly-looking magical beasts that might have once been wolves. The King's Guard had kept open the canyon's mouth and could retreat or receive reinforcements that way at any time. The scouts said it was apparent that General Coalfinder was trying to advance to the trailhead to provide safe passage for the king and his contingent.

The king asked if it were possible to sneak around to the east and rejoin the main host. The Dwarves immediately began to protest as they were looking forward to a fight.

"No, no, that is not what I meant," exclaimed the suddenly defensive king. "We will kill every last one of the enemy before us. What we need is to let General Coalfinder know we are here."

This satisfied the warrior Dwarves, and a young Dwarf from Knolt's staff volunteered to move quickly east and then north to approach the King's Guard from the west. He was tasked with taking several quickly written notes by the king and sealed with his royal stamp. This would let the general know where the king was and could plan accordingly. With an admonishment from Knolt to stay safely away from the enemy, the young runner moved out.

Knolt added some further information from his scouting mission. "The evil army came down the steep closed-in side of the valley below. I have only heard the name Devil's Valley to describe that valley. It was called that because if you went in the valley entrance and were followed, there was no way out unless you were the devil. It is what is commonly called a box canyon. Now, apparently, the Orcs and other evil ones have carved an entire road down one side of the canyon. It is an incredible road that I find hard to believe was created by such evil and rather useless creatures. I suspect it is magical.

"I also was able to gain some elevation to the west and find a bit of a clearing. What amazed me was the organization of the evil creatures. I believe they are being led by something that has great magic and can control those evil beasts. What that might be, I have no idea. Perhaps it is some powerful Orc Wizard. Anyway, they are keeping the entire valley covered with unnatural darkness. This darkness provides comfort to the evil creatures and sucks confidence and hope from our people. We must destroy the evil magic and level that part of the battle. I will take Greentea and two guards for each of us, and that will be our mission. We will go to the western edge of the valley floor, and we will use magic to help in any way we can."

King Hjalmarr, realizing what Knolt had in mind, interrupted the old Dwarf. "Perfect. The bulk of our group can head straight down the path we have been following and engage the enemy directly. We will fight our way to the bottom and then slip hard to the right to connect with the front line of General Coalfinder. This should pinch the enemy between us on the south side of the valley. One last thing, I think you should all know what young Greentea has told me. She believes that the wounded we sent back down the trail did not make it. She believes that they were ambushed and destroyed."

Knolt interrupted. "She is correct. I too have felt the aura of those souls. In fact, I believe that's what stopped me on the trail several hours ago. It was the last warning somehow sent by those brave souls just before they were destroyed."

Hjalmarr nodded gravely. "Let us avenge their deaths by destroying those that have invaded our lands. Even though Devil's Valley is a small corner of Ngarzzorr, it is still our hard-won land, and, as king, I plan to defend every last inch of my land."

The king ended his speech with a look so fierce that many of the Dwarves dare not look him in the face. The eager warriors began to prepare to move out. No Dwarf ever backed down from a fight with the hated Goblins and Orcs. Excitement permeated the air as Knolt and Greentea moved out with their small contingent. Hjalmarr would wait till the moon was high in the sky to commence the battle. This would give Knolt time to get in a position far to the west and north of where the main battle would be. Knolt knew that speed and stealth would be the key to taking out the Wizard of the Orcs. He just hoped that the nagging feeling that he was missing something was wrong.

Greentea followed Knolt as the old Dwarf sped through the heavily treed mountainside. It was now dark, and the partial moon provided some light, but other than that, they were traveling blind. The four guards and Greentea used a small rope to string from one to another. Knolt laughed at them, and somehow, he seemed to be able to see just fine. Greentea could feel the magic aura of the small Wizard as he used whatever magic he could to ease his way. Greentea was amazed at the energy of the old Dwarf. Knolt seemed to relish this situation and was glad to be in the middle of it all.

After several hours of tracking through the wilderness following Knolt, they suddenly halted. Knolt called them together and surprised them all by proposing that they separate. Knolt said, "Greentea and two of the guards will continue in the direction they have been traveling. You will reach an easily defined road that the evil creatures have made in just a few minutes. Greentea needs to use her magic to alter the natural surroundings to hide the road."

Greentea suddenly knew exactly what to do. She and Knolt had practiced this several times on the trip down the mountain. Knolt started to head out when Greentea reached out and grabbed him. "What are you going to do?" asked the young Druid.

At first, Knolt seemed annoyed and then realized that Greentea deserved to know. "We will head down the trail and try to find the Wizard of the Orcs. I will destroy them and then head for the far north side of the mountains and look for clearing to the east and greet the rising sun. I have a bit of a surprise for these evil creatures." In a flash, Knolt and his two guards were gone.

What the two Dwarf guards thought at this moment was later a tremendous joke amongst the Zopfarn Dwarves. One of the youngest and least trained cleric Dwarves was left alone in the wilderness in charge of two experienced members of the King's Guard. Greentea Gravelt would begin her legendary life in this situation. She had no real idea of her unique magic, and she and her two guards were far from any help. Plus, they were surrounded by enemy troops in the middle of the night. Truth be told, all three were scared to death.

King Hjalmarr Zopfarn did not wait as long as Knolt told him to. The temptation to attack those evil creatures was too much even for the wise king. They moved out about two hours after Knolt left. The king had promised four. Hjalmarr and his small contingent moved quietly and carefully down the mountain. They had complete surprise on their side. The Goblin troops guarding this trail never even got an alarm raised before the king's troops destroyed them. Seventeen Goblin guards were killed in the initial assault. The king's troops engaged a contingent of twenty Orcs before they were fully awake. Seven died before they got out of their tents, and nine more were beheaded as the Dwarves formed up a V-shaped front and began to sing their favorite song of war. The remaining four Orcs actually got their weapons raised before they were finished off by the angry, attacking Dwarves.

Down the trail, the final few hundred feet and out onto the valley floor went the charging Dwarves. In the lead was Hjalmarr. So frantic was this initial rush that the others had to yell above the din of the battle to turn to the right. The king realized he was going too far the wrong way, corrected, and made a strong turn. This confused the Goblins and Orcs rushing to wake up and jump into this battle. Turning to the right led the king's troops straight into a pack of the evil wolf-type creatures. The wolves woke up ready to fight. The surprise was gone, and Hjalmarr slid back into his command position for the offensive. The king had killed seven Goblins and at least nine Orcs during the initial rush, far more than any others, as his fury was amazing to behold. Many of the evil creatures would not fight again for several minutes from fear of the wild-eyed Dwarf king.

The offensive progress of the king and his group slowed down, but fate was good to them. The scout they had sent to meet up with General Coalfinder had done his job perfectly. Several hundred of the best fighters under the general were awake and listening for the attack from their king. Hearing the song of battle by the king and his troops was the signal for them to attack. The coordination worked out perfectly as the Goblins and Orcs were extremely slow to react. The wolf creatures, later to be called Scree by the sound the Orcs made to call them, were difficult to defeat and put up a good fight. They had a vicious nature and long, sharp teeth. It took about an hour to destroy all the creatures between the king and the general's camp. Losses by the Dwarves were minimal as they found new hope and energy, knowing their king was returning to lead them.

General Coalfinder and King Hjalmarr met on the field of battle with a hug, and a general cheer went through the entire camp, knowing that the king was safely back. The king quickly relayed the story of finding Knolt and the battles they fought on the way up the mountain. The cold anger the Dwarves had at hearing that wounded troops were destroyed assured the outcome of the upcoming battles.

The battle raged on as the evil creatures showed amazing recovery ability and countered the offensive. A large group of Orcs seemed different than any the Dwarves had ever seen. They were well trained and well armored, and they held firm in the center of the valley. The Dwarves found the going difficult against these creatures. The general quickly briefed the king on the difficulty of these particular Orcs. The king had never heard of such a creature, and being night, he would not see them until morning. Then the general briefed him on the perpetual darkness that the Orc Wizards had created. The morning had not come for the last four days, and the troops were very weary of the perpetual gloom.

The king and his full contingent were back together, and the battle for Devil's Valley began in earnest. The king and his small band had surprised the evil creatures, and on both wings, the line of the Orcs and Goblins was ready to fall. However, the center of the line has held by the large Orcs. They flew a battle flag that could be seen as a black worm with giant red eyes even through the gloom of the day. None of the Dwarves had ever seen such a battle standard from a group of Orcs. The pressure applied by King Hjalmarr and General Coalfinder was causing a slow but consistent retreat by the Orcs of the Black Worm. After three hours of pitched battle, the king called off the bulk of the offensive. Even the creatures seemed ready for a break, and both sides backed off from the battle. Many good Dwarf warriors did not live to see the end of this battle. Casualties were many on both sides. With the break in the battle, the Orcs waited for their Wizards to block the sunrise, and the Dwarves were hoping that dawn would bring bright daylight to lift their spirits.

Chapter 10

MAGIC AND WAR

Greentea Gravelt and her two guards, Katowe and Burntop, went forward as instructed by Knolt. Soon, they came to the road made by the Orcs, and Greentea was amazed. It was at least five feet wide and was cleared of all vegetation. No other road existed like this one except for the well maintained roads of the Mounty Republic. Greentea had no idea about those roads, and all she did know was this road did not feel "right" or "natural" to her. Coming to her barely trained magical senses, she applied her magic to this road and its construct. What she felt was incredible. This road had not been made by hardworking evil creatures. This road was made by magic . . . Magic that was dark and abused nature was the method by which this road had come into being. Greentea found the abuse of nature disgusting. She was almost ill as she examined the magic construct that so violated what she knew of her magic. She immediately began to alter the magic to recreate the natural feel. Large sections of the road started to disappear. The guards panicked as they could not believe the road was disappearing before their very eyes.

The road offended Greentea's sense of nature. She felt the small animal path that the road had followed, and she left that in place. The rest she altered. First, a few hundred feet of road, then more and more of the evil road was changed. Greentea went slowly, changing back the altered landscape. She did what felt right, and her magic flowed from the ground and the air into what she was doing. The two guards looked on in utter amazement. During this time, Greentea Gravelt had her beard altered to a dark green color that would never change during her life. Suddenly, as it started, Greentea felt the magic and stopped. She knew not what she felt, but it scared her, and suddenly, she let out a scream and began writhing in pain on the ground.

Greentea was being magically attacked, and the pain she felt was incredible. She felt the evil of the magic being applied to her life force. She knew she was doomed. Nothing in her training had prepared her for such a direct attack of dark magic. Surprisingly, the creature attacking her had never felt Druid magic before and was somewhat uncertain how to finish destroying the invader. This slight uncertainty is what saved Greentea. That, and quick action by her two guards. Burntop quickly decided to get back into the nearby heavy forest, so he picked up the screaming Dwarf and rapidly carried her back into the woods. Unknowingly, he saved her life by leaning Greentea against a tree.

All things in nature have a feel for all other things in nature. No human or any other creature except for a Druid could possibly understand the way nature's objects know about other natural objects. Usually, all things in nature ignore the others unless they are trying to help or hurt them. Then they sometimes react in surprising ways. The Druid causes nature to open up to those appropriately gifted. Greentea did not know it, but all of nature had felt her attempt to put things back correctly, and trees could help. The tree she leaned against was a healthy pine tree in the prime of its existence. It was nothing for the tree to shield the evil powers searching the mind of the Greentea. The tree had appreciated what the Druid had done, so the tree provided a shield that blocked the intense pain the Greentea was feeling.

All Greentea knew was . . . It had stopped. The pain and power of the evil magic had been intense. She was leaning against a tree with the two guards looking at her with amazing looks. She did not know what to say as Katowe realized that the screams might have alerted the enemy. He instructed Burntop to stay with Greentea, and he quickly scouted the immediate area. Katowe came back soon with a report that no one was around, and the road was gone in the immediate area. Greentea was feeling better. She was able to stand up. She was careful to avoid using her magic again as she was frightened of what had happened. Greentea had never felt such powerful magic. She knew that it (whatever "it" was) was aware of her. She did not want "it" to find her that way again as she knew "it" could destroy her.

Greentea explained to her guards what she thought had happened to her and that she would have to be careful with further magic use. Absorbing that bad news, Katowe led them across where the road used to be and began to climb the mountain on the other side. They had not gone too far when the first lost troops of Goblins started wandering through the woods looking for the lost road. In fact, Greentea had returned to nature about a mile of the magical roadway. The retreating creatures were lost without the road to follow. Greentea and her guards spent some time carefully attacking the retreating Goblins. Greentea's guards were experienced warriors, so lost, wandering Goblins were easy prey. Finally, finding a relatively clear spot high in the mountains, the three Dwarves waited, wondering how things were going with their friends and their king. They expected to wait out the cold night, avoiding any more enemy troops.

Knolt had left his two guards near the spot where the magical road opened out onto the relatively open valley floor. They found a heavily wooded area with a steep mountain behind them to await the return of Knolt. Shortly after Knolt left them, the two Dwarves watched the road suddenly disappear. Several times over the next hour, wandering Orcs and Goblins would venture into the small, forested area looking for the road. It was easy pickings for the warrior Dwarves to destroy the small enemy troops.

Knolt quietly drifted through the sleepy camp of Orcs and Goblins. The front line was several miles away. These reserve troops would be called upon in the morning. Magically shielding him would make him noticed by the Orc Wizards while the others in the camp would never know he was there. This was what Knolt wanted. He felt confident he could magically get out of the camp and properly identify, and hopefully destroy, the Wizards.

The first Wizard to identify Knolt was on the south side of the encampment. The Wizard noticed the magical force and tried to examine it magically. This told Knolt who it was. The Orc Wizard realized his mistake just a bit too late. The spell, sent by Knolt, was a simple one. It would merely take away the Wizard's ability to cast spells for several hours. The south side of the valley would see the sunrise. Examining the Orc Wizard's mind allowed Knolt to learn what he needed to know. What he found out was good—there was only one other Wizard, and it was bad—it was a very powerful kind of Wizard. The Orc Wizard was a very weak-minded creature and could not even identify mentally what the other was. This was concerning to Knolt.

The other Wizard was on the north side of the encampment. Knolt went to send a similar spell to the first but was successfully blocked. Then Knolt felt the power. The magic had stirred things up, and had Greentea been using magic, she would have felt the disturbance in the magical fields of Wyndliege. Knolt was completely exposed and had to use some of his most potent spells to run and hide. He made it to the north edge of the camp and then was hit with the full force of magic against him. Knolt quickly realized that the Wizard on this side of the valley was no Orc. For the first time, Knolt saw (using his enhanced night vision that he had used all evening) what he was up against. Knolt was very scared; he could not defeat this creature magically.

Rising up, less than one hundred yards away, was a black figure. Tall, maybe eight feet tall, and very gaunt, wearing a tattered, flowing black robe was a Balrog. Six long arms with long skinny fingers that turned into short whips appeared out of slits in the side of the robe. No face was visible in the dark hood, and nobody seemed to be under the black robe. Knolt had only seen one other Balrog in all his long years. He needed a moment to think. He dodged behind a large boulder, and that bought him the time he needed.

Balrogs were creatures of the Far North and were magical creatures capable of head-to-head magic battles with the best of the Wyndswept Wizards. In the past, many wondered if the ancient evil Wizard Syterion had attempted to raise the dead, and the result was the Balrog. Anyway, Knolt ran through what had worked in his last battle with the black evil before him. Then he remembered.

Stepping out from behind the rock, Knolt was hit with the expected wave of magic. It was dark, evil, and powerful. Knolt shielded himself and sent a wave of magic at the evil mind of the Balrog. Knolt loaded every pleasant memory he could remember. A warm summer's night, pleasant-smelling flowers, beautiful gardens with a small, nice stream. The Balrog exploded with magic, changing all the pleasant sights, sounds, and smells with evilness and badness. Knolt sent more pleasant thoughts, and the creature continued to change them. Almost immediately, the Balrog lost the offensive. Knolt ignored all the evil and just kept sending magical waves of kindness and goodness.

The Balrog began to scream out in pain. Knolt had taken control, but the Balrog could not be destroyed, and eventually, Knolt would wear down, and the Balrog's allies would destroy him. The army of Orcs and Goblins were so afraid of the Balrog that none would go near the small Dwarf despite the noise of the fight. However, one Snow Yeti stumbled forward to grab the small Dwarf, thinking it would be easy to pick up the Dwarf and crush him. Knolt could not have been happier to see the Yeti. The dumb giant was easy to fool, and Knolt had an idea. Fighting off another wave of kindness by Knolt, the Balrog did not realize his peril until it was too late.

The giant Snow Yeti picked up what it thought was the small Dwarf and crushed it in his massive hand. At that point, Knolt reversed his appearance spell, and the dumb Yeti looked down at the crushed Balrog in his hand and watched as the Dwarf ran off into the woods. The Balrog was not destroyed, but it was rendered useless until it could return to his home in the Far North and collect another garment. The black robe provided the needed form to allow the Balrog to use magic. If one had wanted to destroy the Balrog, the six arms would have to be caught and burned in an extremely blistering fire. The arms started the long crawl home. No one noticed.

Knolt knew this, but that was for another day. He magically disappeared as soon as he hit the nearby woods and stayed that way for some time as the Orcs and Goblins gave chase after him. Eventually, Knolt made it back to his two guards, and after giving the appropriate congratulations for their work in the woods, led them to a clearing high up on the mountains that faced east. Knolt explained his plans to the excited Dwarves, and the three happily began the climb that they would complete just as the long night gave way to sunrise.

King Hjalmarr used the break from the battle to return to his royal tent and plan for the next stage of the battle. He planned to lead his people once again, and this time, he planned to be in full royal armor. He knew his warriors would respond to their king like no other. He prepared for the total destruction of his enemy. He just hoped Knolt could somehow defeat the Wizards who were blocking the sunrise. The king knew that under daylight, his people would rout the evil creatures. He planned his attack to begin at dawn.

Greentea and her two companions spent a long, cold night dodging lost groups of Orcs and Goblins. Two of the evil Scree smelled the Dwarves, but Greentea risked enough magic to confuse the creatures of nature. The two warriors with Greentea ambushed several small groups of Goblins and even got two wandering Orcs. As sunrise neared, the small group reached the tree line far up the mountain. The towering box canyon walls rose above them. As the light grew, Greentea noticed the unnatural road cutting through the rock walls of the mountain. With a quick explanation of what she planned to do to the road, she got the soldiers moved to what she judged to be a safe area, and then she began.

Greentea knew that whatever magical being had attacked her

earlier would do so again when she started to destroy the road up on the side of the mountain. She felt she had to risk it to cut off further entry into Ngarzzorr by the creatures. Greentea had no idea the Balrog was destroyed by the magic of Knolt and the giant hand of the dumb Yeti. All she knew was she could be destroyed by using this magic. However, it did not stop her from sending out the spell to reverse the evil road. Greentea sent the spell quickly and was amazed at what happened. The road disappeared, and a giant rock slide began high on the mountain.

Greentea and her two guards fled down the mountain as fast as their short, heavy Dwarven legs would take them. The whole mountain rumbled and shook from the force of the rockslide. Knolt and his companions noted the shaking and rumbling, and Knolt jumped into the air with a fist pump and shouted, "She did it!" The confused looks on the two guards gave way to smiles as they realized what had happened. Greentea Gravelt had shut the magical exit for the evil creatures. Now, only the devil himself could escape Devil's Valley.

Dawn gave way to a spectacular sunrise punctuated by an impressive display of light refraction by the always colorful Knolt. Knolt magically created prisms in the sky to refract the sunlight as it shone brightly down into the valley. The sudden light after days of darkness and the obvious magical display informed all the combatants that the magic tide in this battle had turned in favor of the Dwarves. The light refracted spectacularly over the valley. Many Orcs and Goblins were shielding their eyes from the intense light to the point they could not, and would not, fight anymore.

The attack by the king in his full, shining armor and his highly trained, if inexperienced, guard was too much for even the Orcs of the Black Worm. The day was long and bloody. The retreating evil creatures had nowhere to go. This was not the maneuvering and swordsmanship of battles between the Mounties, Dwarves, Humans, and Elves (at least in the past). This was a brutal battle to the death by the angered Dwarves and the dispirited, evil, sunlight-hating creatures of Wyndliege. Greentea had destroyed the road, Knolt had destroyed the Balrog who was their leader, and now the king of Clan Zopfarn, shining brightly in the sunlight, in full armor, led his troops on the final offensive that destroyed the rest of the evil creatures.

Greentea and Knolt met up high in the mountains to the west. Once Greentea knew the Balrog that had caused her so much of a problem was destroyed, she immediately set about wiping out the magical abomination of the rest of the road. The magic that Greentea sent out was so powerful that the retreated creatures were scared back down to the valley floor—only to be destroyed by the king's troops.

Knolt, with a beard rapidly changing to every color of good and happy that he had, led the group of six around the main battle lines and, using a little magic, right into the middle of the king and the general's area. Removing the magic was quite the scare to the personal guards of the two powerful Dwarves, but it was a very happy reunion.

Greentea and Knolt were greeted as heroes by the king and General Coalfinder. Many of the Dwarves had no idea of the role the two wizards had played, and fate would be such that many Dwarves would not know for years how important the two were in the battle of Devil's Valley. Knolt and Greentea took leave of the king and the general just as both received a messenger from the king's sons. The news was incredible. The king's sons, Ronjit and Ragnar, had won a huge battle against the Mounties near Beardly. The clever boys had planned and executed a fantastic strategic plan that had defeated the troops of the Mounties and had secured a huge swath of land south of the city of Beardly. More importantly, a trade route to the port town of Rockypoint was now opened. The runner said the sons were calling on their king for reinforcements as they expected a strong counterattack by the Mounties.

Leaving Hjalmarr making plans to go to the aid of his sons, Knolt led Greentea to the finding of Hludowig. The old Dwarf was tending to wounded Dwarves. Knolt immediately came to the aid of the overworked cleric. Knolt had healing powers far beyond any current Dwarf, and soon, the most serious had been treated and were on their way to being healed. Greentea was shown some magic of her kind that assisted all involved. Once again, with a little training from Knolt, Greentea's incredible powers were displayed in her form of magic. Pain relief through certain herbs seemed more powerful when administered by the Druid Dwarf.

Knolt was happy to have met up with his old student, and they drifted off to discuss the state of the clerics. For the first time in several days, Greentea went off to her own small tent she had left just a few days prior. With a bit of time to be alone and think, Greentea marveled at how far she had come. Yet, she was still so alone and so powerless to survive in the big wide world.

Greentea's thoughts were jumbled. She knew that Knolt could really help her in training as a Druid, but she still had not resolved how she would live. She knew that she did not belong with other Dwarves. Dwarves enjoyed a life of mining and making wonderful weapons of war and jewels over hot forges deep in their mountain homes. Greentea enjoyed walking through green forests, picking wildflowers, and enjoying the beauties of nature. It scared the young Dwarf that she was so different from the only life—and everyone—she had ever known. What could she do? What *should* she do? Dwarves could not move freely throughout Wyndliege as the Mounties, enemies of her kind, controlled most of the land. Elves, she had been told, were closest to her in appreciation of all things natural, and the Elves were all slaves of the Mounties. She knew very little about humans, but what she knew was not promising for one of her calling. What should she do? Where should she go? What would become of her? These were the questions she kept coming back to. She could find no answers as she drifted off to sleep.

Chapter 11

CEDRIC

Far to the north and east of the Dwarves of Ngarzzorr, Jari Elmflock ducked down behind the outcropping of rock at the base of the Herrick Hills. The large caribou herd had stayed further south than usual as winter had finally begun to lose its hold over this land. In another week or so, the herd would move rapidly north on the annual migration to their summer grounds, where new additions would be born. Jari thought that one more from the herd could be added to the table of his adoptive family. He knew that the Herrick family appreciated his hunting, but they really did not need what he brought to the table.

He had been taken in by the Herricks long ago, and his debt to his Human family was tremendous. A long time ago, his queen had sent him to study the strange monastery of the Far North of Wyndliege. Jari often thought about what could have happened to him if the instructions of his queen all those years ago had not taken him away from his people.

North of Ngarzzorr was a range of small mountains that separated Lake Sterb from the Darson Desert. Built into the largest mountain was an ancient structure that was occupied by a religious sect. This sect recruited both sexes from every known race, Monks, to come and serve their god and their beliefs. Not one of the four goodly races had ever gained an understanding of the Monks' purposes. No one, that is, until Jari Elmflock, rode up to the monastery over five hundred and eighty years ago and was invited in.

For reasons he could only guess at, Jari was welcomed in, and as events transpired, he watched the Monks record history. Jari learned much about the reason and purposes of the Monks. Fortunately for Jari, much was going on in Western Wyndliege as the Mounties went to war, conquered the Elves, defeated the Humans, and drove the Dwarves northward. The Monks suddenly became very active, going out into the world and recording history as it happened as this was one of their purposes. Even Jari could never learn why. Whenever the Monks sent out emissaries, they asked for, and received, help and protection from the Herrick family. Soon, it just felt right for Jari to settle with the Herricks, as he did not understand the Monks' devotion to their god, and he had lived there ever since. Of course, he really had nowhere else to go.

Jari studied the caribou with the eye of an experienced hunter and soon located the animal he would take. As the animals grazed on the broad steppe, the spring grasses had grown enough that Jari could move close to the herd. Soon thereafter, Jari raised his ever-present bow and fired. As usual, his aim was true, and the animal fell, dead before it hit the ground. A few of the others scrambled a few hundred feet before settling down and resuming their grazing. Most of the herd never noticed anything until Jari came out from his cover and let out a yell, sending the startled caribou rapidly moving away from the intruder.

Jari quickly went to work on his kill and made the carcass transportable by assembling a dragging sled he had brought with him in his oversized pack. With a quick look to the sky to judge daylight, he made off toward the town of Herrick. Arriving at the entrance gate at dusk, Henry Herrick, the youngest child of the clan's leader, Cedrick Herrick, greeted Jari with excitement. Henry ran up to Jari and breathlessly told him that a Monk had arrived around midday and was to have dinner with them tonight. Jari and all the others of the Herrick family knew what this meant.

Cedrick Herrick, a large, barrel-chested man with a very tanned and sun-aged face sporting a full beard, sat quietly in his study, thinking about what would transpire later this evening. For as long as anyone could remember, when a Monk came and visited the great Herrick family compound, it could only mean one thing: history was about to be made in the world. The chosen Monk and a Herrick family member would go out into the world, and the Monk would record the history, and the Herrick would provide for the protection of the Monk. Never, in the thousands of years of this arrangement, had the Monk and the Herrick failed in their appointed tasks. It fell to Cedrick to choose who of his people would accompany the scholarly young Monk who had presented himself to Cedrick earlier that day.

Cedrick secretly longed for this to have happened when he was a younger man. His father and grandfather had longed for this moment. Now, the moment had come, and Cedrick knew it was his duty to choose who of his family would undertake this journey. Survival was always tough in this far northern climate, and the Herricks had long succeeded by being well trained. The training that all members of the Herrick family received prepared them for survival in and around the family lands and prepared them for the chance to accompany a Monk.

Cedrick's thoughts wandered as he, unsuccessfully, tried to focus on the momentous decision he must, as leader of the family, make in just a few hours. Long ago, the Herricks and the Monks made the arrangement that when the chosen Monk arrived in Herrick, he or she would leave the very next morning accompanied by his protector from the family. Tradition called for the decision to be announced at a great feast held the evening the Monk arrived. A statue of stone made in his or her likeness lining the great central road of the compound would forever remember the chosen Herrick. There were twenty-three of these statues presently lining the road. Cedrick would start construction of a twenty-fourth tomorrow. The base of each statue contained a small synopsis of the historical event or events that transpired while he or she protected the Monk. Many in the lands farther south would be amazed at the history (long forgotten) written on the statue bases.

Cedrick, stroking his thick beard and rubbing his balding head, had made several lists of names. Many names were scratched out and then written back in. Cedrick had five sons and three daughters. His two younger brothers and sister also had very capable children. His youngest brother could be considered a candidate. He had several cousins who, through outside marriages, had brought much new blood into the family, and there were impressive candidates amongst their children. All told, Cedrick could reasonably name twenty different Herricks who would be terrific representatives. Generally, the age of a candidate would be between eighteen and twenty-six years. Cedrick, at forty-seven, thought that he would stay in this range, and he favored those a little older over those a little younger. Other than those criteria, Cedrick did not know what he should do. Then an idea came into his head.

He called out from his study, and his butler, James Henry, stepped in. "James, please send a runner to find Jari and have him come to me immediately."

"Yes, sir," said James as he sped away to complete his duty. The Henrys had served the Herricks for as long as anyone could remember. James was as much a close friend as a butler to Cedrick.

Cedrick smirked at James's formality and went back to the task at hand.

James opened the door to the study, and in walked Jari, still in his hunting clothes. Cedrick motioned for James to stay in the room and for both Jari and James to take a chair. The three men sat comfortably, and Cedrick asked Jari about his hunt. Jari told the story of his morning and confirmed that young Henry had met him at the gate with the news. Cedrick turned serious as the subject came back to what must be done tonight.

"Jari, James, tonight, I must make the most important decision I will make as head of this family. I would like your most thoughtful and honest input."

James replied, "Cedrick, it really must come down to your second son, Marcus, or your brother, Kelvon's, son, Paul, or Arthur

James Herrick, your sister's son. We must stay with a male as this chosen Monk is male, and it would be wrong to mix the sexes."

Jari chimed in, "Those three, or maybe . . ." and here he paused for a moment, "Thaddeus Herrick. It is too bad this one is not female. Your eldest daughter would be perfect."

"No, not Thaddeus," said James. "I like your youngest brother, but he is just a bit too careless and daring. Wow. I just remembered, isn't Paul injured right now?"

"Yes, Paul has been tending to a sprained ankle. I cannot consider him. I forgot about the rule that the choice must match sex," stated Cedrick. "So, you two have named four and with injury and, I agree about Thaddeus, we rapidly get down to two. You guys have made this somewhat easier. Let me give you some more names, and you give me your reasoning behind why they should not be considered. Let me start with my oldest, Cedrick Jr."

"Well, let me start by saying that young Cedrick would probably do a fine job, and he will be most disappointed not to be chosen," stated James. "But he is more cut out to be the next leader of this family. He will take your job someday. With that, he will be satisfied."

Jari nodded in agreement.

Cedrick went through several more names, and between Jari and James, certain weaknesses were pointed out for each candidate. It seemed that either Arthur James or Marcus would be the choice. Both James and Jari were careful to point out the relative strengths and weaknesses of the two finalists. They understood; this was to be Cedrick's decision.

Herrick was more than just a town. It was really a walled city far to the north of any other settlement in Western Wyndliege. While dominated by the powerful Herrick family, the city called Herrick was probably five thousand people and was considered a part of the Darson government. All walks of life were contained inside the safety of the walls built by the family Herrick. All races were welcome, and here was one of few places that Mounties and Dwarves both came to trade goods. Huge caravans of goods rolled up the Darson road and the road from Whiterock to be traded in Herrick. The leaders of both the Mounties and the Dwarves knew better than to cross the powerful Herricks. This allowed for needed goods to be traded from one warring faction to the other and back again. The Herricks were fair in what they taxed, and almost everyone profited from the arrangement.

The castle, if you could call it that, of the Herricks was a solidly built stone building. It was well designed to withstand the long, cold winter but was not spectacular or flashy. It was, however, very large. The main dining area could easily seat several hundred, and the raised dais would seat several dozen. On this night, it was full. The guests and the many party crashers were in full party spirits on this momentous night. Cedrick, sitting at the head of the table with his wife to his right and Cedrick Junior to his left, could not take his eyes off the special guest of the evening. The smallish young Human Monk in full robe was obviously intimidated by the large number of rapidly intoxicated guests. Dwarves were downing their mead, and Mounties were drinking their fermented drink that was very potent. Cedrick was very glad to see the whole place surrounded by the soldiers of the Herricks. Many guests would never know just how safe that hall was on this night. The Herricks' powerful secret would protect them all tonight.

Jari, as was usual, was not present. He would not show himself at this kind of event. Many would not like to see him.

As dinner was served and taken away, Cedrick rose to start the business of the night. All who were there anxiously awaited the announcement of who would represent the Herricks. To start the formalities, Cedrick asked the young Monk to step forward. The hooded and robed Monk with a youngish face looked very small next to the large, broad-shouldered, pot-bellied man that was Cedrick Herrick.

Cedrick's booming voice rang out over the assembly, quieting those in the back. All looked at the raised dais with anticipation.

"Today," spoke the powerful Cedrick, "one of our clan will

be asked to accompany a representative of our dear friends, the Monks of the Stone Abbey. For several centuries, the Monks have sent their chosen one out into the world to record the histories of important events. Never have the Monks been wrong in anticipating that important history is about to occur, and never have they failed to have a magical scribe record that history. The Monks have decided that we are at such a time in history. We are lucky to be alive at such a time. Always, the chosen Monk goes out into the world with the protection and guidance of a member of our family. And always, both the Monk and the Herrick family member have returned successfully."

At this point, wild cheers broke out as Cedrick's pronouncements were what they had come to hear, what they wanted to hear.

Cedrick continued almost yelling. "Now, the Monks have made their choice in the young man beside me, and I must choose who of my clan is most prepared and most capable to be the protector in this historic undertaking. I would ask these final five to step to the front of the room: Paul Herrick, Thaddeus Herrick, Arthur James Herrick, Marcus Herrick, and Cedrick Junior."

The five young men all made their way to the front of the room to thunderous applause. Thaddeus was already stumbling drunk, Paul had a very noticeable limp, and the other three looked extremely nervous. The crowd was shouting and yelling to express their feelings about the final five.

Cedrick let this go on for a few moments before he spoke again. "All right," he boomed, "now, we will begin to narrow down these fine candidates. Paul, you are quite qualified and would have been considered more seriously without the ankle injury. With it, I must disqualify you."

Paul bowed graciously toward his leader as he knew this to be true. He gratefully left the dais, and the yelling and shouting from the crowd began anew.

Again came the booming voice of Cedrick, "All right, Thaddeus . . ."

Cedrick got no further as Thaddeus fell flat on his face, too drunk to stand.

"Get him off the stage!" yelled the ashamed Cedrick. "Brother of mine or no, he is not to represent us on this day!!"

The young Monk, who had been stoic up until this time, had an unmistakable look of relief. The final three would be just fine from what he could see and from what he had been told.

For the first time, Cedrick was able to continue without yelling. "Now, there are three fine candidates left. It is a very difficult choice from this point on. It is with great pain that I must announce the next to be eliminated will be my eldest son, Cedrick Herrick Junior."

An audible gasp ran through the assembly. Many had assumed that a father would choose his eldest son as a matter of course. Few knew just how important this decision was to the Herricks. Many of the older members of the clan looked at each other and smiled. They knew the choice was in good hands, and the future was also.

"Cedrick," continued Cedrick Senior, "you will someday replace me as leader of our people, and in that, you will be satisfied. This task is not for you, not at this time. You will continue to work on the skills you need to one day replace me as our leader. In that, you must find solace."

Cedrick gave his father a look that showed he was disappointed in not being chosen but that he may have understood better than any could have anticipated. The two Cedricks came together for a hug right in front of the assembly. The crowd broke out in wild cheers, and now the decision was down to two.

Arthur James Herrick had watched the whole affair in great amazement. He was a Herrick only because the family kept the Herrick name even when married. His mother, Cedrick's sister, had sent him here when it was time to start his training. She had not lived in the compound for over twenty years as she had married a Wyndswept man and lived with him in South Landsend. Arthur (or Jim as he preferred to be called) was not as smooth in many courtly ways compared to the almost royal-like sons and brothers of Cedrick. Cedrick Senior was like a god to Jim, and he could not believe his fortune to be in the final two.

Jim lived not in the main house as was his right, but in the training center. He only had a small chest with a few personal items and a cot covered in animal skins in a small room. The drafty training center building had become his home, and there were none better than him in battle with weapons or hunting skills with the exception, possibly, of his friend, Jari.

Jim Herrick looked at Marcus, and the two of them shared a quick smile. Jim felt strongly that Marcus would be chosen, and he wanted Marcus to know that there would be no hard feelings. He was surprised to see a similar look from Marcus, The two were not real close, but respect was earned in the tough training that the young Herricks went through. These two were among the best in that training, and the respect was mutual.

As the crowd continued to cheer, Cedrick took a moment to look over the two young men. He knew that he would not have any difficulty defending his choice either way. His second son was the picture of a fighting noble. He could represent his people in the halls of the Presidential Palace or before the throne of King Hjalmarr in the Great Blancfrought of Whitehall. He would protect the young Monk against all dangers with ease. The young Jim (even Cedrick knew that preference) was the epitome of the rough-and-ready Herricks of the early days. His half Wyndswept size allowed him to be among the largest Herrick ever. It also made him unbeatable in contests of weaponry and the hunt. The smile inside of Cedrick showed on his face.

Many in the crowd, seeing the sudden smile appear on the leader's face, settled down. They knew the time was now.

Cedrick suddenly knew what he would do. The weight of what had happened over the last twenty-four hours had made him forget who and what he was. His choice was made. He decided right then that they would all go out. A small skeleton crew would make sure that the outsiders all got settled back down in the town. The rest would go out.

Cedrick asked for a moment from the crowd, then stepped off to the side with his brother Andy, Cedrick Jr., and James Henry. The four men whispered for a moment amongst themselves, and then the other three scattered amongst the crowd spreading the word. Cedrick walked back onto the dais.

"Now comes the moment you have been waiting for," announced the leader of the Herrick clan, "but first, I must ask our guest if he has any reservations about either of the final two."

"No, sir," was the rather timid response from the overawed young Monk.

With a smile at the chosen Monk, Cedrick went on. "With great pride, I announce that the representative of the Herrick clan will be Arthur James Herrick!"

The crowd went nuts. Marcus was the first to reach Jim, and the two youths embraced in a hug as several others charged the two finalists. Everyone was congratulating Jim when Cedrick fought his way through the crowd and whispered in his ear. "Tonight, we hunt."

Jim could only smile. Never had he been so happy.

Jim, Cedrick, and the young Monk soon escaped out the back of the great dining hall. The Herricks began to empty the great dining hall and prepare for the night. Cedrick took the two youngsters to a room beside his study and told them to spend a few minutes getting to know each other. Then he left the room.

As Cedrick shut the door, the extreme silence of being in a very loud place and suddenly, in a very quiet place, took over.

The young Monk, more sure of himself in this quieter place, walked over to Jim and said, "I suppose I should say congratulations to you. I have never seen anything like that as the Monks meditate in silence to make decisions. Anyway, my name is Calvin."

"Nice to meet you, Calvin," replied Jim. "I am Arthur James Herrick, but please, just call me Jim."

"OK, Jim, you must call me Cal." Cal was amazed at the pure size of Jim Herrick. At over six and a half foot tall, blond hair, and clean-shaven, Jim showed much of his Wyndswept heritage. "We must leave tomorrow morning as tradition dictates, but we have no real hurry as things are not moving very quickly right now. My superiors have given me a name and a place to start. From there, we go where God will take us."

Jim sized up the young Monk by noting that, while smaller, the Monk was a sturdy-looking Human. With dark hair and a square chin, Jim expected that this man could hold his own. "All right, Cal, why don't you get some sleep, and I will get my stuff ready to go in the morning," he said.

"Sunrise tomorrow then?" questioned Cal.

"Yup, sunrise. Nice to meet you," said Jim as he walked out of the room.

Cedrick could feel the excitement throughout the halls of his palace. The leader of the family had not called a hunt for a long time. Spring had come to the Far North, and it was time for the Herricks to run. Hibernation was over.

As Cedrick came out into the late evening, he saw that most of his family, male and female, were there. The Henry clan had also come out, and although somewhat smaller than the Herricks, he could feel the excitement in them also. Cedrick walked through the crowd, and many congratulated him on his decision for the Protector. Even his wife was able to have a word with him finally. Although a bit upset that her sons were not chosen, she could not deny the wisdom of his choice. He could feel the weight they all felt regarding the pressure of the possibility of failure in the job of Protector. That pressure would now belong to Jim.

The Herrick family walked the main road of the town to the main gate. Many stopped at different statues to pay homage to those of the past. Many were staring straight ahead, anticipating what was about to happen. The Henry family walked slightly behind the Herricks, but they were no less excited.

Complete darkness had settled over the land as the chosen guards opened the gate to the town and let the procession through.

Then the gates were closed behind them. Jim, hurrying to catch up, snuck through as the last man.

The Henrys walked away to the south. The Herricks walked to the north. James Henry and Cedrick Herrick stood watching the two groups walk away.

James said, "We will meet here one hour before sunrise."

"One hour before sunrise it is," replied Cedrick. "Hunt well."

With that, James Henry turned toward his departing clan and ran two steps as fast as he could, then began the transformation. By his fifth running step, the sleek form of the mountain lion was running full speed toward his clan, and they, hearing loud cat sounds, all began to run. Soon, a sizable group of large cats was running south through the wooded hills near Herrick.

Turning to the north with a broad but terrible smile, the form of Cedrick Herrick became one of the great grizzly bears of the north of the world. The grizzly that was Cedrick joined the rest of the bear form Herricks as they went hunting.

The last to change was young Jim. He could not believe how this day had turned out, and, as proud as he was of his accomplishments, he could only roar as the giant man turned into the giant white polar bear that he really was.

Chapter 12

JIM AND CAL

Jim Herrick quietly returned to his tall, lanky, human form shortly before the appointed time of one hour before sunrise. After
a night of being in his natural state, his mind had cleared, and
he felt better than he had since the last time he had transformed.
The Herricks carefully guarded the secret that had made them such
a powerful force in the Far North of Wyndliege. The ability to trans-
form into animals was seemingly isolated to these Humans that
lived in the Far North.

When the Mounties had driven the majority of Humans to
Darson, the Herrick leaders had carefully and diplomatically directed
most of the displaced Humans to settle in the Darson River basin to
the north and east of the city of Darson. The few that settled farther to the north were generally independent types that braved the
harsh winters of the Herrick Region. Cedrick was extra careful and
went to great effort to keep their secret from almost everyone else
in Wyndliege, especially the other Humans. The common man did
not generally know this secret, but most leaders were aware of the
strange talent of the changelings.

As a great polar bear, Jim generally did not run with the others, and this night had been no different. The polar bear form was
unusual but not unknown amongst the Herricks. The form suited
those with Wyndswept blood quite well. The large physical size of
the Wyndswept tended to be the mighty polar bear in the Herrick

clan. As he changed back to human form, Jim felt the regret that all Herricks felt when losing the extraordinary animal senses they are given as a bear. It passed quickly as the human attributes came to the forefront, and he concentrated on being as human as possible.

Jim passed through the entry gate before the others were back and quickly went to his small room in the training center and gathered his few things. He had enjoyed the previous evening, and he had little time to reflect on what it all meant to him. The excitement of being chosen had begun to be replaced by the tremendous responsibility he now had to live up to. Never had a Herrick and a Monk failed in their duties, and Jim did not plan to be the first.

Cedrick led the others back in at the appointed time, and as the sun rose on another day in Herrick, all seemed as normal as the day before. Cedrick felt the tremendous comfort and relief of a night in his natural form. One night as a bear always made him feel wonderful, and he would sustain a good mood for many days. As his thoughts turned to his duties, he realized what a momentous decision he had made the day before. He was truly pleased with his decision, and he hoped that young Jim was up to the assignment. His first job was to see the two off on their adventure, and his second job was to get workers on the needed statue of a giant polar bear beside all those other bear statues in his city.

Calvin Williams, the Third Order Monk of the Stone Abby, had rested very nicely in the comfortable room provided by the Herricks. He was glad to be done with all the selection process and was pleased with the choice of his Protector. The Monk was able in arms, but he knew that protection was the job of the Herrick. The Monk's job in this unlikely pairing was that of leader. He was to go to the right place, at the right time, and get in writing all the important historical facts that were about to take place. In the past, the Recorder Monk (as that was what he was called) had always followed the instructions of the Grand Masters of the Stone Abbey to a successful conclusion.

Like always, the instructions were very vague. The Recorder Monk would have to follow what leads were placed in front of him and decide where to go. Much prayer was uttered, and the pious Monk relied upon his prayers, some gut feelings, and seemingly divine interpretation more than instructions on what to do. Somehow, it had always worked out perfectly.

After his morning routine and prayers, Calvin left his room, and the posted attendant guided him to a place where he could have breakfast. The large number of Herricks moving around surprised him as he figured that the merriment of the night before would slow up the large Herrick men. However, nothing of the sort was seen by Cal, and he was joined shortly in his meal by Cedrick and his sons.

Cedrick Herrick Junior laid out the plans for a procession to the front gate. It would begin in about an hour and would be direct and to the point. The Protector and Recorder were being sent out on their historic mission, and the idea was to honor them but not overly celebrate. He also gave a rundown of supplies they would send with the two adventurers. Cal was amazed at the vitality and energy that all the Herricks seemed to possess. He was impressed that none of Cedrick's sons were visibly upset at the choice of the night before.

Jim Herrick did not eat much breakfast as his nerves were beginning to bother him. The tremendous pressure on him was setting in, and he wanted to get on the road. He was down at the front of the main building checking the packhorses long before any but the servants had arrived. Jim met with and said goodbye to many of his friends as they came to see the great exit processional.

When Cal arrived at the place where the march was to begin, he was surprised to find Jim already there. The young Monk did not know what to make of the giant man who would be his protector. The same could be said for Jim and how he felt about the scribe who would be leading him.

Cedrick and his immediate family led the procession. Jim and Cal were in a place of honor, but the Recorder and Protector would go on foot as was tradition. They seemed diminished among the armored men and women and decorated horses of the family Herrick. The people of the city had turned out, and many in the crowd were only just now receiving news of all that had happened. Many cheers and well-wishes were directed at Jim and Cal. Everyone seemed sur-prised at how fast this event had happened, and the crowd was a bit late and somewhat subdued by the dawning realization that they were witnessing a rare and important event.

Cedrick made a well received and very short speech wishing them well. The procession participants peeled off to one side or the other, and Jim and Cal proceeded to the city's exit as trumpeters sounded off with a flourish. With that, Jim and Cal walked through the gate of Herrick and went off to record and, in their own way, make history.

Cal made a turn south, and Jim, leading the packhorses, fol-lowed. They continued this way for a while as neither man spoke for quite some time. The awkwardness between the two made small talk pointless, and each had many thoughts to sort out.

The city of Herrick had been left behind as the road south went through a wooded country. Tall pine forests had been cleared for the making of this section of the road that ran south to Darson City. Both men knew that they must go to Darson to get papers to travel through the Mounty lands. That was an obvious first step, but it did not satisfy the curiosity of Jim about what instructions the Recorder had received from his superiors. It was his right to know the instruc-tions, and that was what broke the silence.

"Cal, let's pull over for a short rest. I need to repack this horse as it's about to lose its load," spoke Jim, breaking the long silence.

"Sure," replied Cal. "It looks like there is a large, open area at the bottom of this downhill stretch. Let's stop there and take a break. I think we should go over what I know and what we must plan for."

They reached the bottom and found a lovely mountain lake in a pleasant meadow. Many groups had camped in this spot before, and they rapidly hobbled the packhorses and started examining what the Herricks had given them. After a review of supplies that Jim figured would last several weeks, they began to talk.

Cal spoke first. "My instructions are vague in many aspects and very clear in at least one instance. As I left for Herrick, my advisor told me to start by acting on what was clear, and, hopefully, the rest would work out. My first instruction is to seek out a Dwarf named Knolt. They believe he will be traveling to North Landsend."

"Well, that is very clear," said Jim.

Cal then went on. "The part that is not so clear is the next part of the instructions. I am told to assist those that are trying to 'start the changes,' and that he has begun, and he will change it all."

These words made no sense to Jim. "What does that mean, and who is 'he'?"

"That is certainly the hard part. I think my superiors don't know who 'he' is. It was suggested that it might be two different 'he's.' The last part is equally difficult. 'I am to watch for the treachery from the east as all leads back to that.'"

Cal sat quietly as he finished. Jim pondered the words carefully. He wanted to commit the three instructions to memory.

Jim broke the silence. "Was there anything else?"

"No, but we must not read too much into the words at this time," spoke Cal. "Remember, the words that are most puzzling to us now may be clear later, and those that seem simple now may be more difficult later. History tells us that we would not be sent out at this time unless big events were about to happen. We are tasked with following those three clues until they are resolved."

"I know that well," replied Jim. "I was taught that the role of the Protector was to be ready to follow the lead of the Recorder and protect all at all times. I am ready and willing to follow you till the very end."

"Thank you," said Cal. "You give me comfort in saying that. We are to travel to Darson and get papers to travel to North Landsend. It was emphasized to me that we must move along, but there was no need to hurry. I was instructed to pray on everything that we encountered for clues to the puzzles and solutions that would surely come."

No sooner had Cal finished this sentence when a group of highway robbers attacked the two travelers. The group of six thieves had camped around the opposite side of the lake and had been harassing travelers to and from Herrick for the last several weeks. Had Jim and Cal had time to listen to the tales of the traders who traveled this road, they would have heard stories of the frequent attacks in this area.

The robbers saw the small party of two men with several heavily loaded pack animals leaving Herrick. They thought this would be easy pickings.

They were very wrong!

Two of the thieves made for the animals, while three others came in, running full speed and yelling that no harm would come to the travelers if they gave up the supplies. Had they known that Jim Herrick was here, they would have had second thoughts, but they didn't know who they were attempting to rob. The two headed for the animals were very effectively cut off by the quickly drawn sword of the Monk. Sword practice was mandatory for any who could be chosen as Recorder. Cal had excelled at self-defense practice, and the two robbers were effectively stopped cold by the young Monk. However, it was apparent he could only hold them off for a short while.

The three running and yelling never had a chance. Jim quickly pulled out his two short swords and began a dance of death to those that would oppose him. The first charged so hard that a simple deflection of the sword and a quick swipe practically removed his head, and that thief was dead before he hit the ground. The second thief was so off balance trying to slow up from the mad run that Jim simply snapped his short sword through and removed the hand holding his weapon. The robber screamed out in pain, only to have the scream cut short by Jim's second sword entering his throat. The third man got under control but was no match for the enraged Herrick. Jim had been the best fighter in the entire training stable of Herrick fighters. They took great pride in their training to be fighters, and Jim had always had the best work ethic, and the result was on display. After a short parry, Jim dispatched the robber with a fatal blow to the body and quickly finished the job by stabbing the poor man through the heart.

Jim looked around and noticed the sixth man charging in from behind Cal. Before the man could reach Cal, he was suddenly lying dead on the ground as a giant polar bear had crushed his head with one swipe of his paw. The other two, who were gaining on the fighting Monk, were suddenly presented with what must have been the most frightening thing they ever saw. It was also the last thing they ever saw. A giant bear leaped over the Monk and attacked the two with all the ferocity of the battle. The seven-foot bear rose on its back paws, and the powerful front paws destroyed the men in seconds. The attack was over as quickly as it started. Cal observed carefully as the Protector ran off into the nearby underbrush and stepped back out as Jim Herrick.

"Nice work, Recorder," stated the heavily breathing, blood-covered Jim. "You were fantastic with the sword."

"Thank you, Protector. You were as amazing as could be. Your changeling abilities are well known amongst the Recorder trainees, but to see it in person is much more impressive than I ever imagined. I will pray for you."

Jim was very relieved that Cal had known the secret of the Herricks. That could now be in the open between them. Jim was also embarrassed that the two travelers were off to such a poor start on their journey. Six men were dead, and even though they had been attacked, all Herricks hated to kill other men. No matter the situation, the Herricks believed in using justice to penalize criminals. In this case, Jim had acted out of anger at not being prepared for anything on the road. He knew better. In the wilds of Wyndliege to not be adequately prepared could get you killed, and the widely traveled Jim Herrick well knew that.

Cal was also concerned by the lack of precaution the two had exhibited. He was the leader of this expedition, and he had not done as he had been taught by his family first and the Monks later in life. As a leader, the Recorder was supposed to be the brains to the brawn of the Protector. In this situation, the brawn had saved them, and Cal felt very stupid.

While the two travelers were thinking about everything they had done wrong, they almost made another mistake. Jim figured it out first.

"Cal, we had better check the area and make sure that is all of them."

"Right. Let's get ourselves organized and check out this area."

They moved around the lake and quickly found the camp of the robbers. It seemed deserted. They began to check out the three small tents the men had used for shelter. The second tent checked by Jim revealed the prisoner. She was a young woman no more than twenty years old by Jim's guess. She was bound and gagged. Jim quickly cut her bonds and removed the gag. By this time, Cal had checked the third tent and found nothing. He came at Jim's call, running into the tent just as Jim removed the gag.

"Calvin!!" screamed the young woman. "Thank God, it's Calvin!"

Cal took a closer look at the woman, and suddenly, he was hugging her very tightly. Tears streamed down his face. "Cathy, how on earth did you get here? What happened?"

The words poured out of Cathy. They had left home several weeks ago as she wanted to see the monastery and visit Cal. She had been sent here with a large group of her father's troops, and these awful men had attacked them. They killed all the troops and had taken her hostage. The robbers (who were also killers) had decided that she could cook and clean for them. They had not treated her too badly, but would not let her go. She was their slave. One of them had tried to rape her, but the others had stopped it because they did not want her pregnant. Every time they went out to steal and murder, they would tie her up until they got back. This time, instead of the thieves returning, she was released by Jim, who called out to Cal.

Jim was very confused by this, and his look must have said as much because Cal quickly filled in the bit of information Jim was missing.

"Jim, meet my sister, Cathy Williams."

Chapter 13

CATHY

Cathy told her story in full to Jim and Cal, and they, in turn, told her what had happened to them. She had no idea who or what the Recorder and Protector were but was impressed when she found out that they would travel all over Wyndliege. She was a very pretty, slightly built blonde with a naturally bubbly personality who quickly recovered from her ordeal. The two guys knew how lucky she was to be alive.

Cal decided that they would camp where the robbers had set up camp and would watch the road to flag down a traveler to take a message to Herrick to come and identify the now-dead criminals. The authorities of the weak Darson government could take care of that situation. The always energetic and industrious Cathy quickly went through the packs of the robbers and identified the stolen goods. Cal carefully recorded all on paper for the authorities to return what they could. Cathy also found several personal items of hers, including a bundle of her spare clothes. She also recovered a few items of her former guards and packed them carefully away to return to the next of kin that she and Cal knew all too well.

The sadness with which she packed away the belongings of those that had died when she had lived was tough for Jim to watch. He found her to be a very attractive young woman, and he had to bury those feelings as he was the Protector.

Cathy had heard the story of the attack and how Jim had

protected her brother and had destroyed those that had kidnapped her. She found the large, light-haired young man attractive, but she had been through a horrible ordeal, and she needed to figure out what was next for her.

Cal and Jim had properly secured their campsite and carefully observed the road that afternoon when a merchant caravan of Mounties, hurrying to make Herrick by nightfall, came by. Jim stopped the merchants, and Cal gave them a note to give to Cedrick Herrick from Jim Herrick. The merchant recognized the large Jim and promised to get the message to Cedrick.

Finally, Jim and Cal were able to sit down at their campsite and make a meal. Neither man had had anything to eat all day. They were worn out and starving. Cathy came to the rescue as she had prepared a fine meal from their supplies. She was also very hungry. The three of them sat down and had a much-deserved dinner.

That night, Jim took the first watch, and he was not surprised to have visitors in the form of bears. The note to Cedrick would have certainly caused some commotion amongst the family. Marcus Herrick and a slightly gimpy Paul Herrick arrived and were pleased to find Jim on the watch. They transferred back to human form and carefully listened as Jim relayed the events of the day. They were very glad that Jim and Cal were unharmed and very critical of the carelessness of the travelers. Jim took their criticisms in stride. He had made and learned from mistakes before, and he would do so this time. Marcus and Paul sent Jim off to bed. They said they would watch the rest of the night and stay till just before morning.

Cal slept through the night. When he awoke, he found Jim standing watch in the exact spot he had been in when Cal went to bed.

"You didn't wake me for my watch."

"No, I slept also. Marcus and Paul had the watch, so we both had a full night's rest."

Cathy approached the two men and asked, "Could we talk about what's going to happen with me?"

Both men turned toward her and looked her over. She had been a prisoner for almost two weeks. She was half-starved, overworked, dirty, and generally, a mess. She looked like she needed a week in Herrick to recover from all that had happened to her. But she had a look in her eyes that made them both stop from making that statement.

Cathy looked determined to do something, and they could not possibly know what she had in mind.

Jim spoke first. "Would you like to go back to Herrick? I know that Cedrick would put you up until arrangements could be made for you to see the monastery, and then you could decide what you want to do next."

Cal hit close. "Or you could travel with us to Darson, and then we could send Dad a note to come to get you."

Cathy then spoke her mind. She had been up most of the night thinking about her life and future. She had seen the two bears come up to Jim and change into men. She was not as amazed as other humans would have been, and it determined her future for her as far as she was concerned. "Jim, let me talk to you first. Do you know who our family is?"

"No," replied the puzzled Protector.

"We are the Williams of the Williams River. Does that help?" asked Cathy.

"Yes, that explains a lot to me. Cal, you never said anything to me about your family. Your dad is King Henry Williams," said the suddenly smiling Jim.

Cal replied, "Well, we had just met, and I figured we would get around to all that soon enough. Anyways, I committed to my God through the monastery. I was, after all, fourth to the crown. Cathy, my younger sister by only a year and one-half, was fifth."

Cathy interrupted, "Well, then, Jim, you know that my father can be a hard man, and he will not take it lightly that his troops were killed. The man who destroyed those robbers will be well rewarded and much honored by my father. You are the Protector. Do you have time to be properly honored by my father? To hurry that process will insult him, and I bet you two cannot have the delay."

Cal moaned slightly. Jim shuffled and lowered his head, slightly embarrassed and a bit taken aback by all this information . . . Information he knew to be absolutely true.

Cathy continued. "I left home to visit my brother, but, most importantly to me, to see the world outside my father's castle. It worked out that I did not see much, and I still want to see the world. Could you please let me go with you? I think that three would be easier than two on watches, and I could help by preparing meals."

The almost desperate, hopeful look on her dirty face, the pleading look in her brilliant green eyes, and the emotional manner in which these words poured out had Jim immediately in favor of her accompanying them.

"There are many instances of the Recorder and Protector traveling with others in the history books," said Jim. "In fact, there are many instances of several people helping the Recorder."

Cal knew he was outnumbered. "I think we could use a cook," he mumbled and drifted off to begin breaking camp. He had much to think about.

Cathy quickly proved her worth as the travelers made their way south to the city of Darson. She gladly took her watch and helped break camp daily. She kept her word at preparing the meals as both Jim and Cal were awful at meal preparation. Both men tried to help with meals and proved that anything either of them cooked was utterly inedible. It was rapidly a joke amongst the three that Jim volunteering to cook was considered a threat to their health. In truth, Cal may have been worse.

In the wilds of the land south of Herrick, the three travelers followed the much-used road to Darson. The route followed a small stream up from the lake to a narrow, rocky pass. While not very high, the pass was very noticeable, and the views from the summit were very enlightening. To the east, one could see the seemingly endless desert of central Darson. This desert was not easy to cross, and few did so willingly. To the west, the great Whiterock River flowed, and beyond the river, the heavily forested land of the

Dwarves. Straight ahead to the south was the narrow canyon of the small stream commonly called Borman Creek.

Borman Creek picked up just past the pass formed by several small areas containing natural springs. Several of the springs were hot springs, and several natural baths had been formed out of Human-built small dams. The three travelers took full advantage of this area, and Cathy was able to get enough privacy to bathe thoroughly, and thus, she could finally wash her bad adventure into the past. Beyond the springs, the creek flowed into a narrow canyon. This area was always an adventure for travelers, and Darson authorities keep several active, armed patrols to maintain safety through this area. Going around the small canyon was difficult as the land on both sides was rugged, broken land, containing recent lava flows with jagged edges and unbelievably difficult terrain.

Beyond the several miles of canyon, Borman Creek opened out into the plains and farmlands north of the city of Darson. The three were well received through this land as the word of the destruction of the thieves spread in advance of them. Those robbers had terrorized this area, and the Protector and Recorder were treated as heroes.

Soon enough, the three travelers entered the busy port city of Darson City. For the first time, they came into contact with the Republic of the Mounties.

Cathy had never been to such a large town and was very insecure about the noise, dirt, and generally overcrowded city life. Cal had been there before but did not like the busy city very much. It fell to the more experienced traveler, Jim, to lead the group through the city. He knew where to find safe, honest stables for the pack animals, clean lodging, and good food during their stay in Darson. Any Human who had to deal with the Mounty authorities usually found frustration in getting travel papers, and Jim was no exception. He filled out forms explaining who they were and where they were going. The bored Mounty authorities filled out the paperwork and generally scoffed at the titles of Protector and Recorder. The fact that Cathy and Cal were from the Williams family caused some stirring of the bureaucracy, which was the main reason the approval came through in only three days.

During their stay in Darson, Cal and Cathy went to the house that their father kept in Darson. The king would often travel there to meet with the Human leaders, and he had a very respectable residence maintained by a few of his employees. The employees were stunned to see two of their king's children visit them. They offered to take care of the prince and princess as per their status, but both Cathy and Calvin turned them down. The two of them both wrote long notes to their parents, explaining all that had happened. The employees at the residence were stunned and saddened by the deaths of so many of His Majesty's troops, and a runner left immediately with the notes and the story.

With travel papers in hand, Cathy and the two men stocked up on supplies and started their journey to North Landsend but unfortunately their Mounty issued papers were making them go to the city of Litteville first. The well-traveled roads of the Republic made for easy travels south on the Liege Road to the Litte River and then west to the vast Mounty city of Litteville. In Litteville, even Cal was uncomfortable with the size of this city. Cathy was amazed and even somewhat scared at the number of people and buildings in such a small area. Both recovered quickly, but it was Jim who had the experience to get the proper paperwork so they could move on. However, the titles he gave to the authorities provoked no response, and the Williams name meant little here. It looked like a several-week delay was probable in this very large Mounty city with thousands and thousands of Elven slaves.

Cathy found the Elves very intriguing. She had never seen any of enslaved race and quickly realized that the people she saw were not aware of themselves. Most visitors realized this quickly but did nothing about it. Cathy could not do that. She spent much of her time during the lengthening spring days walking the wide streets of the city. She constantly tried to talk with the Elves as they went about their duties. She found them unfailingly polite and impossible to hold in a conversation. They were extremely preoccupied with their assigned tasks. Cathy found this disturbing and tried to talk to Jim and Cal about them.

"They look so sad and downtrodden," stated Cathy to the two men over dinner. "I want to find out about them and what they would like to do. They have no ambition besides what they are told to do by the Mounties, and that seems so sad to me."

"Cathy, do not speak of that," hissed her angry brother. "We are guests in this country, and we need to respect their society."

Jim took a different route in this discussion. "We just need to get our papers and move on. Cathy, the Elves have been this way for many years, and who is to say if they want to change? Leave them alone, and we can get on the road soon enough."

Cathy left the discussion very distraught but decided that her brother and his friend knew best. She stewed for two more days before the course of their journey took a vastly different turn, and the Elves were soon not a worry for her anymore.

Jari Elmflock had followed the three travelers until they had reached Darson City. He had observed them from a careful distance and had caught glimpses of a few bears that were not natural also following them. Jari wished that he could go with them. He sadly turned back after they had reached the safety of the city and headed north to his adopted home in Herrick. He was over halfway back when he decided to look in on her. He had not seen her for a few years, and although he wished to be with her, he could not.

He entered the monastery through a side entrance. The doorkeeper recognized him and suppressed her surprise at the visitor. The female wing of the monastery had a central receiving area, and this was where Jari was directed. He had lived here for a while and was very comfortable with the customs of the Monks.

She arrived, wearing her robe pulled over her head. Jari could not see any of her face as she always looked at the floor, but his memory of her filled his mind. He had no trouble seeing her that way. They talked to each other, but no words were spoken aloud. They could hear each other's thoughts.

You still wish to go out, don't you? she asked.

Yes, I feel trapped by these circumstances, and I wish to try something—anything.

I know. We have long suffered. Soon, our time will come again. Things are changing faster now, and the Monks have had to move. I will allow you some minor duties now. She outlined a small part for Jari, and he was thrilled.

Chapter 14

ACKNOWLEDGMENTS

Jim, Cal, and Cathy dined together every day at the small inn where they were staying. They were in the large city of Litteville. The Mounty proprietor was a round-faced, portly man who served the Humans and all his guests with a bustling style that wore out his guests. He was full of great cheer, and he entertained all his guests with many bad jokes. He constantly told, and then laughed at, his own jokes with a hearty, high-pitched laugh. His dour wife mainly stayed in the back, preparing meals. She was very good, and the fare was much better than the three travelers expected. The two rooms they had were sufficient and comfortable. Cathy's room was very small, but it gave her some much-needed time alone to regain confidence in herself and obtain some much-needed rest from all she had gone through. Cal and Jim had a two-bed room with a working desk. They spent much of their spare time planning the next portion of their journey and studying maps of Western Wyndliege that Cal had brought from the monastery. They never knew where they would wind up, so they studied their maps very carefully.

On the tenth day of their arrival in Litteville, papers were delivered to the travelers. The contents could not have surprised them more.

Jim opened the note, read it, and then passed it to Cal. Cal read it carefully and then set it down. Without saying a word, Cal stepped out of the room and went to get Cathy from her room. The young woman followed her brother into the men's room. Jim had picked up the note, and he read it aloud to Cathy as Cal pulled the door closed.

"Arthur James Herrick, Calvin Percy Williams, and Cathy Rose Williams are commanded to meet before His Most Magnificent Magi Vonn. Meeting to be held at the Magi conference room in the Presidential Palace, Haleport, Republic of the Mounties at noon tomorrow," read Jim.

All three were aware of whom the Magi was and how important he was to the government of the Republic. Cathy spoke her greatest fear. "I hope that my talking to the Elves has not got us into trouble."

Her brother quickly replied, "No, Cathy, the Magi would not summon us if that were the problem. He would just have us arrested and tried in the very organized Mounty system. I believe he may have heard our titles and wants information."

"That," commented Jim, "is the one thing he will not get from us."

The three travelers awoke early. After a quick breakfast, they made their way through Litteville to the great bridge that connected the large city of Litteville on the north shore of the Smelter River to the unbelievably huge city of Haleport on the south bank. Both cities were built on the lands that made up the mouth of the great river as it flowed into Bane Bay. The great river flowed into many channels, and the two cities seemed to have developed every habitable piece of land in the delta of the river. To add to the number of waterways, the Litte River flowed south through Litteville into the Smelter less than two miles from the bay. Both cities had been well laid out, and the two cities had traded extensively since the Golden Era. Many felt the Golden Era had started when the Great Bridge was completed, connecting the north and the south of Western Wyndliege.

Crossing the bridge was an experience for all three as even Jim had never been to Haleport. The Great Bridge was a giant stone structure over a mile long and wide enough for about thirty people to walk side by side. It crossed the river by jumping from island to island. Five main islands and two very small, man-made islands created the supports for each arc of the bridge. The bridge was not straight as it had different angles to land on the available islands, but it cleared the river and was great for trade between the cities as the mouth of the Smelter was difficult to navigate. The silt that flowed down the river and the tides from the bay made for many problems to ship goods by water.

The three were amazed at the many carts, hansoms, and carriages hauled back and forth across the massive bridge. Commerce of all kinds was moving in all directions, and the Mounty military was scurrying in all directions on who knows what errands. Elves, heads down, were going mindlessly about their assigned duties. The whole was a picture of unorganized confusion. Loud noises, yelling, and cursing were the directives of most people. The three Humans were just trying not to get run over as they crossed the bridges.

The huge city of Haleport was immaculate and orderly. The streets were broad and well organized. The flat lands at the mouth of the river and the bay quickly rose into small hills. The roads went straight up and down these hills, making for beautiful vistas in many directions at the top of each hill. Houses and buildings were built into the sides of the hills and were painted a variety of bright colors. The effect was dazzling.

The centerpiece of the city was the Presidential Palace. The palace was the largest building any of them had ever seen, and they were all intimidated that they were going inside that monstrosity.

Vonn had arranged for the meeting to be in his conference room on the third floor of the Hillcenter. It was a magnificent room that would help to impress his visitors. He knew that he probably would not get the information he wanted as he expected that the travelers did not know the answers. He and Jules had read about the Recorder and the Protector. He was familiar with who they were and where they came from. He had heard about them when they were in Darson City, and he had ordered them to be sped on through to Litteville. His staff of apprentice Magicians kept a careful eye on anything unusual in the travel requests in the Republic. Fortunately, one of his staff had questioned the titles, Recorder and Protector, and mentioned it to Jules.

Vonn watched the three enter his conference room, and he knew the room had its effect on the nervous travelers. He observed the large man, obviously the Protector, and noted the Wyndswept blood in him. The hooded Monk was the Recorder. He seemed to be very within himself despite the nervousness. Vonn expected him to be very tight-lipped. The surprise to Vonn was the young lady. She was a pretty girl, very blond, and was obviously of a well raised and educated upbringing. She was also noticeably very intimidated by these surroundings. Her bearing was not that of a princess but that of a scared little girl. Vonn found himself wondering if she was pretending to be less than she was, or was she really that sheltered.

Vonn's staff had provided the Magi with a complete dossier on each, and he had read and committed to memory every factoid of their background. He knew the Monk was the brother of the girl, and they were both raised very well by their parents, who happened to be the only capable Human king and queen. The Protector was a bit more of a mystery, but that was true of most of the Herricks.

Jules, beside him at the twenty-foot-long table that stood raised about five feet above the floor level, had also studied the dossiers, and he was comforted by her presence. The three travelers had to look up to see the Magi and his assistant. Behind the Magi was the beautiful tower with the statue of the Mounty. The effect was terrific.

Jules opened the meeting by introducing the three guests, herself, and a lengthy introduction of Vonn stating his accomplishments and titles.

After the introductions, Vonn sat quietly and studied the three intently. Finally, he spoke. "Welcome to Haleport and the

Presidential Palace, Recorder."

"Thank you, Magi," replied Cal. "We are honored to be in your presence."

Cal knew enough from his studies to know the proper responses in this situation. Jim most certainly did not.

"Welcome to you also, Protector, and you too, Princess Cathy. We are honored to have you visit our city on your journeys," stated Vonn. "My assistant, Jules, and I are very aware of who you are and what your journey entails. We assure you that we will do everything in our power to help you accomplish what it is you have been sent out to do. The Republic only asks that, in return for assistance, you keep us informed about where you go and what you are looking for."

This sounded very reasonable to Cathy, and she began to relax a bit. However, what her brother said next amazed her and scared her more than just a little.

"Honored Magi," replied Cal, "we are pleased to hear that you and the Republic will assist us in our endeavors. However, if you know who we are and what we are to do, then you must also know that we will never inform anyone of our destinations or assignments."

The Magi and Jules had expected just such an answer but hearing it was a shock, and it was confirmation that these really were the Protector and the Recorder. They both faked great offense at the statement from Cal. Generally, anybody else in front of this powerful man would have immediately told them everything they knew. Vonn knew he could have his visitors put to death for not answering his questions, and from the response of the young lady, Cathy, he could tell that she did not know anything about the Recorder and Protector.

Cathy was never so scared in her life. Her brother had just told the second most powerful person in the world that he would not answer his questions. Had he lost his mind?

The Magi then spoke in a raised voice. "Do you know that I could put you to death for such an insolent answer?"

"Yes," replied Cal quietly, "but you will not. The sacred duties of Recorder and Protector will allow us to walk out of here with your support and acknowledgment of who we are. You know, or you should know, that we know so little that our information would do you no good. You also know that delaying us will not stop history from happening. Our coming is the harbinger of change, and you want to know as much as you can so you can bend the change to your purposes. Sorry, Magi, but we just record the events that will happen, and any attempt to change or alter the events will not work. Additionally, if you have really studied our history, and I expect you have, you would know that I receive my information through prayer, and what I could tell you at any one time would not help you. The information comes as it comes."

Vonn knew the quiet Monk was right. He was defeated in his attempt to gather any information from these two. He tried a different tactic.

"You will be followed everywhere you go in the Republic. I will personally track your every step," yelled the infuriated Magi.

"OK," was the simple reply from Cal.

Jules chimed in. "Recorder, you will not be given the papers you need. We will hold you up every step of the way. You will be frustrated at the sluggishness at which Mounty bureaucracy can move. With a little information, Vonn will make your papers ready at once at every stop along the way. No delays."

Jim had been very quiet just listening to this exchange. He knew the rules of the Recorder and Protector as well as Cal; he was just not comfortable in this environment. Cal was very comfortable. His father was a king. A politician's training had been given to all the Williamses, and a Recorder's training had added to that for the intelligent Cal.

Cal spoke. "Magi Vonn, Assistant Jules, let me be perfectly clear. Our roles as Recorder and Protector have bound us to the rules of what we are. Jim and I have, for several years, been trained for this journey. Many of my fellow Monks and many of Jim's relatives train for a decade or more for the honor to be Recorder and Protector.

Our superiors chose us for many reasons, not the least of which is to maintain the rules. While we are very new to our roles, we are both comfortable that you will assist us as so many have done in the past. We do not change anything. We do not affect anything. We really don't do anything but record history as it happens in front of us. I remind you, Magi, never have we failed."

Vonn had read everything he could and had consulted with Lojzue La Yellow about the Recorder and the Protector. He knew that further attempts to delay the two in front of him were useless. Lojzue had very clearly told Vonn that they would not know anything useful and would not tell him if they did know. He told Vonn to get to know them and then let them go. If what they were doing involved Vonn, they would find him. Vonn knew this meeting would come to a most unsatisfactory conclusion as far as he was concerned. That had never happened to him before in this great hall.

Vonn spoke again, but this time very calmly. "You have passed the test. I acknowledge that I believe you are a pious Monk of the Stone Abbey chosen to be Recorder and that you are a shape-changer of the family Herrick chosen to be Protector. I will also pass the test of a government representative who will not delay you on your destiny. Good luck to the Recorder and Protector, as I pledge not to interfere without cause."

The three travelers quickly made their way out of Hillcenter and, after sightseeing in Haleport, made their way back to the small inn in Litteville. It was no surprise that a large package was waiting for them with travel papers to North Landsend.

Vonn and Jules talked for a long time in the private sitting room near their lodgings. Vonn opened up to Jules about his belief that the magic of the land was changing.

"The land will be less responsive to our efforts to call up magic," stated Vonn. "The time of using the magic of the land is fading very slowly, and it is failing. We must master other types of magic, and that is why I have been sending you to the library so often recently. I feel that the strange magical wave I felt recently came now because of this change. I feel that the wise Monks have sent out a Recorder at this time because of this."

"What do we do?" asked Jules.

"We attempt to learn," replied Vonn.

As he said this, they were interrupted.

President Taver Wrigger finished his meetings for the day and went to find Vonn. He wanted an update on the three travelers from the north. He found Vonn and Jules in Vonn's sitting room, and he barged in as only a president could do.

"Ah, Vonn, could I have a word with you?"

"Yes, certainly, Mr. President. Jules was just leaving."

"She can stay. I want both of your opinions on these supposed Recorder and Protector peoples." The always present temper of the president was rising.

Vonn started, "I firmly believe they are who they say they are. They would risk death not to tell me anything."

"They *should* be put to death," exclaimed the excitable leader.

"What good would that do? They would die, and we would still have no answers about their purpose," replied Vonn.

"I know, but why can't they at least tell us something? It ticks me off that they are so tight-lipped. You told me they know very little right now and that the Monk will pray on what to do next. How could that possibly work?"

"I do not know, Mr. President. It is the way of the Recorder and Protector. Do we want to follow them?" asked Jules.

"Yes. I want a squad to travel with them and keep them out of trouble. Vonn, what the hell is going on? Tell me now!"

Vonn paused for just a minute. That was too long for the temperamental president.

"I demand to know what it is that you are hiding from me, Vonn. I have sensed it since our public meeting on the failings of the magic. We are all too scared to admit that we are afraid of what might come next. We are all sticking our heads in the ground because we do not want any bad news. I am president of this great country, and I do not plan to see it fall without a fight."

The rant by President Wrigger gave Vonn time to think. Vonn signaled for Jules to leave, and they waited while the able assistant gathered her things and left.

Vonn began, "Taver, we are now living in a time of change. What that means, I don't know. Our magic is fading. We must acknowledge that. We can bury our heads in the ground as you so aptly put it, or we can fight it. I am choosing to fight. There are other magics that are different from our magic. I am attempting to learn about them. It may take several generations for the magic to fade so that any but the strongest notice it, but things are happening that lead me to believe that we may live to see this change."

"Do you think these three are part of the change?" asked the president.

"Yes. The Stone Abby Monks sending out a Recorder, our recent magical failures against the Dwarves, and the recent strange magical wave . . . It all adds up to things happening. In fact, I think more is happening that we don't know about. We must be ready for anything and everything," replied Vonn.

"What about the offensive we are planning against the Dwarves? I remember your support is what led us to this."

"Don't change any plans right now. This will take a few years to sort itself out. We are best served by remaining strong, and that can be achieved with a great victory over the Dwarves."

"One more question, Vonn. You previously said the Elves would not change during our lifetime. Do you think their coming now may have something to do with the Elves?" President Wrigger visibly shivered as he asked this question.

"I don't know, Taver. It is the question that haunts me night and day," said Vonn. "We would be defenseless against them if they came out of the spell rapidly and completely. They have multiplied to huge numbers, and so many are still alive who would remember from before the spell. If the spell breaks, we would have them leaderless for a while, but they would eventually go to the Dwarves for help. The greedy Dwarves, for a price, would probably help orga-nize and arm them. Also, I don't know how well the Republic would function without our slaves doing the work. It is possible that we might be better off without having to support all their mouths to feed. The biggest problem could be the retribution on us from the newly freed Elves."

The president and the Magi sat in silence for a few minutes, thinking about what could happen to them and their country should the magic fail completely. Neither man knew any life other than the one they had, and such drastic changes were beyond their comprehension. Finally, the president stood up and, with an angry gesture toward the Magi, said, "Make sure it doesn't happen, Magi, or your head will be the next for chopper's blade." With that, the angry, scared President Traver Wrigger stormed out of the Magi's rooms. He had a war with the Dwarves to prepare for!

Chapter 15

THE BLACK PINE TREE

Greentea Gravelt woke with a start. Yesterday had seen her people defeat the evil army that had invaded the Dwarven land of Ngarzzorr. Her uncle, the Wizard Knolt, had defeated the evil Balrog that was leading the Orcs, Goblins, and other evil creatures. The army had rapidly finished off the rest. Now, it was early morning, and the Dwarven camp was unusually active. Her dreams had been disturbing. She was wandering through strange lands in her dreams, and none of the places she went to was a home for her. It had made her sleep restless, and it was making her very groggy this morning. She was amazed at the rustle and bustle of busy Dwarves clearly preparing for something. She was going through her morning routine when Hludowig came by her small tent and told her what was going on.

"Good morning, young Druid," stated the cleric. "Today, we break camp. The battle of Devil's Valley has ended. The king is headed to visit his sons on the front lines near Beardly. All the camp will go with him except for you and Knolt. You and he will travel alone to the tree that talked to you."

At this news, Greentea felt the fear of being all alone in the wilds of Ngarzzorr, with only the old Wizard with the colored beard for protection. This sounded very frightening to her, and she mentioned this to Hludowig.

With a friendly smile and small laugh, the cleric continued.

"With Knolt, you will be protected better than this entire army protecting our king." With that, he hurried away.

Greentea was soon joined by two of her relatives that Knolt had sent to help her prepare for the journey to the Black Pine tree that had "spoken" to Greentea. Her stuff was packed in no time, and she grabbed some breakfast from the nearest mess tent. She had no sooner finished her last bite when she heard Knolt across the large tent set up for food preparation.

"Youngster, where are you?" yelled the now-red-bearded Dwarf. "We must be on our way. Time's a-wastin', and I want to talk to that darn tree today. There you are. Are you ready? Can you find that same tree? Can we make it in one day's hike?" The questions came so fast, Greentea had no idea which to answer first.

"I am ready when you are," tried Greentea in answer. It seemed to work.

"Great, glad to hear it. Let's hit the road before this huge army trips over itself trying to get moving," stated the old Dwarf very loudly.

Several of the regular army Dwarves mumbled something about respecting the power of the army, but Knolt paid them no mind. He was excited to be on another adventure, and he always attacked an adventure with great energy.

Knolt and Greentea headed out early on a perfect spring morning and were well on the way back to the tree before the advance scouts even got away from the main group of the king's army. Knolt was very truthful in how long it took the large group to get moving.

The trip with Knolt was an ongoing learning experience for Greentea. He put her through several exercises to teach her more about her true calling. She was exhausted before lunch at the constant use of her Druid magic as they traveled. The Wizard drove her unmercifully in her magic exercises. She was also trying to maintain a sense of where they were going as she tried to lead

Knolt to the right tree.

Knolt was in a very talkative mood, and he entertained Greentea about stories of the old Druid Dwarves and their assistance to the Elves. In her exhausted state, listening to his stories was a welcome respite from Druid magic. He finished his story, and she was looking around for the proper direction to go when Knolt asked her if she could use her magic to find the path to the tree. She looked up with a puzzled look, and Knolt laughed at her expense.

"Young Druid," began Knolt, "you stated that the tree attempted to speak with you and left you a message in your head. That was a powerful magic that was used to impart that message. Reach out with your magic and feel the source of that power. You may be able to feel it still."

Greentea stopped and looked around. She then reached out her magical ability like she did when finding the path up the mountain. Her practice was paying off as she immediately felt the power of the magic that the tree had used to impart the message. She could also feel other, older magic uses and even a few that she had used when she came through here a few days before. She also could feel some magic being used by Knolt.

Feeling the magic used by the ancient Wizard was a powerful experience for the young Druid. His magic was many times more powerful than any she thought could exist. As she found his magic, he put his blocks back up, and she was tossed aside from his thoughts.

"How did you do that?" exclaimed Greentea. "I could feel your magic for a moment, and then you hide it from me."

Knolt chuckled a bit and then said, "That is to remind you of how far you still have to go. It is a simple spell to hide your flow of magic, but it takes great power to maintain that spell when you are working with others. You will develop that skill soon enough, but for now, I will not teach you that skill. Did you find the tree?"

"Yes, I did find it, but I also read that you found it, and we have been following the correct path all along."

"That is correct as I located the tree last night and calculated that with an early start, we could reach there today. That is why I am pushing us to get there."

By skipping a dinner break, the two Dwarves soon stood in front of the ancient Black Pine tree that had attempted to communicate to Greentea just a few days earlier. Knolt walked all around the tree several times, and Greentea could feel powerful magic working between Knolt and the tree. Suddenly, Knolt broke off the powerful communication and quickly asked Greentea to set up camp and get dinner ready. With that command, Knolt walked up to the tree and put both arms wide around the tree as if to hug it. As soon as he got as much of his body touching the tree as he possibly could, he melted into the tree and was gone from Greentea's vision.

Greentea was utterly shocked! Knolt was gone. She had no idea what to do, so she decided to follow Knolt's last command. She set up their things in a small clearing near the big tree. There was no magic coming from the tree that Greentea could feel. She tried a small Druid spell of listening to birds and animals, and even that was very weak. The magic just seemed very weak since Knolt had entered the tree. Greentea was very surprised and a bit frightened.

Greentea was preparing a meal as Knolt had instructed when she felt the rush of magic come through the small clearing, and moaning came from the tree as Knolt appeared much the same as he left. He fell from the tree as if pushed away. Greentea rushed over to him and found the old Dwarf lying beside the tree, snoring.

Knolt slept through the rapidly approaching night and well into the next day. Greentea kept a vigil over him, wondering if he would reawaken. She did not sleep much and ate even less through the night. Finally, around noon the next day, Knolt woke with a start.

"Did you get dinner fixed" was the first thing Knolt asked, "like I told you to?"

"Yes, but that was yesterday. You slept all night and much of today."

"Oh, well, I am hungry. What do you have?" stated the grumpy Wizard with a very red beard.

Greentea found some dried meats and started to prepare another meal. While Knolt munched on the meat, Greentea worked on making a soup out of some vegetables and rabbit meat that they had brought along. Soon, they had both eaten, and Greentea wanted some answers from Knolt.

Greentea asked the question that was really bugging her. "Did you find out an answer to my message, 'he comes'?"

Knolt answered slowly. "It is not as simple as finding an answer. The message is a part of a command, and you are the intended recipient of that message. I expect if you could have done what I just did, you would have received a lot more information. But you are not ready for that yet, so the voice speaking through the tree has given me a message that I must keep secret from you. As it states, 'he comes,' and the 'he' is probably the person who caused the wave of magic that set off the communication through the tree. I have been given enough instructions and have deduced enough on my own to start this adventure."

Knolt grabbed Greentea by both arms and looked deeply into her eyes. "You are the center of much that will happen, and you must continue to improve your magic abilities. You must be strong! You are not destined to live your life in the safe caves of Whiterock, and you may wander the world for many years to find the place you belong. But there is a place out there where you belong. I will lead you for some of that time, but our paths may part before you find what you want and need."

These words hammered into Greentea. She knew the caves of Whiterock were not for her, and hearing that there was a place for her was wonderful. Her doubts that there was a place for her was replaced by the optimism of youth. All she had to do was find her place in the world. She had no idea of the great pain and change in her world before that would happen!

Knolt and Greentea stayed by the Black Pine tree the rest of that evening and made plans for the adventure that Knolt insisted they undertake alone. Knolt pointed out that they needed to hurry, and traveling with a large party was very slow. Also, Knolt wanted to take a different route than he expected Hjalmarr to take. Knolt planned to go straight south to the Smith Tunnels, through the tunnels, then turn west along the Mowkers River and maybe catch a log raft down the river to Rocky Point. The king would go through the foothills to near Beardly. There, the Dwarves maintained a recently created Dwarven stronghold that was the southernmost outpost of the land of Ngarzzorr.

Knolt spent much of that night and much of the next few days showing Greentea how to protect herself in the wilds of Wyndliege. He taught her how to scan the area for threats magically and use Druid magic to warn her of any invaders, human or animal, that might come too close to her and compromise her safety. He showed her how to provide a fire while protecting the plants that were so precious to her calling and how she could survive using her magic to provide food and water in emergencies. He even showed her how, at night, he could construct a clear dome over the two of them so they could sleep every night without fear. Greentea found this dome construct to still be far above her abilities. She did not know that only Knolt, amongst Wizards in Western Wyndliege, could actually make a protective dome large enough and strong enough to protect overnight.

Greentea began to feel very close to the old Dwarf with the multicolor beard. His grumpy demeanor began to be somewhat humorous to her. She found him wonderfully endearing when he was trying so hard to be patient with her when she was slow in learning something. She found herself listening much more closely to his advice and really trying to make his beard turn a happy color, like silver or gold.

The days of slowly traveling south through Ngarzzorr headed for the Smith Tunnels were some of the best days of Greentea's life. She would wake early and fix the old Wizard a good breakfast. She had learned that he loved to eat delicious meals. Then she would break camp and load the two packhorses they had taken from the King's Guard. She would listen carefully to what Knolt wanted her to work on magically, and then she would work all day on refining magical skills. Knolt was mostly happy with her progress, but he would often seem to be upset with things. Occasionally, Greentea caught a look of concern on Knolt's face. She would ask what was wrong, but the only answer he would give was that he wished they had more time.

After a week of steady but unhurried travel, a line of small mountains appeared directly in front of the two travelers. From Knolt's planning, Greentea knew that this was the mountain range that divided Ngarzzorr from the land of the Mounties. While not tremendously high in elevation, this mountain range was very steep and challenging to go over. One could go to the east and go around the range near the confluence of the Ngarzzorr River and the Mowkers River, but this was many miles out of the way. Another route was the one the King's Guard had taken, and that was through the tunnels near Beardly. Knolt had chosen not to go that way for fear of delay in traveling with Hjalmarr.

The third way, the way Knolt had chosen, was through the Smith Tunnels. The tunnels had been carved through the mountains eons ago by peoples no longer remembered. The tunnels had a reputation of being a confusing labyrinth. It was rumored in Whiterock that no one could go through those tunnels. All Dwarves had a sense of where they were when underground. Most Dwarves spent all their lives deep in the tunnels and caves of their home, and to get lost or even confused was very rare. For any Dwarf to be uncomfortable or confused underground was a testament to how rare the Smith Tunnels were. For some reason, maybe ancient magic, even a Dwarf could not find their way through them. Because of the strategic importance to Ngarzzorr, many had died trying to mark the way so others could follow. Fortunately for Greentea, she had never heard any Dwarf discuss this subject, so she had no fear of what lay ahead. She was just going where Knolt led her.

As the small mountain range grew ever closer, Knolt pushed Greentea ever harder in learning about the power and the limits of her magic. She improved daily, but Knolt was not to be satisfied. He knew that he needed years to train the young Druid properly, and he probably only had a few months at best. Knolt was very concerned about how to get to where he knew they must go. He even wondered what adventures would delay them trying to get there. He had little concerns about passing through the Smith Tunnels. After all, he held the key!

Chapter 16

HUCKENDUBLERS

The trail that Knolt and Greentea were on was not much more than an animal track. At this point, neither of them traveled as one would expect, and the trail was mostly unnecessary. Greentea moved around and through bushes and trees, bending her magic to fit whatever plant or tree was there. She was seldom visible to the human eye. Knolt used all sorts of magical devices to remain hidden from all in their path. Greentea would even use some of her magic to keep the two pack animals in tow.

Knolt would often use magic tricks to speed them along or slow them up, requiring Greentea to find ways to use her magic to keep up, keep the animals moving, and keep track of the crafty old Dwarf. It was a game they constantly played as Knolt tried to fool his young trainee magically. Much to his pleasure, it was getting more difficult.

The mountains were looming ever closer when a spring storm came over the mountaintop from the southwest and hit Ngarzzorr. Rain fell in buckets as the Dwarves played their magic games, both getting wet, then magically, finding ways to avoid the rain and drying out. Greentea found she could magically move from tree trunk to tree trunk using the pine canopy as shelter. Knolt simply had the rain miss him, or occasionally, he would create a magic bubble around his upper body. Both wore out earlier in the day than usual, and they set up camp for the tenth night since leaving the king's host.

Knolt was in a talkative mood, and he told Greentea that he felt by tomorrow, they would enter the tunnels. She was relieved to hear that as the rain made necessary a lot of tiring magic usage. Greentea found an opportunity to ask a question that had been bothering her.

Knolt was grumpily talking about the weather, the king, the Mounties, magic use, and anything else he could grump about when he brought up the Mounty Magicians.

Greentea took the opportunity. "Knolt," she asked very quietly, "what makes the Mounty Magicians so powerful?"

The old Dwarf stopped his rambling and glared at the youngster. "Who told you that?" he snapped, his beard shading toward an angry red.

"It is commonly talked about by all the clerics. I got tired of hearing about how we needed to work harder to be as good as the Mounties."

"The fools!!" yelled Knolt, his beard going redder than Greentea had ever seen it. "They are teaching that to all the young clerics?"

Greentea could only manage a slight nod. The spring rain had stopped, and a quiet settled around the nice, warm campfire they had burning. Knolt, with a wave of his hand, removed his magical shield over their camp.

He glared at the young Druid Dwarf for a few seconds and then fell into silence. Greentea could see that he was steaming mad but had no idea why.

After a few minutes that seemed like forever to Greentea, Knolt continued. "Young Greentea, my dear relative, the best hope for our people in many, many years. Please, forgive me for yelling. This is shocking to me. If ever I get my hands on those fools or that so-called king of ours, I will shake some sense into their foolish heads. This may be the biggest mistake our people are making. If you never believe anything else I say, please, remember that the Mounty Magicians are no more powerful than any Dwarf cleric, Human shaman, Witch or Wizard, or Elfin artist or Wizard."

"But . . ." started Greentea before his look quieted her.

Knolt continued. "All those who work magic use one of three types. Air magic is the oldest and most advanced. It required the use of certain words in the ancient language. Very few can use this magic anymore. I believe that I may be the only person of any race in Western Wyndliege who can use air magic, and I am very, very limited in what I can do.

"The second magic is fire magic. Many can use it in various ways, but few have much control over it. For example, a Human shaman in Darson can somewhat use fire to predict a paying customer's future. The fire can give hints to those that can use it. Sometimes, it is just a carnival game with no magic in use. I have at my disposal a more advanced use of fire. I and certain others can use it to travel to other planes of existence to meet and discuss things in powerful environments. Fire is often a method I use to communicate with others I do not understand. I know this sounds complicated, but I am not always sure who or what is communicating with me. I never know if it is the truth or not, but it always seems to wind up being truthful, but not in the way I first understand the communication. Sometimes, I am given information through the fire, much the same as the Black Pine tree was the method used to reach you after the touch to the magic.

"The third magic is land magic. It was said during the Golden Era that only Western Wyndliege has land magic. The magic of the land is what all the clerics, the Magicians, and the Wizards use. Some in all races use it better than others. But, and most importantly, no one race uses magic better than another race. Therefore, the Mounties use the same magic as our foolish clerics. They are not stronger or better than us. They just are in a better place to use it. The magic seems strongest around the Bane Bay, and as you get further away, the land magic weakens. The Mounties' great advantage was the healing magic. That is elementary magic, and for some reason, it works best for the Mounties. Dwarves can cast an identical spell on Mounties and achieve the same results. This I know for a fact as I have done it. But it does not work to heal the Dwarves or

Elves and is limited on Humans." Knolt ended this long story with great sadness on his face.

Greentea sat quietly for a long time, absorbing what Knolt had said. When she spoke, what she said surprised both of them. "My magic comes from all three. Mostly, I am using the land, but the others are there. I have felt them. That is what makes Druid magic so powerful!"

Knolt nodded. "Your insight serves you well. Go on. I want to hear what you say on this."

"You are a Druid also, aren't you, Knolt?"

"Yes, Greentea, I am, but I am more."

Finally, it all clicked together for Greentea. "Knolt, you have all the magics! You could do what a Stone Elf could do. You could do what a Druid Dwarf could do, and you can be a Wizard, an Artist, a Magician, and a Cleric. Whatever else there is, you can be that!"

Knolt chuckled. "You are very close. I have the magic of all those, but I can only be Knolt. I cannot wholly be any of those, but I can pick and choose parts of any and have some use of what is chosen. I am, I think, unique. I spent many years as a youth trying everything and found this out. I then searched everywhere I could go to find something similar. Nothing came close. I am now very old, and I feel my time may be coming. This may be my last adventure as I feel death creeping into my old bones."

"You can't die, Uncle! You must spend some years training me and helping me find more Druids and some Stone Elves and whatever else I am here to do," exclaimed Greentea.

This startled Knolt. "Where did you get the idea that you must find other Druids and Stone Elves?"

"I . . . d . . . don't know," stuttered Greentea. "It just suddenly seemed like something I am supposed to do. Ever since I left Whiterock, I have looked for where I belong and what I am supposed to do. It just seemed like that is what I have been looking for . . . a purpose."

Now, it was Knolt's turn to pause and think. "You may be right; you might go on that search. I must say to you that the chances of success are slim, so you must not despair if it turns out differently than you plan."

Both Dwarves went to bed that night with many thoughts in their minds.

The following morning, Knolt talked only about getting to the tunnels and out of the miserable weather. Something about his abrupt manner made Greentea feel that the conversation of the night before was now off-limits. The rain had let up, but a cold front followed it, and the temperatures had turned sharply cooler. They broke camp early, and they both started the day just simply walking along the small path. This path turned sharply uphill, and they wound their way into the foothills of the mountains. The trail wound through a small valley and up over a small saddle in the foothills. As they cleared the saddle, they first heard the noise. It sounded like the death screams of a large animal being taken by a bear or large cat from a distance. Both Knolt and Greentea ignored it the first time, but the second, then the third time they heard the noise, it was unusual. They both began to use magic to cover their movements.

Around a sharp bend in the path, they came upon a very well developed road running north and south. This very much surprised Knolt. He had no knowledge of any developments near here. This was southern Ngarzzorr, and he thought it mostly undeveloped. Knolt quietly instructed Greentea to use magic to hide, and then they heard the strange noise again. This time, it sounded like men screaming, and then an odd pounding and scraping noise, followed by a tremendous banging occurred. The banging was accompanied by a shake that felt like a small earthquake.

The two Dwarves made the way toward the noises, using all their best magic hiding power. Finally, they reached a point alongside the road where they could look down into the small settlement. It was obviously an outside Dwarven town. Knolt looked on in amazement as about fifty Dwarves were dressed in full battle armor. The war exercises they were doing were unlike anything Knolt had ever seen.

Ten Dwarves would all put a very large piece of armor on their heads. This headdress was about twenty-five feet long. Ten head areas were spaced equally along the length of the headdress. Each Dwarf warrior would put his head into one of the ten head areas, and the headdress would rest on his or her shoulders, and clever straps wrapped under the arms to secure the strange head covering. The top of the headdress was the most amazing part. Swords and axes and blades of all sorts had been attached at various angles. The ten Dwarves would then lower their heads and, making the most awful screaming noises, charge the setup enemies. Scarecrows that were full-sized and shaped like an enemy had been set up and were taking a tremendous pounding.

The Dwarven warriors would charge through the enemy scarecrows and then smash headfirst into the side of the mountain. The collision with the mountain was incredible, and the Dwarves were stunned momentarily and then retreated to where they started. Then the next ten would take the place of the first and repeat the process. Knolt thought he had never seen anything so ridiculous.

Suddenly, Knolt looked to his side and realized that Greentea had dropped all magic and walked down the road toward the Dwarves. Knolt was in a panic, and he quickly put his magic over her. Greentea turned toward him and said, "It's okay. I know what this is, Knolt. These are the Huckendublers!"

Simpson Hucken was a smallish Dwarf that had come up with the idea of the strange headdress. The battles against the Mounties had been going poorly, and Simpson had an idea. He took the idea to his dear friend, Cynthis Dubler. Cynthis was one of the kingdom's best armor designers and a great blacksmith. Deep in the bowels of Whiterock, the two Dwarves designed and implemented their unusual idea. The headdress would go onto some of the fiercest, most reckless, and undoubtedly brave Dwarves in the kingdom. The idea was to train the chosen Dwarves until they, with no heed to their own welfare, would lower their heads and charge as one into the front lines of the enemy. The armor they would wear to protect themselves on their lower bodies was the best Cynthis could create. She worked her forge for several weeks till she had created the headdress and the heavy armor. King Hjalmarr and his sons, Ragnar and Ronjit, had loved the idea, and they sent General Wyot Stonehead to oversee the operation.

When the Dwarves had been chosen, the heavy training began. In Whiterock, the Dwarves had put up with many inconveniences over the years, but never had anything been more bothersome than the crazy training program of Simpson Hucken. General Stonehead was at first intrigued and, soon, a huge supporter and leader. The newly named Huckendublers would train night and day. The screams and crashes and banging of the routines drove all the other Dwarves to protest to their king. King Hjalmarr had decided to move the noisy group elsewhere and called General Stonehead into his chamber. Much to Hjalmarr's discomfort, the general showed up with all his troops in tow. The group had forsworn cleaning or bathing until they would go into battle. The overpowering stench of the group made Hjalmarr realize he must take action.

Hence, the now-famous Huckendublers, over three hundred strong, had been shipped across the kingdom to be closer to the battles per orders. The truth was, it was the furthest from Whiterock that the king could think of when the overpowering smell was in his chambers. General Stonehead achieved a new level of fame amongst the younger Dwarves itching to fight the Mounties. The general, Simpson, and Cynthis recruited enough able bodies to create five teams of Huckendublers.

The move across the kingdom had occurred over two years ago, and now, Greentea and Knolt were walking into the new town of Huckendubler. Simpson Hucken was watching General Stonehead put his five well trained teams of soldiers into training action. The smoothness of the attack and the incredible power of the ten well trained Huckendublers and their twenty battle aides, and thirty swordsmen and archers, was an amazing sight to the smallish Simpson. As Simpson saw the two Dwarves walking into town, his heart soared. He was awaiting the call to, at long last, go to battle, and he hoped the two Dwarves were coming with that news.

Knolt watched the crazy actions of the Huckendublers and their insane battle plan of simply lowering their heads to about waist high and charging recklessly ahead. The support group followed and flanked the ten leading the charge. The Dwarves flanking the ten in the headdress had the most dangerous jobs. The most obvious way to foil the crazy attacks was to attack the flanks and drop the end Dwarf in the headdress. Cynthis had thought of this and had created a solid steel side panel with handles to allow the Dwarf next to the last Dwarf in the headdress to help hold up the end of the heavy device. The muscles developed by the Dwarves in their two years of training were incredible. The Huckendublers were the strongest and best-trained fighting unit Knolt had ever seen. General Stonehead had his troops ready to go to war.

Greentea, while not knowing much about warfare, had excellent olfactory glands, and as she and Knolt approached the training soldiers, she almost passed out from the smell. She also noticed the smallish Dwarf off to the side and knew that this was the famous Simpson Hucken. Practically the entire city of Whiterock had come out to watch the strange group leave. Simpson had made a ridiculous speech that Greentea had heard many mock. The speech was that "his group was going off to change forever how Dwarves approached warfare." He pompously proclaimed that "the Huckendublers would be the greatest heroes of the kingdom and that they would win back Luul Almas for Clan Zopfarn." Ignoring those that mocked Simpson, the troops marched out of Whiterock, led by the impressive General Wyot Stonehead, with their heads held high, and none in Whiterock other than the king and his top military advisors ever heard from them again.

Knolt noticed the stare of Greentea in the direction of the small Dwarf and headed toward him. Knolt bowed at the waist in the traditional Dwarven greeting. Simpson returned the greeting. Simpson spoke first. "Do you bring orders from the king?" he asked excitedly.

Knolt was a bit taken aback by this question. His beard changed several colors as he gained his footing. Simpson Hucken was stunned by the realization that he was in front of a Dwarf of magic.

"What kind of a greeting is that?" barked the now-perturbed Knolt.

The fast-approaching general tried to get involved. "I am General Wyot Stonehead, leader of the Huckendubler unit of the Zopfarn army. Please, welcome to our small community of Huckendublers." He finished with a bow of greeting that only those of the military seem to make perfect.

"I am Knolt, and this is Greentea Gravelt of Whiterock. We are travelers passing through to the Smith Tunnels," announced the old Wizard Dwarf.

Perhaps no other words could have brought more silence to all of the Huckendublers. Living next to the entrance had made the soldiers fear the place. Hearing the proclamation by the old Dwarf stunned the group to silence. Knolt then added, "And all of you really stink!"

The whole group immediately started laughing.

The general took command of the situation, and after more introductions, barked out several orders and instructed Knolt, Greentea, and Simpson to join him in the command center.

The main group of Huckendublers returned to thier training, and the named Dwarves made their way to the largest of the three wooden buildings that had been constructed. The command center was a rectangular building with the main entrance facing the main road. The part of the building near the road was a meeting room with good maps of Wyndliege on the walls and a large table with about a dozen chairs around it. The military efficiency with which the general's men moved rapidly made the travelers very comfortable, and good food and drink were provided.

The disappointment shown by Simpson when he found out that Greentea and Knolt were not coming from the king to call them to battle made the preliminary small talk somewhat uncomfortable.

As all were relaxing, Knolt relayed to the general about their travels, and the general filled Knolt in about what they were and how it all started. He had just explained the pledge not to bathe and the king's sending of them here to train when in rushed the dirtiest Dwarf Greentea had ever seen.

Cynthis Dubler came to the meeting from her forge, where she and her assistants were always busy making the armor for the troops. The way Cynthis drove her and her team had allowed the Huckendublers to be incredibly well prepared. All that hard work by Cynthis and the pledge not to bathe until engagement in battle made for an unbelievable smell that not even the general could ignore.

"Throw open the door and all the windows," commanded the general as soon as Cynthis arrived. It really was terrible, and Knolt's beard was shining bright red in anger.

"You fools," shouted the diminutive Wizard Dwarf. "You do not bathe because of some ridiculous pledge made two years ago, or so, and you wait for a call to battle that the king has no intention of making. The battles rage less than five days' march to the south, around Beardly, and yet, here you sit. Get off your butts and march south, find some enemies, and put this experiment to the test. Then go take baths and rejoin the king's troops as proud members of the Zopfarn army!"

The tone of Knolt was immediately offensive to Simpson and Cynthis, and they both began to protest Knolt coming here and saying such things about them. They took it very personally. General Wyot Stonehead took the comments by Knolt in a different light. Greentea would never forget what happened next. The general stood and drew his long sword and held it out across the table, pointing at all four other Dwarves in the room. This silenced the feeble protests and complaints coming from Simpson and Cynthis. The look of fury on the general's face made all of them, except perhaps Knolt, fear for their lives.

The general pointed the sword directly to the throat of Simpson Hucken, and the general told him to shut up. He pointed the sword at Cynthis Dubler's throat and told her to shut up. He went by Greentea with a look that Greentea would never forget and then stopped with the sword pointed at Knolt's suddenly brilliant blue beard. The look the general had on his face would have caused a lesser man to run for his life. Knolt looked the general in the eye and began whistling an old Dwarven fighting song.

Dwarves had long sung or whistled songs of joy as they marched to battle. No Dwarf feared death from fighting, and whistling or sign-ing was a way of showing that this was the thing they most wanted to do. Go to battle! The general joined Knolt in whistling, hesitantly at first, and then with more gusto. The sword never moved as the two Dwarves, one an ancient Wizard who had seen many, many battles, and the other a younger general who had been preparing troops for a long time to go to battle, finished the familiar whistled tune. The four soldiers serving the five in the room had come in as they heard the whistling. Now, a silence settled over the room, and the tension was palpable.

Never taking his eyes off the eyes of Knolt, the general spoke. "Coming here and saying such things breaks every rule of common Dwarf decency, and I should run you through, but I hear the truth of what you speak. We will march to battle. We will go to glory on the fields of Beardly. Do what you will, Wizard Dwarf. You say you go to the Smith Tunnels, and in my eyes, you will only find death there. A shame that, as I would speak to our king about your treatment of us here and request that you be banished from our clan, should I ever lay eyes on you again. The king does not allow visitors in his kingdom to treat their host so rudely. Go, Knolt; go to your death in the tunnels!!"

As the general finished his speech, he rapidly sheathed his sword and began barking orders to his men in the room. Simpson and Cynthis rapidly walked out of the room, and the general and his men began running around, barking orders to break camp and preparing to leave. As they left, all could hear the loud, raucous laughter of Knolt as if he had just heard the funniest joke ever. Knolt laughed so hard that he could not catch his breath. Greentea was concerned about the sanity of the old Dwarf, who was her mentor and protector. All she could do was sit alone at the conference table and wait for what would come next.

About the time Knolt and General Stonehead were sitting down to have their contentious meeting, King Hjalmarr Zopfarn was sitting down with his two sons to discuss the battle situation near the town of Beardly. Beardly was a small but beautiful city that had existed for more years than any could remember. Ancient Humans had built Beardly, and the last monarchy had been the Beardly family, but that line had died out long ago. When the Mounties had conquered the Humans, the people of Beardly retreated into their town, and the Mounties had ignored them. Beardly survived because it was far enough to the north and had little strategic value to the Mounties. That changed as the Dwarves settled Ngarzzorr and looked for trading paths to the south. The Zopfarn Clan worked for years to build a road from Whiterock to the Dwarf tunnel connected to Beardly. Near Beardly, under the mountains, was a small Dwarf settlement that the Zopfarns maintained in natural and formed caves that faced the Mowkers River valley. It was a large cave and allowed the Dwarves to hide troop movements from the Mounties. The primary goal of the king and his sons was to open the lower Mowkers River valley to the trading post of Rocky Point. If this could be accomplished, then the Dwarves could trade with the Wyndswept, who were always docking trade ships at the small but usable port at Rocky Point.

As Beardly backed up to the towering mountains of Ngarzzorr, the plains to the south were fertile lands that had seen the battles between the Mounties and Dwarves over the last several decades. For a long time, the Mounties had kept the Dwarves locked against the mountains. Only four weeks prior, the previous battle had seen the Dwarves break out onto the plains all the way to the north bank of the Mowkers. The main routes to Rocky Point were open to the Dwarves for the first time in many centuries, and the Dwarves would desperately attempt to hold this new line.

This victory led to the public meeting with Vonn the Magi in front of the president and Congress of the Republic of the Mounties. Now, the Mounties were increasing troop strength to push the Dwarves back into their caves. This buildup had caused the king to come south after the adventure with Greentea Gravelt.

Hjalmarr and his warrior sons had sent out scouts who had reported back that the Mounties were preparing for a large return strike. This was expected, and the confirmation from the scouts led to planning by the Clan Zopfarn.

Ragnar Zopfarn, the oldest son of King Hjalmarr Zopfarn, was by all accounts the strongest Dwarf fighter currently alive, with the possible exception of his father. His full black beard had been at the forefront of every significant offensive push the Dwarves had made for many decades. His wounds had been many, but his skills at fighting had always kept the injuries minor. If Ragnar was the brawn of the Zopfarns, his brother, Ronjit, was the brains.

Only a few years separated the brothers in age, and for many decades, they had been organizing the troops of Dwarves that protected their peoples. Ronjit was always thinking of the master plan that only he seemed to know. He had opened trade for the Dwarves into the far northern town of Herrick and had designed and built the road to Beardly. The clever tunnel near Beardly was a masterpiece of defensive construction. The Dwarves could come and go through the tunnel as they chose, but the route north was easily defensible as the Mounties had spent years and many lives trying to breach the south entrance.

The entry from the south was uphill, well into the tunnel that passed through the very steep mountains. Ronjit had designed the tunnel to have large openings off the main path that all contained round rocks the size of the tunnel. The Dwarves would retreat past the openings and then release the huge boulders from the side entrances.

Seven years ago, the Mounties staged a large, sustained offensive that pushed the Dwarves back into the tunnel. As the Mounties pushed the offensive into the tunnel, for the first time ever, the first steep side tunnel was passed, and the Dwarves released the first large boulder. That boulder was rolling at a tremendously fast pace before roaring into the main path. The boulder left no room for escape as it fitted perfectly into the main tunnel. The first boulder crushed every Mounty who invaded the tunnel. The Dwarves never had to release a second, and the Mounties never again tried to invade the Ronjit-built tunnel.

Ronjit had further enhanced his fight-planning reputation during the battle over a month ago. Ronjit had moved nearly five hundred Dwarven troops way west of the Beardly plain. By having the troops move only at night, they had surprise on their side when on the fourth day of the direct offensive from the tunnel, the five hundred attacked late in the day from the west. The setting sun provided cover until the brave five hundred were closer than expected. The Mounties had already fought a long battle that day against the Ragnar-led main force when the Ronjit-led flanking maneuver hit. The Dwarves, of course, did not know of the healing problems the Mounties' Magicians were having. All they knew is they hit a softened Mounty line and overwhelmed the troops. The Mounties were in full retreat for several miles until the Mowkers River, and darkness allowed the Mounties to recover. Troop reinforcement for the Mounties was able to move in overnight, and the healing went better that far south. The following day, the Mounties held a line from just south of the Lower River Bridge to a point along the Beardly River south of its confluence with Smith Creek. Ronjit was the hero of the battle.

Now, King Hjalmarr and his sons were planning on how to hold their gains. Ronjit had spread an excellent map of Wyndliege north of Bane Bay. He spoke first. "Our weak point is up here!" Jabbing his stubby finger at the area east of the tunnel, he said, "We are spread so thin up here to the north. We are prepared for an attack down south by the river, and we are dug into the central plains, keeping the roads west open. But if the Mounties attack up near the ancient forests of the foothills, we could get overrun and outflanked."

"We could move there, and you and Ragnar could go back to

your commands," suggested Hjalmarr.

Ragnar objected. "No, Father, you must move to the center with the King's Guard. Ronjit and I will flank you, as it should be!"

"But your troops are the most battered," countered Ronjit. "While admiring your incredible abilities, your troops, and even you, got battered before we made it to the battlefield. Ragnar, you must at least take some fresh troops the king brought and any others we can move here to prop up the north line."

"I agree," stated the king. "All the fresh troops will go to the north under Ragnar. Ronjit will hold the south. My guard and I will take the center. We must hold this line for the summer. We can open up trade and make life miserable for those bastard Halflings."

The king of the Dwarves had spoken, and that was final.

Chapter 17

SMITH TUNNELS

For the second time in less than two weeks, Greentea left an army of Clan Zopfarn Dwarves to go off into the unknown with the crazy Wizard Dwarf, Knolt. He was her distant relative and had taught her quite a bit of Druid magic. He always seemed to have more advice, but he had just been quite rude to her clansmen, and for a Dwarf, that was considered highly inappropriate. Greentea had been raised in the ways of her people, and the rudeness of Knolt was different from the clannish Dwarves in Whiterock. She had second thoughts about going to the Smith Tunnels, and she told that to Knolt.

"Well, girl, you want to know about yourself, don't you?" asked the clever old Dwarf.

"Yes," answered Greentea.

"Then gather up some supplies from these smelly fools. They can certainly spare it, and we will get you many answers. The Smith Tunnels promise to reveal much about you, if you are brave, strong, and quick on your feet. I expect we will come out on the other side much more enlightened about our quest and what is going on in the world today. Actually, I expect you will find some of this adventure educational, and it might even answer some of the questions you keep asking yourself."

No speech by the old Wizard could have raised her curiosity more. Greentea asked for and got supplies from the army, and they were on their way before General Stonehead had even started his army moving south.

Greentea and Knolt were forced to leave behind the two pack-horses. They both had to carry a pack with needed supplies. Like all sturdy Dwarves, this was not a major inconvenience for them.

The entrance to the tunnels was less than half a mile from the settlement of the Huckendublers. Walking side by side, the old Wizard Dwarf and the young Druid Dwarf walked into the gloom of the Smith Tunnels.

The path was gloomy but wide and well made. Knolt used his powerful magic and created a nice light globe to surround them. Greentea soon made her first observation about the tunnel.

"I am surprised, but this tunnel was not Dwarven made," she observed.

"No, it was made by others; Humans, I think, mostly. It is ancient and very different. I even believe that some work is still being done somewhere in this complex," stated a hushed Knolt.

Something in his tone told Greentea not to ask any more questions, so she remained silent.

The path split off in many different directions, but it was not confusing. The main route was not in doubt as it went straight through the mountain, never turning and with little elevation change. The Dwarves called it a "wet tunnel," with many signs of water dripping through the route. Underground water is like spring water and is usually very good to drink. Several times, Knolt stopped and got out his old, battered traveling cup and took a drink. Greentea did the same. Except for the silence, it was much like all their other travels.

Finally, they reached a point where the paths became confusing. Several similar-sized routes took off from a central area about thirty feet in circumference. Knolt hesitated for just a moment before taking one path the led slightly down and to the right. This path ended about one thousand feet down it. Then they returned to the central area. Again, in silence, Knolt started down the path that went slightly down and to the left. Eventually, it ended, and they had to return to the central area. This time, as they entered the central area, Knolt turned toward Greentea with a strange look on his face. His beard had turned very black—and then he disappeared and took the light with him.

Greentea was not frightened as all Dwarves were used to the absolute blackness of the underground. She was slightly irritated at this game that she thought Knolt was playing. She found in her pack the needed items to create a light and was about to strike the flint when she felt the cool breeze. Now, she was beginning to feel strange, and the hair stood up on the back of her neck. She reviewed in her mind the look on Knolt's face and the black beard. It struck her as very odd, and her senses went very alert.

The cool breeze that felt unnatural had her feeling a deep fear as she realized that her magic of the Druid sect was practically useless in the rock tomb of the cave. Then she saw it. It was huge, maybe seven feet tall, with a slight glow of dark red. It was more shadow than form. It was carrying something that anyone or anything would recognize—a long sword with a glowing red edge. The long sword was definitely *not* a shadow. The sword was all too real.

The dark red shadow loomed over her and grunted something in a language she had never heard before. Two other shadow things appeared out of different tunnels. They drifted into the central area. The first one raised his sword as if to swing it and cut off her head. As it did this, she heard a small voice—Knolt's voice—from far away, whisper, "Use your magic, fool." The surprise of Knolt's voice and what she had heard did not register immediately, and she would have been too late, but she had one instinct left that *did* save her life. She dove for the floor, causing the first sword swing to whoosh above her neck. Before the second sword could swing, she called up the ancient magic of the Druid Dwarf.

This magic requires items from nature such as trees, plants, or animals to work best. In a cave, under a mountain, she did not expect much for her magic to reach. Never in Whiterock would her magic work well. In the Smith Tunnels, her magic found something vital to her magic touch, something of the natural world. She went to it as she would when moving from tree to tree. As she went, all three sword blades sliced through empty air.

Greentea was gone.

She felt herself moving faster and faster. She had closed her eyes from fear as the swords had swung at her head. Greentea really did not know if or why she was still alive. To test this, she opened her eyes. She found herself sliding down a dimly lighted shaft. It sloped down at a constant rate, sliding her ever faster and faster. This time, she closed her eyes to concentrate on her special magic. Doing this allowed her to feel the natural items that her magic had reached out to when she was in trouble. Somehow, this provided her a moment of comfort during this long slide. She did not know how, but in the Smith Tunnels, her magic had, momentarily, saved her life.

Her immediate problem was sliding down a sloping tunnel only slightly larger than her body. At first, she had been sitting up sliding, but as the speed had picked up, she had been forced to a prone position. This was a good thing because of the narrowness of the chute. Before Greentea could really analyze her predicament, she blasted out of the tube, crashing into the most interesting creature she had ever seen.

Hundreds of similar yet widely different creatures surrounded the first creature. They all had two very short legs. Their bodies were very round and much longer than their short legs. Most of them had more than two arms at the top of the body, and the arms did not seem to grow from the same spot like most animals. They had round faces with perfect, almost too smooth skin and seemingly no facial hair. The shape of the face would have reminded Greentea of a very fat, portly Human man if she had ever seen one. She had not. They had round, plump cheeks, deep-set eyes, almost perfectly round noses, and a mostly bald head with no visible ears. Greentea had no idea whether they were men or women or just what they were.

The creatures all shared the same basic features but their differences were incredible. They varied widely in size, color, and girth. The skin on some was smooth, wrinkled on others, except, of course, for the face. Age was impossible to tell. Some were short and wide. Some were very, very tall. Many different colors were visible, but most were a shade of brown. However, white and red were also present. It was impossible to imagine, but Greentea suddenly realized they resembled trees. Living creatures that had humanoid heads but were as varied in shade and size as trees in nature. Her Druid sense helped her to this conclusion and confirmed it.

As she used her Druid abilities, the creatures began talking to each other in a very strange, slow-sounding language. Her magic was affecting the creatures, but she had no idea if that was good or bad. She also had sudden thoughts about Knolt. Where was that old Wizard?

That thought was rapidly blown out of her mind as the creatures all reached out to her magic at the same time. The creatures with questions, comments, and complaints magically pelted her. The words were all Druid Magic sounds that she could understand perfectly, but she was overwhelmed and could not sort out who or what to answer first. She also was not sure she could respond to the various tree sounds that she was hearing all at the same time.

The treelike creatures began to make her understand some of what was being mentally pelted at her. She suddenly realized that they were aware that she was a Druid and that it was not strange or unusual. In fact, they were expecting something from her, and that something was very important to them. Greentea Gravelt suddenly was aware that these strange creatures expected her to do something, and if she understood it correctly, that something was to lead them somewhere. It was very confusing for all involved and not for the first time Greentea wished Knolt was there.

Knolt hated leaving the young Druid like this, but he knew she had to face the Twigbots alone. He had much to do here, and he was anxious to start. The three dark-clothed men appeared as he had expected, and he magically disappeared by floating to the top of the underground room and watched from there. Knolt had confidence in what would happen as soon as Greentea stretched out a tentacle of her magic. The men would recognize it and find a way to send young Greentea to her first destination. The trapdoor in the floor surprised Knolt a little, but he knew where Greentea would wind up. He chuckled to himself about how he would have to ask her permission to leave before this was all done.

Knolt stayed invisible to the eye, but the three men now took notice of the second intruder. The leader spoke. "Who visits our home with a young Druid Dwarf?"

The second responded, "Well, Javit, I seem to remember the smell of this one's magic. Our old friend Knolt has brought the Twigbots what they most desire. Why don't you come down and talk with us, you silly Dwarf?"

The second speaker finished this statement with a slight laugh and removed his head covering, revealing a tall, black-skinned Human man. Knolt magically reappeared, floating above the three men's heads, and then floated down to the cave floor with a big smile creasing his face. The other two men revealed their faces similar to the first. The three tall, Black men and the short Dwarf greeted one another like the good friends they had always been.

These men were Dondlings. Knolt had long maintained a good relationship with these Humans. Knolt had long known of their unusual ability to identify all races by any magic that they used. Even though the Dondlings were known to have few magical skills compared to others in Wyndliege, they could immediately recognize magical usage and type.

"Javit, Samson, and Stonkill, what a pleasure to find you all healthy and still protecting your home," said Knolt in greeting.

"Yes, we're still at it, even though times seem to be changing. Do you bring us tidings of what is going on outside? Even though we have large communities in Darson, Beardly, and North Landsend, we have little word of the movements of the Dwarves and the Mounties," stated Javit.

"I have some news that I will share with as many as you can gather. Is old Merrium still carrying the burden? Is Jongel still your leader?" inquired Knolt.

"Always questioning," laughed Javit. Turning somber, he continued. "No, Jongel passed across the river of death eight years ago. I am now the head of the Dondlings." He stood tall as he made this pronouncement, and Knolt and the others could see his pride in his somewhat new title.

Javit continued. "We have many here as we hear of an escalation in the war. Our Beardly folks are concerned about a negative outcome for the Dwarves. In addition, we must tell you of Merrium. Let us go to Central Hall, where we will share stories."

The three tall Dondling men and the old, short Dwarf walked through the confusing labyrinth of the Smith Tunnels. All four knew the way equally well. They talked as old friends do of many things from the past. Arriving at the appropriate place, Knolt took his leave of the men and went to the same small quarters the Dondlings had always reserved for their great friend and supporter.

Knolt was refreshed, fed, and ready when, about three hours later, the runner came for him. He was anxious to learn what he could, then get over to Greentea, and see what she had accomplished. As he walked into the Central Hall, Knolt always had to stop and gape at the incredible size and beauty of it. It was a natural cave with thousands and thousands of gems glittering from natural light that filtered down through fissures hundreds of feet deep. The natural light somehow made its way to the cave deep underground. The cave was several hundred feet high with a rounded dome roof except on one side, north, thought Knolt, where a small stream fell out of the wall about halfway up and landed in a small pool before winding its way out of the hall further into the mountain. The natural light, the beautiful waterfall, the sparkling gems just hanging out of the walls, and the large, flat floor made Central Hall one of Knolt's favorite places in Wyndliege.

Javit had gathered up approximately seventy of his subjects to attend this meeting. This was a lot to be in the tunnels, and that made Knolt curious.

Javit started the meeting. "Greetings to all who are here present today. We have a visitor from the north. I am happy to announce an old friend of the Dondlings. Knolt the Dwarf is here to talk with us about news from the Dwarves of Clan Zopfarn."

Knolt knew enough of their ways to realize it was proper for him to share first. He told of the birth of Greentea and his knowing she was a Druid at or near her birth. He told of his leaving Whiterock, expecting that he would need an outdoor place to train the Druid. He spoke about the long wait and finally getting her to his mountainside home, only to have experienced the magical wave from North Landsend before she arrived and the Black Pine tree giving her a message. He told of his conversation with the pine tree and what he thought he needed to do from that. He also revealed what he knew of troop movements from the Dwarven side.

As Knolt finished, a young Dondling arose and began to tell her tale. She was from North Landsend, and she related the story of the young Jackrol Tiller and his touch to the magic. Knolt shivered at her description of the strength of the touch to the magic of the land. Never had he heard of such magical power. To learn it was a student not yet trained in magic made the wonder of his feat even more impressive.

The second and third Dondlings to speak talked of things going on in Beardly and Darson, respectively. To Knolt, this was not important to his plans, but the size of the upcoming battle was amazing to him. King Hjalmarr had picked quite a time to leave Whiterock and visit his sons. The battle won by his sons had scared the Mounties, and they were planning to strike back. The Mounties were planning an enormous war effort to retaliate against the Dwarves.

The next speaker was to be Javit. By now, many of the Dondlings left the hall, and Knolt remained with only Javit and his closest advisors in the great hall. They moved to the President's Alcove off to one side, and with this small amount of privacy, continued with the storytelling.

Javit told of the significant events nearly eighteen years ago. Merrium completed her task, and the young Wyndswept man, Jackrol Tiller, was the Chosen. Few things could have surprised Knolt more than a Wyndswept receiving the great gift.

"Why on earth was the Chosen a Wyndswept? Surely, there must be a mistake by he who makes no mistakes," interrupted Knolt in a loud voice.

The others present all lowered their heads. Interrupting a story was very impolite to the Dondlings. Javit gave his old friend a pass. "Yes, Knolt, we were distraught, and many called for an investigation. The note sent by Merrium was proper in all aspects, and the messenger was questioned in this very room, with all of us here using our truth magic. It was Merrium, and per orders, she gave it to the young Jackrol Tiller. There can be no doubt that it was so ordered, but the questions remain . . . Why now, and what will the gift do? Three thousand years, we carried the secret of the First. Three thousand years, many generations of us, we lived to see one old lady complete a task . . . Our great civilization set aside to maintain one secret. Now it—the great gift—goes to descendants of those that hurt him most."

A lengthy silence followed this statement and, for most, very sad. Knolt took in all that he had learned, and a plan came to his mind.

"Javit, what would happen if the Dwarves win this upcoming war? Would not the way be open to North Landsend?" asked Knolt.

"Yes, the land route to the sea would be open, and your Dwarves could trade directly with the Wyndswept. Rocky Point is tough but fair to travelers. With some care, Dwarf traders could make the sea journey to North Landsend," replied Javit.

"I'm not talking about trade. I'm talking about getting my young Druid friend there. She must meet up with Jackrol Tiller as I believe that to be a part of her destiny. It could be possible if this battle goes poorly for the Mounties," stated the now-excited Knolt.

"Great. All we have to do is defeat the damn healing magic, and we can overrun the thousands of Mounty soldiers. No problem there, right, Knolt?" said the suddenly bitter Javit.

"Sorry. We have all suffered from that evil magic for way too long. But much of what is going on leads me to believe that things are changing. Will you continue to sit on the sidelines now that your task is complete, or will the Dondlings once again rise and be a force in what happens in Western Wyndliege?" asked Knolt.

"We wait for one more sign. That sign will trigger us to action. Until then, we remain vigilant."

It was the answer expected by Knolt, but he had to ask the question. They all knew that it would end this way; then Knolt took his leave of the Dondlings.

Chapter 18

TWIGBOTS

Never had Greentea felt anything like the cacophony of magical noises that the strange creatures directed at her. She could not even stand up because the noise was so loud and uneven. It was clear to her that the creatures were trying to talk to her. She could pick out words and small phrases, but none of it was coherent thought. Finally, she let out a piercing scream . . . and all went quiet.

An organized movement by several of the things caught her attention. It was undeniable that they had made a path for her to walk through. Greentea stood up, and she quickly checked herself over for any injuries from her long fall down the chute. She was sore in many places but otherwise unharmed. She began walking down the path cleared by the strange treelike creatures. Greentea also carefully shielded any use of her magic to avoid the confusion of a moment ago.

The ground she was walking on was very damp and muddy. Soon, her boots were making her labor to pull them up out of the muck on each step. A nervous murmur went through the creatures, and Greentea could clearly tell the murmur was telling them to keep the path drier. How she could tell that she was not sure, but sure enough, the route became much drier land. Moving easier on the dry land, Greentea rapidly advanced across the vast, underground cavern, and moving on the ever-higher ground, she could look back and see the vast underground lake that occupied most of the lower cavern. Most of the creatures stayed near the lake or the small stream feeding the lake.

As Greentea advanced farther up the strange path made by the creatures, she noticed the small stream noisily tumbling down the side of the cave and forming a little pool before flowing on to make the small stream flowing into the lake. Around the small pool were five enormous creatures and an oversized empty stone chair carved out of the cave wall next to the tumbling water.

Greentea stood staring at the chair, and the five large creatures stood staring at her. Greentea knew the chair was for her, but questions tumbled through her mind. No answers could she get until, with a start, she remembered that she was blocking her magical powers. She rapidly removed her block, and she heard a creature say, "She seems not to be responding now, but there is no mistake . . . She used Druid magic."

Greentea had no trouble understanding what was said, even though it was spoken in a tree language that no other being could possibly hear. She did not know how to respond in the language they were using, so she finally just spoke. "I hear you now. I was blocking because of the noise that hit me when I first came here."

The creature just to the right of the stone chair responded in a very high-pitched voice but using the common language, "Welcome, Master Druid. We have long awaited your return. Where have you all gone?"

The question puzzled Greentea but hearing her own tongue relaxed her tremendously. "I don't know how to answer your question, but I will tell you all I know. I am a Dwarf. My name is Greentea Gravelt, and I have some unique skills that have been called Druid Magic. My Druid Magic skills have not been born to my people for many, many years. A fellow Dwarf by the name Knolt led me to the Smith Tunnels. He is a relative of mine who is helping me learn to be a Druid."

This statement caused quite a commotion. Greentea could hear the words "Druid" and "Knolt" often repeated. The commotion amongst the creatures was stopped by the creature to the right of the chair.

"Silence. I must have silence," commanded the huge creature. "Welcome, Greentea Gravelt the Druid. We live to serve you. All Twigbots, the Fathers of Trees, serve the Druid Dwarf who sits in the king's chair. Please take your chair, Greentea Gravelt the Druid, and lead us. We have long waited for those in power to bring us another king. Knolt is the name of one who could bring us another king. We will accept you and only you!"

Greentea was now more puzzled than ever, and she was ready to scream at Knolt—if she ever saw him again—for putting her in this position. The Twigbots were already making more noise. She could hear them wanting her to sit in the chair. The force of Druid and other magic aimed at her was awesome. With no other choice, plus she was tired of standing there being confused, she promptly went over and sat down in what was obviously the king's chair.

The result was incredible. The Twigbots immediately began to celebrate in their own fashion, and the intensity of their joy struck Greentea. Her magic picked up the immense atmosphere of excitement.

The huge Twigbot to her right leaned toward her and said in the common tongue, "I am Strif. I last served Leafbright the Druid before he went to fight the battles against the Mounties. Since then, we have had no king to lead us. Leafbright made us stay while he went out, and we were very sad by him leaving us. Then nothing—no one was assigned to replace him. We have very little information from the outside. The Dondlings don't come down here very often."

Now, Greentea's confusion soared ever higher. She thought carefully before asking her next question. "You seem to know Knolt. Has he ever been your king?"

Strif then did what could only be interpreted as a laugh. "No, Greentea Gravelt the Druid. Knolt is a leader on the outside. He directed us moving from Haleport to here when the Mounties and the Dwarves went to war. Knolt said the queen wanted us here, to be safe until the war was over. Then we heard the Elves were having struggles with Mounty magic, and evil spread over the land. Twigbots just stay here until Druids and Elves move us back to the outside. We want to go back to Jarven and Haleport. Can you take us?"

Before Greentea could answer any more questions, the Twigbot to the left leaned in and interrupted. "Strif, we must remember, the king may want to rest and feed. They do it so differently than us. We must remember how to keep the king strong."

Strif responded to this by telling Greentea about a small alcove not ten paces from the chair that housed the king. Greentea immediately wanted to check this out, so she jumped down from the chair and headed for the alcove. This movement elicited a response from the Twigbots as they all lowered their heads and arms in a sort of salute to the king. Greentea was amazed at the motion aimed at her and quickly headed for the little alcove, which turned out to be a really nice room with comfortable lodging for a Dwarf. The little corner was hidden from the view of all the Twigbots. It had running water from a small wellspring out of the wall. Surprisingly very little noise from the Twigbots invaded the small room. Greentea quickly spread out her pack and had some dried meats to satisfy her hunger. Feeling better, she decided to lie down on a stone bed (preferred by Dwarves) and get a little rest.

Greentea woke with a start. She had expected to lie down for a moment and think about her predicament. Instead, however, she had fallen asleep. She wondered if her fall had shaken her a little more than she thought. After the rest, she was no closer to answers for how to convince the Twigbots that she could not be their king. She was a young Druid, not very well trained, and she was certainly not taking them anywhere. Again, she wondered where Knolt was. She needed him to help her with some of these answers.

The five giant Twigbots around the pool were all glad to see Greentea walk back out and take her chair. The population of Twigbots again all gave the lowering of the head and arms salute. Greentea was very charmed by them, but now, what should she do?

Strif again came to her rescue. "Perhaps Your Majesty would like to approve part of the plan for the celebration for your coming here. Proop, here," gesturing to the Twigbot to her left, "and Joomb," looking at the one next to Proop, "have laid down some plans."

Joomb immediately described events that would last several days and end with a party in the Central Hall if the Dondlings would allow that. Joomb wanted to know if Greentea Gravelt the Druid could talk to the Dondlings about using the Central Hall.

Again, Greentea was utterly lost with this talk of Dondlings and Central Hall, but to calm Joomb down, she said she would ask. She also explained that while her name was Greentea Gravelt, it would please her if they just used Greentea. This seemed to delight all of the five Twigbots surrounding the pool.

Then Proop came to his part of the planning. "Would Greentea the Druid be inviting any guests to the celebration?" he asked. Proop seemed to be strangely nervous asking this question of Greentea.

Greentea responded, "Only Knolt, if I knew where he was."

The five Twigbots surrounding the pool all did a shaking of arms with a sound that could only be called laughing. Strif said, "Your Majesty is teasing us, of course. Knolt is talking with the Dondlings. We all feel him up there talking with the Dondlings. Don't you feel him, Greentea the Druid?"

Greentea felt stupid for about the thousandth time since she came to this place. She reached out her powerful Druid Magic and immediately felt Knolt and several other powerful beings. Instantly, she knew they were the Dondlings and that they were the ones who had attacked her. They were mostly blocked, but Greentea knew he was there, and he would be there to find her soon.

Using her magic had another unintended response from the Twigbots. They all seemed to be basking in her using the Druid Magic. She could feel them trying just to touch the edge of the magic. She decided to test this by giving some of her magic to Proop and Joomb. They both responded immediately. They screeched out in what Greentea thought was pain. Both screamed, "Not me, please.

I am not worthy, Your Majesty." Nevertheless, it was done, and both Proop and Joomb dropped a nut-looking thing from one of their many arms. The Twigbots were silent for a moment, and then, one by one, they kneeled on one knee, a very awkward movement, and lowered their head and arms in a gesture that could only be a salute.

Greentea looked up at Strif for an idea of what to do now. She could see the tears in the eyes of the huge creature. Greentea wondered what had just happened. She wondered if this was really going to go badly for her. She thought, *Well, this might be the shortest reign ever by a king.*

At that moment, time stood still for Greentea Gravelt. The huge Strif was crying, and Proop and Joomb were staring at the little nut-like thing that had fallen from their arms, and all the other Twigbots were in a kneeling salute. Right then, Knolt walked in and, with a golden-colored beard, said in a loud voice, "Well met, Twigbots. It has been long since I have seen you. I see you have seated your new king, and she has started producing. What are the plans for the coronation? The Dondlings will all be there, and, of course, we will use the Central Hall. I love a good Twigbot party!"

The chaos of the next few minutes was one of the strangest things Greentea had ever seen. Knolt walked up to Strif, grabbed two of the largest arms, and danced with the large, short-legged creature. As long as the Twigbot feet stayed in the water, they could move with exceptional grace and ease. Several of the Twigbots began singing, and they had the most amazing voices Greentea had ever heard. Just like that, the subjects of King Greentea the Druid were celebrating the first newborns (as the two nutlike things hatched to reveal baby Twigbots) to their group in over two hundred years.

Knolt eventually, as the singing and dancing continued, pulled Greentea into the small alcove and explained to her what had happened. "I went this way to allow you to take your rightful place as king of the Twigbots and to have discussions with my friends, the Dondlings. The Dondlings are a group of powerful Humans that live spread around Darson, Beardly, and several other places. The Dondlings have protected the Twigbots since I had gathered them up and brought them here at the instruction of the High Elven Queen Gavriel before the fall of the Elves. That was over two hundred years ago.

"The leaders of the Dondlings have long hidden in the Smith Tunnels, and they have watched over Twigbots. The Elves and the Druid Dwarves had always been the protectors of these strange creatures. The Dondlings have served as the protectors of the Twigbots and will do so until you assume the role of king."

Knolt continued. "Don't worry; you can handle the fairly harmless tree peoples. They serve a very specific and unique role in our world. You will enjoy learning about them and what they can do to make the world better. Also, as you accidentally discovered, only through Druid Magic will the strange creatures reproduce."

Knolt paused for a moment before continuing. "The Smith Tunnels were built and belong to the Dondlings. They did not want it to be used to the advantage of either side in the long wars between the Dwarves and the Mounties. These black-skinned Humans killed any trespassers into the tunnels. A few trespassers surrendered and were put to work in the northern part of the tunnels where the Dondlings were mining. Those captured were treated well but not allowed to leave.

"The Dondlings," explained Knolt, "were waiting for certain signs before choosing a side and joining the battle. One sign was the return of the king of the Twigbots, and there are several more. Be careful judging them until you know the whole story, and do not underestimate them.

"One thing would stay their hands regarding trespassers, and that was Druid Magic. Once you attempted to use your magic, they smelled it and sent you to the Twigbots. They smelled me and greeted me as a friend, even though many years had passed. When and if they join the wars, they will make a difference!"

Greentea had many questions about why she was to be the king of the Twigbots. Knolt explained, "Actually, the king of the Twigbots does not do anything as far as leading. The Twigbots only need water and protection from those that would harm them. They are the Fathers of Trees. They formed all the trees in the world and set nature to reproduce the trees naturally. The trees that Twigbots form are very special, and very few that they formed are left. Certain groups want to destroy any trees that Twigbots make because of things they can and cannot do. You can learn this on your own later if you are so destined. I will not help you with this, and I warn you that to use the power of the Twigbots can be perilous. The relationship between the Elves, the Druid Dwarves, and the Twigbots is complicated. You will walk many paths before you come to use the fun-loving creatures that are now your subjects."

This led Greentea to have more questions than ever, but not a word would Knolt add about the tree people.

The party of the coronation was a great event. The Dondlings went out of their way to make Greentea feel welcome, and Knolt went into his small quarters and was rarely seen. The Twigbots could only be a few hours out of the water, so the actual ceremony was short and to the point. Greentea was given a small scepter to signify the position. The party after was fun as the singing Twigbots must have been well known to the Dondlings as they asked for song after song. The Twigbots danced their strange feet in water dance until even Greentea could enjoy the swaying tree people. Proop and Strif stayed close to Greentea as much as possible. Greentea wondered about this until one moment she was left alone, and the pounding of Druid and other magics from the rank-and-file Twigbots came screeching into her head. Greentea could not believe the noise they made and how it affected her. When Strif came waddling over next to her, the noise lessened, and Greentea realized that he (?) was blocking that magical noise. She asked, "Strif, are you protecting me from all this magical noise?"

Strif hesitantly replied, "Yes, Your Druid Highness. We are aware of the discomfort that our king hears from our magic."

"Why does it do that?" she asked.

"We are not sure. The magic noise we generate is a problem for almost every user of magic from all races. It is one reason we need a king to protect us from those that would do us harm. It is effortless for us to block the noise from one Druid as long as we are next to them, but we cannot turn it off. The Dondlings do not seem to hear it, with a few exceptions. Elves sometimes hear the magic noise as music and love it; therefore, we have usually been around the Elves. A few Elven artists seem to be bothered by the noise, and things have occasionally gone bad for us." Strif gained confidence as he told this story to Greentea. Suddenly, he was teaching his new liege, and he found that energizing.

Using his newfound energy, Strif began quite a dancing effort, with Greentea along for the ride. Despite herself, Greentea found that she was having fun and laughing at the seemingly happy, harmless tree people. She was ready to stay here and relax for a while. Knolt, however, had other ideas.

With a bright red beard and fire in his eyes, Knolt came rushing to find Greentea. He was in a hurry as it was time to go again. He found her smiling and dancing.

"Are you ready to go?" he demanded. "We have been in here long enough, and you will return to your subjects another time." He finished this last with a slightly sarcastic attitude.

Once again, Greentea wondered if going with her seemingly crazy relative was the right thing to do. She was hesitating as she pondered all this when something dawned on her. "Hey, you are not bothered by the magical noise," she exclaimed.

He went through several different facial expressions and several colors of beard before replying. Finally, he just repeated the words, "We have to go!"

She realized that she had so much left to do. First, she had wondered where she belonged in the world, and now that she had become a king of magical beings, she had to go off, wondering again in the seemingly fruitless search for whatever was next. The puzzle of where she belonged had gotten much more complicated as she had several hundred Twigbots to care for. How could she possibly fit them into her future, and how many riddles did she have to uncover about them before she found her answers . . . or any answers?

Knolt watched his young relative struggle through these thoughts, and he could probably guess what most of them were. He did feel a bit sorry for her. She was so young, so inexperienced, and so important. Nevertheless, they had to go. He just worried about how little she had been trained in Magic and how little she knew of the world outside.

Knolt looked his young relative in the eye and said, "Greentea, war has started between our clan and the Mounties. We must be there to do our part, no matter how large or small that turns out to be. We must go! The Dondlings are taking us out of here today."

Chapter 19

CROSSROADS

C athy Williams was tired of this. They had their travel papers and could go directly to North Landsend. That would suit her. North Landsend was a human settlement, and she was growing to dislike the Mounties. Out on the road, the Mounties and their slaves, the Elves, were everywhere. The Mounty troops were moving north. The supply train behind them was growing, and the Elves were being treated, in her opinion, worse than ever. Cal was praying every day, and he was not sure that they should go as previously directed. This indecision drove the impatient Cathy crazy. The giant protector, Jim Herrick, was not in any hurry, and he seemed to be very interested in the military movements of the little people.

Cathy took her complaints to Cal after an overcooked dinner at the tiny inn they had procured in a small village. "Why can we not get moving along? We have been here for three days. The innkeeper is overrun with Mounty troops, and the food is terrible. Let's get out on the open road, and I will cook us some good food for once!" demanded the young woman.

Cal looked up from his prayers. He saw the resemblance to himself in the pretty young lady before him, which brought a slight smile to his face. He was enjoying his younger sister's company despite her occasional complaints. Like most of his family, Cathy was not a patient person. That probably made them successful, as his dad was king of a sizeable human kingdom north of Darson City.

Cal was glad he had taken his calmer, more even personality to the monastery. He was finally clear on what came next. He was amazed at the clarity that came to him as the Recorder. He was told that his prayers would be answered on what to do, and now that he had experienced it a couple of times, he was amazed at how clear the right thing to do became to him as he pondered and prayed on it. He just knew he was correct!

"Cathy, go get Jim. I have an answer."

The thrilled girl ran to find the big protector. When both were seated in the small room they all shared in the village inn, Cal began. "I have prayed much since we left Litteville. We are just past North Junction, and ever since we left that place, my prayers told me we were going the wrong way. I did not know how to interpret this, so I stayed here. My prayers told me not to continue. I remembered from the maps a place called Crossroads, and as soon as I thought of that name, I was told to head there. Then I thought of the Mowkers River, and my prayers were answered. Whatever story I am to record starts there. We are to go to the town of Crossroads. Something will happen there, and then we will continue to the Mowkers River. It is there where our story begins."

Jim leaned his big body back and smiled. Cathy clapped her hands in front of her and said, "Let's pack up tonight and head out at first light."

Without removing his smile, Jim replied sarcastically, "We have no papers to go to Crossroads. Are we to become criminals in this fine Republic?"

Without hesitating, Cal simply said, "We leave tomorrow at first light for North Landsend via Crossroads and the Mowkers River. We Humans have a poor sense of direction." He finished with a big smile, and they all laughed.

Crossroads was a boomtown cut in a deep valley that bisected the Gray Front. The wet springtime weather made all the streets a muddy bog, and the small village had grown to a sizable city staging out the Mounty armies. The troops were streaming from the south to the north. Jim had found out from Mounty troops that the Dwarves had won a battle, and the Mounties were going north to take back what they had lost, and maybe even more. Troops were talking about defeating the Dwarves and driving them all the way back to Whiterock.

Jim Herrick had found that the Mounty soldiers loved to practice their war craft, and a big man like Jim was great practice for the little Mounties. Jim purposefully made his matches closer than needed to get the soldiers to open up and give him information. In this way, he learned much about what had gone on and what was going to happen. The large numbers of troops moving north led him to believe that Cal had been right in this detour.

Cal had insisted on finding lodging in Crossroads, as he felt something would happen here that would lead to the next step. Jim had found some room at an old inn, and even Cathy was satisfied with the service at the rather mean-looking inn. The travelers did not have to stay long as on their third day, Cal received a letter from the proprietor of the inn. The old proprietor, Hans, was a Mounty who seemed to be extra stoic, even for a race known for that trait. In this case, Hans was very shaken up as he handed over the note to Cal.

Cal recognized the seal this time and was not surprised to be called to the tent of the Magi. He gathered up the other two travelers, and they read a note almost identical to the one they received in Litteville. The Magi was in Crossroads, and he requested their presence.

After a few inquiries, they located the large tents of the Mounty command north of Crossroads. The second largest of these was their destination. Again, Vonn and Jules met alone with the three travelers. This time, they dispensed with introductions and got right down to business.

"Have you lost your maps to North Landsend?" asked the Magi in as sarcastic a voice as he could muster. "I am certain that my able assistant could go over maps with you and show you a much-easier route to North Landsend."

Playing this out, Cal replied, "What a kind offer, Magi, but we are not lost at all. We thought that we would like to see the beautiful Mowkers River before continuing to North Landsend. Our papers did not state a specific route, so we thought we had some latitude on choosing a route."

This obviously irritated both Mounties, and they both rose out of their comfortable chairs. Once again, Cathy and Jim wondered if they had gotten in too much trouble with the powerful Magi. Cal continued. "I am surprised to see you so far from your beautiful home in Haleport."

"Enough!" snapped the Magi. "You will answer my questions, or you will die. Are you sent here to spy on us by our enemies?"

"We only come to record history as it happens," replied the defiant Cal. "We are sent out to do a job by our superiors and led by my prayers to God. We have nothing to do with you or your enemies. You will not kill the Recorder or the Protector, and you know it, Magi. You are a well-read, intelligent man who is trying to understand the events happening in the world. You know our presence signifies that important events are about to unfold, and, naturally, you are trying to shape what I record."

Vonn stared at the man in front of him. Seldom in his life had he been spoken to like that! He was always the one in control, and his threats were never empty. This time, they were, and he had been called on it by this smallish Monk from the north. He tried a different approach.

"Jules, order up chairs for our guests. Sit down, everybody. This conversation will take a while. Cal, if I may call you that, please, have a chair. I am trying to understand what is going on. You scare me by your very presence here and now. You are right. My threats are empty, and I will not harm you. I would rather make friends out of you than have you leave and be on the other side of this battle. You have obviously been instructed to be here. I would rather help you than go against you."

Cathy and Jim were visibly shaken by the earlier exchange and were shocked at the change in the Magi. Elves brought in chairs for the three guests, and they all sat around a low center wooden table. Vonn changed his personality and became the perfect charming host. The change was surprising to even Cal. After some small talk of traveling, the Magi got back on to his single-minded task, learning about the Recorder and Protector.

Vonn asked for and received the story of how they were chosen and how they prepared their whole lives for this adventure. Vonn was surprised that Jim had left South Landsend to go to Herrick to train for this, even though he knew the odds of actually becoming Protector was very low. Vonn learned of the thugs they met on the first day out of Herrick and the finding of Cathy. They told their story of dealing with Mounty bureaucracy in Darson and Litteville. In addition, at Vonn's pointed questions, Cathy's feelings about the Elves were talked about.

Jules and Cathy had an interesting discussion concerning the Elves, and while neither agreed with the other about the Elven issue, they seemed at ease talking with each other. Vonn invited the travelers to stay for dinner, and they agreed.

The Magi's fare was top-notch, and after a delicious meal of roasted rabbit and vegetables, the questions from Vonn started again. This time, the tone was friendly, and Cal was much more willing to talk.

Vonn asked, "What do you know of the troop movements?" This question was directed at Jim.

Jim was shocked that he had been called upon. "Well, I have talked with many of your troops and have learned that the Dwarves won a battle earlier this spring. The Republic is throwing many troops at them to defeat them this time. Many of your soldiers expect to chase them back to Whiterock." Jim ended with a big smile.

Vonn and Jules both found this incredibly funny. They both laughed heartily at this statement. Jules recovered first. "Pardon us for laughing. It funny to us how optimistic our troops are. We would never try to invade the land of the Dwarves, as they are very safe from us up north. We just want back what they took from us this spring." As Jules said this, she nervously looked at Vonn, hoping she had not said too much.

Vonn did not respond to her look as he was still softly laughing. He then stated, "You pass a crucial test by telling me of the truth about your training with our troops. We have been watching you three and following your movements. We must make sure that you are not spying for our enemies. I have believed that the positions you hold require certain neutrality in our little war. My president is not as sure, and he wants no mistakes leading up to the battle ahead. Would you answer just one question, Recorder?"

Cal replied, "That, of course, depends on if I can."

"Of course," mumbled Vonn. "Have you recorded anything yet?"

Cal did not hesitate. "No, Magi, I believe I will not record anything until I reach the Mowkers."

Vonn could not believe he had got that much from the Recorder. So he volunteered some more information. "We are going to battle the Dwarves just across the river south of Beardly. Could this be your first recording?"

"Ah, a second question already," said a smiling Cal. "Well, I am certain that something is supposed to happen at the river, and battles are usually historically significant if something unusual happens. That could be it, but I think it is more than that. Mounties and Dwarves have had many battles, and my superiors have not felt them significant in a historical sense."

Vonn was amazed at the information he was gaining, but everything led to more questions. So he tried another one. "So, you really don't know what you are to record. You just know to go to a certain area?"

"A third question after saying just one," said the now teasing Cal. "No, Magi, I really don't know what I will write. I have been told it will be clear to me what to write when I see it. It is clear to me where to go when I pray on the correct words. I must assume that it will be equally clear what to write when it occurs."

Vonn was surprised at the clarity of this answer. It confirmed many things he and Jules had read about the Recorder but did not understand until they heard it said by the earnest young human male in front of them. Vonn only knew one thing to do at this time. "We are following the president of the Republic, Traver Wrigger, to battle. I will be at the head of his retinue of Magicians. I would like to invite the Recorder and Protector and their friend, Princess Cathy Williams, to be my guests as we travel to war."

To say the three travelers were surprised would be an understatement. Cal again took the lead in matters of court politeness. "We would be honored to travel as your guests, Vonn the Magi. You have treated us well tonight, and with your company and my prayers, we may find answers about what is to be recorded. Thank you."

Cathy and Jim were satisfied to be traveling with the head of the Mounty Magicians. They figured that they would be safe and sound in this company. Little did they know that Traver Wrigger and Vonn were fighting leaders, and they would find themselves in the front of the battle!

The process of going to war was slow and tedious. The Mounties were amassing over fifteen thousand troops for the upcoming battle. President Wrigger and Vonn wanted to make no mistakes in the upcoming battles. They estimated Dwarf troop strength at somewhere around six thousand troops, and they had to bottle up the Dwarves against the mountains near Beardly. They had to close the trade routes to Rocky Point and the oceangoing ships of the Wyndswept. If the Dwarves could open that trade route, they could trade their much-desired goods around the Republic. The agreements the Mounties honored with the Wyndswept were very clear about the freedom of trade for the seagoing folk.

Cathy Williams and Jules found that they were fast becoming close. The warrior Mounty admired the graceful finish of the young Human Princess, and Cathy found Jules an older confidante who had many worldly experiences to teach. They spent much time together, which allowed Jim and Cal freedom to do as they wished.

Jim found much to do surrounded by thousands of young fighters training for battle. He had lived in this environment for much of his life, and his warrior skills made him popular amongst the troops as an unofficial trainer of all types of war instruments.

Cal was bored out of his mind and very impatient. Day after day, the Recorder prayed for something to happen. All his prayers would tell him was to go to the Mowkers River. The wet, rainy, spring weather made his waiting even worse as he caught a severe head cold and was miserable for days.

To make matters worse for Cal, he was forever called into meetings with Vonn and President Wrigger. Cal enjoyed the company of the taciturn Magi, but the temperamental president was a different story. Cal had lost count of the times the president had threatened various terrible deaths to the Recorder for not telling him what he was going to record. It was comical to Vonn as he stood to one side and listened to his president and the Monk from the north repeat the same things repeatedly. President Wrigger found it impossible to believe that the young Monk did not know more. The Recorder held back the information he had, as his position required, and the president knew that and was utterly frustrated that he could not know all. As president of his large country, he was not used to being denied, and any who dared usually died at his hand. This smallish, young Human had many secrets, and he knew he could not kill him and learn those secrets from a different source. He had to let the Recorder do his job to find out why he was here. If he had known about history, President Wrigger would have been amazed at the number and quality of leaders of the past that had faced this exact dilemma, and none of them had been able to do anything but let history play out and be recorded.

Unknown to Cal and his fellow travelers, the war had begun. The Mounties had to make every battle last as long as possible. They would engage the enemy in several areas to create fatigue and wounds on the Dwarves. Their best advantage was the incredible healing magic that renewed their soldiers daily. The enemy had no such magic.

In the west and south of the lower Mowkers River valley, over three thousand Mounty troops were pouring across the Lower River Bridge into a small triangle of land bordered by the Mowkers on the south and the Beardly River on the east. This land was where the Mounties had stopped the Dwarves led by Prince Ronjit. It was critical that the Mounties hold the bridge, as the land north of the Gray Front and south of the Mowkers was a vital area of farmland and rangeland that produced much of the foodstuffs in the Republic. If the bridge were lost, much of this area would be quickly overrun by the Dwarves.

Willey Swordsinger and Donaghy Kinched were the generals leading this army. President Wrigger felt strongly that the war could not be won in this area by these armies, but it could certainly be lost. The spring rains had made part of this small triangle of land a bug-infested swamp. The Mounty soldiers had great motivation to break the line of Ronjit Zopfarn and gain higher ground.

Ormarr Caapo and Cadon Arsestrong had about five thousand troops moving north of the Mowkers River toward Smith Creek near the heavily forested country between Smith Creek and the Beardly River. The plan was to get to the foothills of the Ngarzzorr Mountains and outflank the Dwarves by taking the so-called foothills trail to Beardly. The only problem with this plan was neither general had ever been in this area. Caapo's troops were supposed to be familiar with this area, but the patrols that should have scouted the area had been lax in their duties, and no one really knew where to go. This was unknown to all the leaders except for Cadon Arsestrong, and he was not going to bring up his failings. Still, the foothills trail would prove easy to find, and it looked like this maneuver by the Mounties would work.

This left the center attack to the ten thousand-strong troops of Bagatur Rinson and President Traver Wrigger. Finally, as spring turned to summer, the troops marched out of Crossroads and headed north to Fjord. Across the great river and then Rinson and President Wrigger went due west across the fertile rolling hills of this land. The six-day march brought the generals to the small garrison of troops holding the line against the Dwarves. King Hjalmarr

Zopfarn had been steadily pushing the line to the east, so it was almost a hundred miles to the east of the Beardly River when the fresh Mounty troops relieved the tired troops. Scouts for the king of the Dwarves had seen a large force moving westward, stopped the offensive, and retreated to their dug-in lines west of the Beardly River, and waited.

Chapter 20

BATTLE OF BEARDLY—THE HUCKENDUBLERS

President Traver Wrigger and Vonn the Magi had abandoned the Recorder and Protector when they started the quick march to the battlefield. They were trying to lead their army and did not want the extra time needed to alert the Humans. Following a few days later, Cal, Cathy, and Jim were not happy with the Mounty leaders. Even so, there wasn't anything they could do about it.

Cal finally crossed the Mowkers River, and despite reverent praying, no inspiration would come to him. Cathy and Jim had settled into a comfortable day-to-day routine in Crossroads, and now, all that was gone.

When the three travelers arrived at the forward camp, they were amazed that no actual fighting had yet taken place. The Mounties found themselves in the position of waging an offensive campaign. It had been several generations since they had last found themselves in this position. President Wrigger was no fool, and he was not going to rush his troops into a battle that had not been thoughtfully planned. The Dwarves were well positioned with the Beardly River between them and the Mounties. If the president and General Rinson directed their troops to go south, they would have to cross the Beardly farther downstream than planned. No Mounty knew of a safe crossing in that area. If they went north, they would cross Smith Creek and then fight across the rather steep hills and dales of the land between Smith Creek and the Beardly River. The Dwarves were effectively dug in along a line at the top of the rise between the two watersheds.

After careful scouting and a report from General Kinched that the battle in the south was a stalemate, President Wrigger sent over three thousand troops under General Rinson north to cross Smith Creek and try to put flanking pressure on the entrenched Dwarves in that area. The president took upon him and almost six thousand Mounty troops to attack the Beardly River and the well-fortified and well positioned Dwarves. Little did he know he was running into the King's Guard and King Hjalmarr himself.

No word came from the Far North. General Bagatur Rinson sent advance scouts out on horseback to get General Caapo to pull south of the forest and help him. This would leave General Arsestrong to complete the flanking maneuver in the Far North.

The Dwarves were greatly outnumbered. Ronjit Zopfarn had about three thousand troops to battle in the south. The skillful prince rallied his troops well, and the early battles in the south were cat-and-mouse battles that had limited fatalities and did not accomplish much for either side. If Prince Ronjit had known how critical the Lower River Bridge was and how unprotected the land to the south was, he might have attempted a strong offensive and created a bad problem for the Mounty leadership. However, he did not know this, and he knew that a breakout would be bad for the Dwarves, as it would leave the south flank of his father unprotected. Ronjit was content to hold the present line and hope his dad and brother would gain large amounts of land in the north.

General Willey Swordsinger concentrated on the northern tip of the triangle and stretched his presence up the west bank of the Beardly. While this did little to change the battle in the south, it did, eventually, give the Mounties under the president a place to fjord the river and attack the King's Guard from the south.

In the north, Ragnar Zopfarn and his approximately fifteen

hundred troops had very little to do. His scouts would go out every day and survey the land from the foothills to the north to the south edge of the forest. So far, Ragnar had not sent his scouts very far into the woods, and none of them wanted to go there!

Ragnar had one other problem on his hands, and he handled it by sending the Huckendublers to the southern edge of his command. His regular troops wanted nothing to do with the strange group. The spring rains had helped diminish the smell a little, but no Dwarf really wanted to be near the odd group. Ragnar thought that the south edge of the forest would be a good place for them. He knew he would not be outflanked from the south with them there. General Stonehead and his six hundred Huckendublers would protect that direction and send appropriate notice if anything happened.

Bagatur Rinson and his troops engaged in the first battle of significance shortly after crossing Smith Creek just east of where it joined the Beardly. About two thousand Mounties attacked a well dug-in position of Beardly Dwarves under King Hjalmarr. The Mounties charged the hillside, sustaining terrible losses. The Dwarves only numbered about three hundred and were eventually overrun. The Dwarves retreated, and General Rinson pressed more troops over the hill and fought due north along the line. The battle went for nine days, and the Mounties gained about ten miles of the disputed boundary. The offensive ran out of steam as both sides had suffered high casualties. The Dwarves always dished out more than they received in each phase of the battle, but the Mounty Magicians healed many wounds and reenergized the Mounty troops. King Hjalmarr reinforced his northwestern flank as General Rinson attacked in that direction. The king was very concerned about these troops being trapped by the river, as the Mounties would eventually turn to the west. The rough terrain of this land made large-scale fighting difficult other than on the main ridge.

President Wrigger heard of the battle by General Rinson and was pleased. He ordered his troops to the west and commenced his offensive. The president attacked the Dwarves along the Beardly River just a few miles south of the confluence with Smith Creek. The Mounties had brought wooden rafts, put them in the water, and swam behind the rafts for protection. Dwarven archers put many arrows into the river and a few into Mounties. Landing and charging into the woods led to the bloodiest part of the war. The president dumped everything he had into this offensive.

Over six thousand troops attempted to cross on the first day. Several hundred Mounties died in the river, and the Magicians could not help them. On the far bank, the battle was brutal. Hundreds of Dwarves and Mounties fought hand to hand. Many on both sides were killed, and the Dwarves eventually gave ground in the southern part of the attack. President Wrigger himself led the troops on a charge from this established beachhead as the long day reached its final hours. The screaming president and his guard gained almost a mile of ground from the river in an hour of frantic fighting. The Dwarves now knew that the president was in the battle. However, it was still not known to the Mounties who was leading the Dwarves.

To the south, the president's troops connected with the soldiers of General Swordsinger, and the southern flank of the president was secured. The huge offensive had taken an entire day, but by nightfall, the troops of the Republic were safe across the Beardly River.

Cal, Jim, and Cathy watched some of the fighting from a safe distance from the Beardly River. Still, no inspiration came over the Recorder. Vonn and Jules, who were with them, were puzzled at the lack of interest by the Recorder. This was the largest, most complex war either of them had been in, and the lack of interest by the young Monk was distressing. They understood that he was here to record something big, and if this were not it, what was? As the beachhead was established, Vonn and Jules were called away, and the three travelers watched the attack by the president and saw Vonn following him, with Jules protecting her boss. Again, no inspiration came to Cal, and he finally left the small hillside they were on and returned to his camp. Jim and Cathy watched for a few minutes more, and, with a shrug of resignation, they too returned to their camp.

The tired and wounded warriors now used the magic of Vonn and his Magicians. By morning, almost all the Mounty troops were completely rested and healed. Still, the losses were terrible from that first battle. Over nine hundred of the sixty-five hundred soldiers died, and another three hundred were mentally harmed from the fighting. This was the hidden problem of the Magicians' healing magic. Many Mounties could not forget the pain of the severe wounds. The healing magic would fix their physical injuries and remove their fatigue; however, those who could not mentally withstand the pain would have to be sent back to the large mental institutions maintained by the Republic. Neither the Dwarves nor the Humans knew this cost of the war.

President Wrigger raged about the mentally weak Mounties as Vonn performed the healing process on the temperamental president.

"Those damn, weak-minded idiots. I'm going to kill them all to show the troops just how tough a Mounty has to be," raged the president.

Vonn answered, "You are under my care for another hour, Mr. President, and then another battle awaits tomorrow. You will waste no energy on those Mounties who are now mindless!"

Traver Wrigger continued to fume but more quietly as he knew that Vonn was right. In the north, that same night, Bagatur Rinson personally beheaded seven Mounty troops who had lost their minds from the pain. General Rinson lost a lot of respect from his troops for that incident.

The battles now settled into the pattern that many conflicts between the Dwarves and Mounties had in the past. The Mounties would poke and prod, never committing to any significant actions. The Dwarves would try a few large offensives but would always be thwarted by the healing power of the Magicians. Every day, the fresh, healed troops of the Mounties would go against the weary Dwarves. Slowly, but surely, the Mounties would gain ground against the Dwarves.

In the far south, the troops of Ronjit Zopfarn were carefully rotated in and out of the front lines, and they maintained against the pressure applied by the Mounties. In the Far North, the Dwarves still had no enemy to battle. Despite reports of two large armies of Mounties, none had made contact with the Dwarven forces. The western edge of the forest had yet to see a single Mounty troop exit from the woods on that side.

In the middle, the King's Guards were steadily losing ground against the pressure of President Wrigger from the south and General Rinson from the north. The troops of Ragnar were needed to help, and the troops stationed farthest south of Ragnar's army were the Huckendublers. Finally, this strange experiment was going to be tested. What a test it turned out to be!

A week after the crossing was won by President Wrigger, General Stonehead's Huckendublers were engaged on the southern edge of the great forest. General Caapo's army poured over Smith Creek south of the woods after receiving orders from General Rinson to come to his aid. Between General Rinson's north flank and General Caapo's force sat the Huckendublers. Later that same day, General Stonehead received orders to turn south and engage the troops of Mounties led by General Rinson. The general was a veteran of many campaigns, and he did not worry about the seemingly conflicting problems. He immediately sent a dispatch outlining his plan to the prince. He sent seven Huckendubler platoons toward the threat of General Caapo, who was marching due west, and three Huckendubler platoons to harass the northern flank of General Rinson.

Later, he would be admonished for splitting his meager troops, but for now, he had played his cards, and the long-awaited fight for Simpson Hucken and Cynthis Dubler's crazy idea was about to happen. The battles were engaged in the north against General Caapo a day before the remaining Huckendublers could travel south and locate the battle against General Rinson's troops. In the north, the Mounties of General Caapo were from the Land of Seven Rivers, and they were the most inexperienced of all the Mounty troops. Adding to the problem was the pacifist feeling of their general. The battle started poorly and ended worse for the Mounties. They skirted the southern edge of the forest and formed up for the march to General Rinson. They had been marching for less than two hours when the Huckendublers engaged them.

Four of the seven platoons of the hooded Dwarves attacked. The initial wave of Huckendublers was brutal. The Mounties had no idea how to fight the ten-Dwarf front. The head weapons were brutally effective at destroying the Mounty line. Like a hot knife slicing through butter, the hooded Dwarves poured through the Mounties. Two of the four platoons went through over five hundred Mounties before suffering a single wound. The Mounties were destroyed, with over half of the five hundred killed before they could stage any response. The third platoon hit directly into the northern edge of the march, and the Mounties did not even fight back. They immediately retreated into the southern edge of the forest and were not seen again until all hostilities ceased in the battle. The fourth platoon attacked the southern edge of the Mounty line and ran into the most experienced troops of General Caapo. The battle was fierce, and the Huckendublers suffered their first problems.

About fifty Mounty warriors battled around the northern edge of the hooded Dwarves and tried to attack from the rear. General Stonehead knew this would be the weakest point of his strange fighting style, and he was prepared. Just as the Mounties circled behind the hooded Dwarves, he threw the first of his reserve platoons into the battle. Now pinched, the fifty brave Mounties fought to the last Mounty. They killed several of the support Dwarves and even got two of the hooded Dwarves in desperate fighting. However, the Huckendublers prevailed, and the troops of General Caapo were sent into a disorganized retreat, only stopping after crossing Smith Creek. Over five thousand Mounty soldiers were marching with General Caapo when attacked by the Huckendublers. By nightfall of the bloody first day, over seven hundred Mounties were dead, three hundred had deserted to the forest, and two thousand more were injured. The Huckendublers had suffered twelve fatalities and thirty-one wounded.

Never had any force caused more destruction to the Mounties in all the years of fighting. The superior armor and unbelievable headdress weapons were very effective, but amazingly enough, the superior training made the biggest difference. The Huckendublers were so well trained and so well armored that they seemed unbeatable. This appearance of indestructibility had been on the side of the Mounties for so long that having the tables turned was even worse than the considerable battle losses.

General Stonehead immediately sent off another dispatch to Prince Ragnar. The two messages from the general arrived almost simultaneously to the prince. The first infuriated the prince, as he was not happy that the general had split his forces. The second dispatch was so unbelievable that the prince decided to take a small contingent and ride south to inspect the situation personally. He also sent messages to his father and brother about what was going on. This was common as the king and his sons constantly communicated.

Prince Ragnar rode south to intercept General Stonehead going west. The prince guessed, correctly, that the general would follow the three platoons he had sent to find General Rinson's troops on the ridge between Smith Creek and the Beardly River. Prince Ragnar found the three platoons first. Led by Simpson Hucken, the Huckendubler scouts had just found the Mounty army. The prince, preaching caution to Simpson, was thinking of calling for additional troops from his group in the north when General Stonehead arrived with the two new platoons from the battle the day before.

Now with five Huckendubler platoons and his small guard, the prince ordered an attack on the east flank of Rinson's army. Fighting uphill, the prince expected heavy casualties if one of the Huckendublers did not crest the ridge quickly. He should not have been worried. The Huckendublers tore into the Mounties, and the result was much like the day before. The three Huckendubler platoons attacked at three different points along the line, and in no time, they fought to the top of the ridge. The platoons north and south fought toward the group in the middle. The other two who had sat out the day before were again held in reserve. This time, they were needed.

Again, the Huckendublers' initial attack was brutally effective. Several hundred Mounties were wounded, many seriously in the first wave of the hooded Dwarves. Most destructive of all was the well-trained troops protecting the flanks of the strange hooded front. Those in the direct path of the strange hooded ten-Dwarf front were generally doomed. The strong armor of the hooded Dwarves protected them from almost any angle. Those following the front cleaned up those that were run over by neatly beheading the Mounties before they could rise. On the flanks were extremely well trained fighters and bowmen who were well armed, well armored, and very skillful. The front would crush the enemy in the center, and the bowman would fire heavily into those trying to flank the front. After a volley, the best swordsmen in the platoon would attack the edge of the front. If the enemy could get to the rear and attack from behind, they could have some success, as the front could not turn easily.

General Rinson's experienced troops did not panic like the previous day, and the fighting was fierce. General Stonehead found it necessary to deploy both of his reserve Huckendubler platoons to drive the Mounties from the ridge. The five fronts finally lined up together and drove a V-wedge right through the middle of the Mounty army. Reaching the Dwarven troops who were pinned between the Beardly River and the Mounty troops, the prince could get a message through to the battle commander and tell him to attack the remaining Mounties to the north. Prince Ragnar used one Huckendubler platoon to support and lead the fight to the north. The other four Huckendublers secured the ridge and began to fight south. By day's end, General Rinson's army had been split in two and driven back to the point he had first encountered the Dwarves.

It was a massive setback for the proud general.

In two unforgettable days, the Huckendublers had turned the war in the north into a rout for the Dwarves. Prince Ragnar promoted several of the field commanders, Simpson Hucken, and General Stonehead, on the spot. Messages were sent to the king, and the Dwarves celebrated heartily. The threat to the King's Guard from the northwest was ended. Most importantly of all, the aura of the indestructibility of the Mounties was destroyed. They *could* be beaten!

Chapter 21

BATTLE OF BEARDLY—FOOTHILLS TRAIL

President Taver Wrigger took the news of the battle victories by the Dwarves in a bizarre way. Usually, the temperamental leader would fly off the handle at such bad news. In this case, he knew the battle losses would cost two of his political enemies much. He knew that Caapo was done as leader of the Seven Rivers. Mounties were very unkind at the ballot to losers of big battles. As for Bagatur Rinson, the president knew he would fight back very hard at this point to save face. Taver Wrigger planned to have no such setback, and he put his best military leaders to work solving the new battle tactic of the Dwarves.

More infuriating to the president was the lack of activity by the Recorder and Protector. It was driving him crazy, not knowing what Cal would suddenly find worth recording. The president and Vonn had discovered the name of the new fighters for the Dwarves and tried that word on the Monk. "Huckendubler" inspired nothing from Cal, much to the disappointment of Vonn. This caused the president to rant and rave at the young Monk, threatening all sorts of dire consequences if he did not "do something."

With this distraction, President Wrigger and Vonn were slow in planning another offensive. They needed to attempt to break out of the stalemate in the central and southern fronts. This delay gave King Hjalmarr some time to rest his troops and reestablish a strong position. The always industrious Dwarves had dug in along some small ridges in the central plains west of the river and were pre-pared should the president attack again. War was coming!

Greentea Gravelt had left the Smith Tunnels with some re-gret. The experience had taught her much about whom and what she was and what she could become. She and Knolt traversed the southern exit of the tunnels into a dark, dense forest that seemed very old and familiar to the Druid sense of the young Dwarf. She was mildly frightened by the evil feelings the forest maintained for living creatures. Examining the trees made her realize they were very old and very wary about warm-blooded creatures. Evil was not the right word, although any average person would perceive the forest that way. The ancient trees had been harmed many times throughout their long existence. These trees were very capable of communication with one another and those that could understand them. Of course, Greentea could easily understand them, and she rapidly learned to communicate back to them. The trees accepted Greentea because of her position with the Twigbots. The Twigbots, who were the fathers of even these ancient trees and their lan-guages, were very similar.

Knolt was unusually patient with Greentea's exploration of the forest and its sentient trees. He knew that this was an important time for Greentea to understand her Druid powers fully. Truthfully, Knolt understood that she was learning the true power of her type of magic. He had a strong feeling that he and Greentea would be separated for a while, and she would need all she could learn.

Shortly after realizing that the trees could talk with her, Greentea realized that the forest also contained Twigbots! The strange little creatures had a secret opening from their underground lake into the woods. Twigbots would come and go into the forest, doing whatever it was they did. Greentea never did fully understand the relationship between the ancient trees and the visiting Twigbots. As far as she could determine was the Twigbots considered a trip into the forest to be a vacation. Much like other races visit the beach, a lake, the mountains, or the ocean to relax, the Twigbots entered the forest and walked from tree to tree, almost melding their odd bodies around the trunks of the trees. That was why Greentea did not, at first, realize they were even there. The Twigbots would smash themselves against the trees that hid them the best and just stay there for hours. Once they released from the tree, the Twigbot would immediately head back to the underground lake that seemed to be their home. It was a strange mystery to Greentea.

Greentea did realize that if she did not harm the trees, they would treat her with respect as soon as they realized she was Druid and king of the Twigbots. In fact, they asked what they could do to help her! As she had no idea, she just kind of ignored that request.

Greentea would have stayed in the forest for a few more days learning about the trees and the Twigbots, but Knolt realized that there was a war going on that needed his help. He started to convince Greentea that they needed to help their people in a very important war, but she needed no convincing. Greentea was aware that she must help her people if she could. It was the only thing a member of the Dwarf clan of Zopfarn would do—or die trying!

Knolt and Greentea left the forest as the sun set on that early summer day. Upon exiting the forest, the army scouts of Prince Ragnar Zopfarn's army quickly spied the duo. The prince's scouts invaded their evening campsite to "protect" the two Wizards. Knolt immediately wanted to know why they were "invading his camp at dinnertime." The scouts were not friendly to the two Dwarves as they could not figure out how they had got here at this time. The leader of the scouts, a crusty veteran of many battles named Sergeant Preniad, sent a messenger back to Prince Ragnar and attempted to secure the two Dwarves until he could find out what to do with them. The names Knolt and Greentea meant nothing to Preniad. He was a veteran of the southern wars and had only been to Whiterock once in his long life. He also had no idea what to do about the magic of his captives (as he thought of them).

Knolt paid the scouts little heed as he finished his meal and lay down for his nightly rest. Like always, he put up his nightly protective barrier shielding himself and Greentea. Unfortunately, his barrier also contained Sergeant Preniad and two others of the scout unit. The rest of the company was on the outside of the barrier. This meant that those inside could not leave the circle of the barrier, and those on the outside could not get inside. Also, communication through the barrier was not possible. Even more unfortunately, the army scouts inside the barrier did not realize this until after Knolt had gone to sleep. Greentea, of course, saw all this and was unable to sleep, waiting to see what would happen next. She was lying in her night bag, listening to the snores of the old Wizard Dwarf, waiting on the inevitable.

The second in command, Sergeant Tevan, was ordered by Preniad to take the first watch. He, of course, was about ten feet away from Preniad but on the other side of the magical barrier. He began his nightly preparation to sleep and asked who had the first watch. Of course, neither of them could hear the other, and in the twilight of the summer night, confusion was beginning to happen. One scout named Jovell got up from the log he was sitting on, enjoying the small campfire of Knolt. He went to relieve himself and walked into the barrier. The crunching sound Jovell made as he walked face-first into the invisible barrier made Greentea start to laugh into her blankets. Trying to maintain her composure became more difficult as the second in command, Sergeant Tevan, saw Jovell fall down soundlessly (he was outside the barrier) and ran to help him, only to crash even harder. Preniad, finally looking up from his pack, started to yell at his soldiers. Knolt just continued to snore.

Sergeant Preniad was upset at his second in command, Sergeant Tevan, who had, from his limited vision in the dusk, suddenly lay down while on watch duty. A fourth soldier outside the barrier drew his bow and notched an arrow, looking for the enemy that had caused them to have two soldiers down, including the second in command with a profusely bloody nose. Preniad and Jovell began to catch on.

Preniad, drawing his scabbard, asked Jovell, "What happened?"

"I am not sure, sir. I walked right into something, and then the sergeant was headed toward me, and he seemed to run into something also. Strange, though. I couldn't hear or see anything."

"Stay there. I think we have something magical going on here," stated Preniad. With that, he walked over to the snoring Knolt and gave the powerful Wizard Dwarf a swift kick in the butt.

Never in the wildest dreams of Preniad's long service to his clan could he imagine what would happen to him next. Immediately, he felt an electrical shock rifle through his body, shooting his entire body about fifteen feet in the air as the magical construct of Knolt immediately disappeared. Preniad could see flames flying from his mouth as he attempted to scream. The fire appeared to have prancing ponies interspaced with ugly orcs as the flames flew out of his mouth and died away. Then green slime ran from his nose, showering the unfortunate Jovell. Preniad wound up upside down several feet off the ground. Somehow, his ankles were locked together like they had a rope tied around them and then attached to a tall tree that was not there.

Knolt, waking from his sleep, was angry beyond anything Greentea had ever seen. Up until now, she had been having quite a laugh at the unfortunate scout soldiers. Now, she was a bit afraid for them as Knolt was really angry. Quickly, Knolt put the other three soldiers in an identical state to that of their leader. Four members of the advance scout party were hanging upside down, just as several members of the prince's army arrived to welcome Knolt.

The scout Preniad had sent back to report their find had ridden his pony hard and reached the prince quickly. Prince Ragnar had heard about Knolt and Greentea from his father and was anxious to protect them and bring them into the safety of his army. He expected the Mounty troops to be right on their heels. Therefore, he had sent a large party with one of his top aides, General Rockright, to greet them and lead them back to the comfort and safety of his command.

General Rockright had the perfect timing to ride into the small camp just as Knolt removed the barrier and turned the scouts upside down next to Preniad. Preniad still had green slime running from his nose, Sergeant Tevan was bleeding from his nose, and smoke was pouring over the whole camp from the flames that shot out of poor Preniad's mouth. Knolt, with a bright red beard, turned on the arriving troops and looked ready to take on a whole army if needed. He was *that* mad and definitely that able. Greentea, trying not to laugh, let out a yell that stopped all of them in their tracks.

"STOPPPP!!!!!!" yelled Greentea at the top of her lungs. This seemed to activate some of her magical powers, and the force of her words stopped everything immediately. Even Knolt paused. "Everybody, just calm down."

This outburst activated her raw Druid magic, and the soldiers present would later swear that nearby trees and plants moved closer and seemed menacing. Darkness fell as some of the soldiers with the general screamed out loud as the anger and magic of the Druid Dwarf stopped all of them. The plants, bushes, grasses, and trees seemed to send a wave of anger through all the Dwarves, and then it passed, and twilight returned.

"Wow!" was all Knolt could say.

The general wanted to know what was going on, and Greentea began to explain. As she started to tell the story, she was interrupted by a crash as Knolt, his temper cooling, released the four scout soldiers, and they fell on their heads as they crumbled to the ground, moaning but unharmed. Greentea told the story of the night, and the general was angry at Knolt and started to tell Knolt what he had done wrong. By this time, Knolt had crawled back into his bedroll and was trying to go to sleep.

General Rockright was getting very angry at the old Dwarf, and the incident might have gotten ugly if Greentea had not intervened. She told the general that she would talk to Knolt. Greentea went over to Knolt, told him to make a very small barrier around just the two of them, and they would sleep. Knolt did this, and General Rockright and his troops were on the other side of the magical barrier of Knolt. Knolt and Greentea went to sleep, and the army on the other side of the barrier could do nothing with the two clansmen.

General Wilten Rockright never had a longer night in his entire career. Greentea's move to exclude the army men so that she and Knolt could sleep completely fooled him. All he could do was stay on the outside and wait.

He sent several messages to Ragnar, and much to his relief, the prince himself rode out to where Greentea and Knolt were just beginning to stir and fix breakfast inside Knolt's protective cocoon.

Never had Prince Ragnar seen anything like what he saw as he rode up. General Rockright and twenty-five of his best troops surrounded the two smallish Dwarves in the center. The two were happily going about breaking camp and having a light meal before going on a day's march. The old Dwarf even walked behind a bush and relieved himself. Of course, the soldiers stood not five feet away on the side he had gone to, to hide from Greentea. The prince could not hear a sound they were making. Knolt even stuck out his tongue at Preniad, obviously making fun of the scout leader for the kick in the night.

Finally, Knolt took down his magical barrier and addressed General Rockright. "Well, General, I have had a fine sleep, and we shall go wherever you would like to take us. My choice would be to go to Hjalmarr first."

"That is King Zopfarn to you, clansman!" interrupted the prince.

"And who are you?" asked Knolt as he turned and looked at the young man. Knolt knew it was one of the sons of the king even before the answer.

"I know who you are Knolt and Greentea Gravelt. My father told me of you and that you would show up in time to help us. I am Prince Ragnar. Even though we have never met before, I have been taught who you are and somewhat of what you can or could do. My father said we must take you to him if we see you. He also says you are dangerous and powerful beyond what I can imagine, but from what I heard about last night, I am not sure I want to cross the Druid either."

Knolt adopted a much more conciliatory attitude toward the prince. Greentea was surprised as Knolt adopted proper court manners in dealing with him. Knolt asked many questions and provided much information about what they had seen since leaving the tunnels. Upon learning that the Dwarves' scouts had seen a large army of Mounties heading for the trail through the forest, Knolt asked Greentea if maybe she would be happier there. Greentea immediately understood that she could have the ancient trees help her delay the Mounties. She smiled brightly and said she would love to go back and advance scout for the Mounty armies. The prince seemed confused by this exchange, but Knolt whispered in his ear for just a second, and he granted her leave back to the forest if she wished.

Before they parted, Knolt had just a few minutes with her and told her of his plan for the Mounty army. Greentea had similar thoughts, and then she and Knolt said goodbye. Knolt told her he would come to get her when the war was over, and then they would continue their journey to North Landsend.

King Hjalmarr Zopfarn, along with the rest of the Dwarves, celebrated the success of the Huckendublers. He called Cynthis Dubler from the hot forges of the Dwarven holdings near Beardly and Simpson Hucken from the troops to personally honor both of them. The heroes' welcome they received more than made up for Simpson's ridiculous speech when leaving Whiterock. He had proven all that he said true, and the honest Dwarves were more than happy to honor him for all his successes.

Knolt had taken leave of Prince Ragnar and arrived before the king. Hjalmarr immediately put him as the chief advisor to the king! The old Wizard was a masterful war planner (he had done it more than any creature alive), a powerful protector for the king, and, as always, a complete pain in the butt. He complained loudly to the king for calling the founders of the Huckendublers because of their smell. Happily, Simpson had bathed as the battle had commenced. Cynthis was still carrying the smells of working the forge. She was rewarded by the king and immediately sent back to her beloved art. Surprisingly, Knolt and Simpson Hucken spent some time together and seemed to become friends. Knolt even seemed fond of the diminutive Dwarf who was full of strange, outlandish ideas, all of which Knolt seemed to think excellent ideas. The king and his other top advisors thought the ideas at best, dangerous, and at worst, ludicrous.

Simpson and Knolt pushed very hard for a southern offensive to take the Lower River Bridge. Knolt was amazed at the ability of the young, small, and somewhat bookish Dwarf to understand war plans and tactics that he himself had taken a long lifetime to learn. Simpson seemed to realize the immense book of history and knowledge that was Knolt. He wanted to learn as much as possible, and he even put up with Knolt's impatience with the king and his army.

Knolt wanted action, and the king and his advisors were in-credibly cautious and thorough. Knolt was now seeing up close the reason the Dwarves would always lose to the Mounties. The caution played directly into the hands of the healing Magic of the Mounties. Knolt whined, screamed, argued, and pushed as much as he could, but nothing would spur the king and his advisors to move quickly in any decisive manner.

Finally, as the pressure mounted on the King's Guard from the president's forces, a plan of attack was hatched. Knolt hated it from the beginning, but the king himself finally overruled him and threatened he would be arrested if he did not go along. The plan was to feint to the south with a moderate force and attack from the north with the Huckendublers and part of Prince Ragnar's force. Even young Simpson Hucken realized that this left the north wide open should General Caapo reattack or General Arsestrong's troops appear from the north. The plan was also weak as it left the Dwarves exposed to a strong attack right up the middle. Should President Wrigger attack right at the Dwarves, only the king and his guard would be there to prevent a major breakout for the

Mounties. Should the attack create a breakout, President Wrigger could march all the way to Beardly unopposed.

Knolt knew that in the Far North, the Mounties were lost till the war was over. He also knew that General Caapo was not going to defeat the remaining Huckendublers south of the forest. Those two things were not of importance to the old Dwarf. His biggest fear was from the frontal assault. He knew that once President Wrigger figured out the northern offensive was using a large number of troops, he would attack the Dwarves straight in front of him. Knolt did not trust the King's Guard to hold against the experienced Mounties. Knolt guessed, correctly as it turned out, that the King's Guard had grown soft during their extended stay in the safety of Whiterock.

Greentea immediately had picked up on the thoughts of Knolt when they heard about the approaching Mounty army. No way would that army get through the forest trail along the foothills if Greentea and her Twigbots were there and prepared for their arrival. No longer would the fears of being alone bother her again. She would help her people in ways she could have never imagined before. She would stop the Mounty army of the north.

Greentea immediately turned around and headed back to the forest. Once again, she was leaving an entire army of her people, this time alone. The advance scouts rode with her to the forest edge but would go no further. Alone and on foot, Greentea Gravelt walked directly toward an entire Mounty army with no weapons other than her magic and its ability to control the forest environment.

She had allies in this forest. She called to the first Twigbot she came across and told it to lead her to the secret opening. The poor Twigbot was so amazed to be asked to do something for the king that it took several minutes for it to quit doing the kneel-down salute and begin to move in that direction. Several other Twigbots joined in the short walk to the cave opening that led back underground. At the entrance, the noise of the Twigbots began to get to her, so she shouted an order to bring her Strif. Strif and Joomb arrived very quickly and immediately put up their innate block for the young Druid. Feeling better, Greentea asked the two Twigbot leaders if what she had in mind were possible. Their excitement over what she was proposing and their affirmative response to the idea gave her confidence that she could do this.

It was a very simple plan, really. The forest already did not like warm-blooded creatures. Anyone that harmed the forest would not be treated nicely by the forest. An army on the march was not going to be responsible for its treatment of the woods. The army was on a mission to get from one side of the forest to the other as fast as possible. Greentea and the Twigbots had no intention of allowing that.

Two days after the return of Greentea, the forces of General Cadon Arsestrong entered the forest along the well-defined Foothills Trail. A three-day march should have taken the army through the woods and right into the troops of Prince Ragnar. Three weeks later, about half of the Mounty army would stagger out the way they came in. Never would General Arsestrong fulfill President Wrigger's northern flanking maneuver.

Under the direction of Greentea and friends, the forest confused the poor soldiers by changing the trail, making it disappear, and separating the troops. The soldiers were attacked by falling branches, poisonous plants, thorny bushes, and starvation as game was kept out of the reach of the scouts and hunters for the army. Seldom did scouts return as they were often wandering around the forest, lost for days at a time. When General Arsestrong ordered the cutting of trees and burning fires to cut their way through, the forest responded in several ways the soldiers would never forget.

Greentea was really not the instigator of what happened to the army. She did not want the military to go through the forest, but she did not intend to harm the troops directly. The trees, however, once the burning and cutting began, had other ideas. After the trail ended for the third time in a day, General Arsestrong ordered several platoons to cut a path through the forest. The general, sending a soldier climbing a tree and sitting there for an hour to watch the sun's movement across the sky, could determine due west and ordered his troops forward.

The cutting of the forest caused more problems than ever for the soldiers. The anger of the old trees was incredible. Every felled tree crashed on troops, branches were tossed down with regularity, underbrush seemed to grow thickly right where the troops were attempting to get, and worst of all, the underbrush was full of plants that caused rashes and itchiness for the soldiers. Finally, the general found a clear trail, and even though the trees blocked out sunlight, it ran seemingly in the correct direction. The path finally seemed open, and the general ordered a double-time march to get through the forest. The soldiers were happy about this as they all wanted out of this hell.

The general and several hundred of his troops mounted the ponies they had been leading and decided to ride ahead to do their own advanced scouting. However, unknown to the soldiers, the trail had started angling to the right, and they were gaining elevation in the foothills of the Ngarzzorr Mountains. The path opened up as the troops came out the north side of the forest in a steep-sided box canyon. The soldiers had a clear trail in front of them as far as they could see. The problem was the path circled back to the east and entered a tunnel going under the mountain. Yes, they had found the opening to the Smith Tunnels!

The frustrated troops retreated down the trail and into the forest. In a fit of anger, the general spurred his mount to a brisk trot, taking the lead as they reentered the gloomy woods. Just as they entered the forest, the trail peeled sharply right and off of a twenty-foot-high cliff. The leaders of the army, following the general closely, all rode right off the cliff. General Arestrong survived the initial fall, but met his demise by the horse of his personal magician. The Magician, named Sveler, was riding hard to protect his charge when he followed General Arsestrong off the cliff. The unfortunate horse of Sveler crashed into the general as he was rising from the fall. The right front hoof of the horse smashed the skull of General Arsestrong. Sveler could do nothing for his charge, and he had his hands full as every mounted Mounty crashed off the sudden cliff. Many were injured, and the horses all had to be destroyed.

Greentea felt bad about ordering the magic to change the trail to go over the cliff. She had done it only after prodding from the Twigbot leaders. Strif reminded her that this was war, and she needed to help her people in a warlike manner. Removing the horses from the troops would further demoralize the lost army.

The other problem for Greentea was the simple fact that she was alone. Getting food and sleep were real problems. If Greentea was not personally directing the old forest, the trees would take a terrible toll on the soldiers. Many were killed or maimed simply because Greentea tried to get a few hours' sleep.

One significant lesson taught by Strif and Joomb was the use of several different plants in the art of healing. Greentea began to use her abilities to separate various plants into different types of healing. Many hurt and wounded Mounties would later report of the strange Dwarf creature that healed their worst injuries and sent them back the way they came. Of course, her drugs made them hazy and unclear on precisely what had happened.

The Mounties tried for many days to get through the forest, but all trails only led them further and further from the western boundary of the woods. By now, the Mounties knew the forest was after them, and the troops wanted to retreat. To avoid a mutiny, the remaining leaders agreed to withdraw from the forest. Three weeks after entering the eastern side of the woods with nine thousand Mounty troops (about five thousand went south with General Caapo), the troops exited, numbering less than forty-five hundred healthy soldiers. They left with low morale and many threatening desertions about three miles further north from where they had entered. Soon enough, their scouts reconnected them with General Caapo and their supply train. Finally, the starving army was able to organize resupplying.

To the south, General Caapo got reports of what had happened and personally rode north to take command of the remnants of that army and combine it with his Huckendubler-battered troops. From General Caapo's position south of the forest and east of Smith Creek would come the last push by the still nine thousand Mounty strong, "Army of the North."

Chapter 22

BATTLE OF BEARDLY—MOSSY HILL

Knolt knew the battle plan of King Hjalmarr Zopfarn had massive flaws. The king was leaving himself and his private guard open to attack while demolishing the Mounties on his left that were dug in north of Smith Creek. If the Mounties held tough, the crazy but effective President Wrigger of the Mounties would run right through the position of the king and his troops. He also knew it had great possibilities.

Knolt wanted King Hjalmarr to do two things. First, have Prince Ronjit in the south make a push south as the Dwarf offensive started, and, second, have Prince Ragnar in the Far North push to the south to join the large offensive on the king's left. Prince Ronjit would keep President Wrigger from connecting up with the southernmost Mounty troops, and with huge numbers, break out past the king and Prince Ronjit and take all the central plains. Prince Ragnar would secure the king's northern edge and leave the far northern flank to Greentea and the forest.

The king listened carefully to Knolt's concerns, and he did move to have Prince Ronjit start an offensive in conjunction with his. This probably did help with the eventual outcome. However, the king would not move Prince Ragnar. He still could not believe that Greentea could do as Knolt had said. Poor Prince Ragnar . . . His troops were never involved in the final battles.

The morning of the planned offensive arrived with a massive

rainstorm. Early summer was the rainiest time of the year in this part of Wyndliege. The rain made moving the army through the mud almost impossible. The movement of the troops proceeded as planned, only much slower. Hjalmarr was frustrated from the beginning of the troop movements until the offensive finally started two days late. To the south, Prince Ronjit started his offensive on time. This actually confused the Mounties and wound up in favor of the Dwarves.

President Wrigger sat in his advance tent waiting out the massive rainstorm when reports started filtering in. Vonn and the Recorder were there when messages from the south came in about an offensive by the Dwarves. This concerned the president as losing the bridge would be very bad. The following report talked about massive troop movements in the rain to the north. This made no sense to President Wrigger or Vonn. Obviously, this war would be won in the center where the bulk of the Mounty troops was trying to push out into the Beardly plains.

Two days later, the rain let up, and the Dwarves attacked in the north. Led by General Stonehead, four platoons of Huckendublers, and over twenty-five hundred Dwarf soldiers, Bagatur Rinson's position in the hills north of the confluence of the Beardly and Smith Creek was blasted. The retreat was very organized, but the experienced troops of General Rinson fought over every inch of ground. In the south, Prince Ronjit had not succeeded in taking the bridge but had pushed the Mounties back to within a half-mile of the bridge.

President Wrigger responded exactly as Knolt feared. With the Dwarves attacking in the north, the president led a massive attack directly west across the Beardly River. Leading it personally, President Wrigger overran the established lines, and King Hjalmarr was forced to send his personal guard into the battle to keep it from turning into a rout.

The Mounties, under General Rinson, were getting soundly beaten and retreated across Smith Creek. Establishing a new line across the creek prevented the heavily armored Huckendublers from leading the attack. The creek was fairly wide and deep in most places, and the Dwarves would have a tough time taking the Mounties on the other side. This final obstacle for the attacking Dwarves gave enough time for President Wrigger to achieve a breakout to the west.

The rapidly retreating King's Guard was in deep trouble as there was no way to reinforce from the north or the south. They would have to make a last stand to try to stop the Mounties. King Hjalmarr was an experienced Dwarven fighter who knew how to pull victory out of the jaws of defeat. He chose a rise in the plains called Mossy Hill by the locals. Mossy Hill was actually a small ridge that ran from the Beardly River about five miles across the plains of Beardly. The river flowed through a canyon with rapids, and the portal for boats went over Mossy Hill. The road for the portal was a well maintained gentle grade that did not offer many military advantages other than higher ground.

The Mounties could have skirted the ridge to the west, but that would have bought time for the Dwarf troops, and Traver Wrigger wanted to end this once and for all. The Battle of Mossy Hill was fought over two days. On the first day, President Wrigger did not venture to the front lines but tested the relative strength of the various ways to attack the hill. He learned a lot and planned his attack the following day accordingly.

King Hjalmarr watched from the front lines for the first time in the war. He quickly judged that the Mounties were probing the lines to plan the big offensive the following morning. Hjalmarr went into the fight for the first time on the portal road. The Mounties were amazed when they saw the banners of the king of the Dwarves. The red banner with the perfectly shaped diamond below a crown of seven points, each topped by another diamond, was unmistakable. Seeing that unique banner as the king joined the fight caused commotion among the Mounties. They were rapidly thrown back to the base of the grade before Hjalmarr's guard relented and went back to their position at the top.

Vonn and President Wrigger were having trouble believing that the king of the Dwarves had left himself so unprotected against the overwhelming numbers of the Mounties. The president had sent scouts on horseback around the ridge and determined that no other force was behind the Dwarves as he attacked the hills. Vonn estimated the strength of the Dwarves at less than two thousand weary and tired Dwarves. The Mounties had over five thousand freshly healed and rested troops.

The second morning dawned clear and bright. The rising sun in the east provided some cover as the Mounties attacked in force. President Wrigger and Vonn were personally leading the charge. The screaming president was a revelation that morning. No Mounty in several decades had fought with so much skill and brute force. He far outdistanced the accompanying troops. Finally, he had to slow down and drive back a bit for his own safety.

The resistance from the Dwarven army was much stronger than anticipated. Everywhere, the fighting was intense, and many on both sides were going down hurt or killed. Many who went down would rise up injured and continue. Soldiers on both sides fought brilliantly. The Dwarves spent a large proportion of their efforts on damaging the Magicians. This had happened before, and Vonn's Magicians all had protection troops. It was among these troops that the heaviest Mounty casualties occurred. Hjalmarr Zopfarn had planned his last stand, if that was what it was, to be damaging beyond belief.

All morning long, the Dwarves and the Mounties battled. The Mounties had advanced about halfway up the hill, and the portal road was still held mainly by the King's Guard. Taking a break from the front line, Traver Wrigger altered his strategy and personally attacked up the road. Moving a platoon westward gave him room to lead the attack up the road.

The screaming Traver Wrigger led the charge, with Vonn right behind him as his healing Magician. Jules, protecting Vonn, was right there also. The president routed the Dwarves, and for the first time that day, the Dwarven line wavered and began to break. Right then, herald trumpets sounded, and the king's banners were raised. King Hjalmarr Zopfarn appeared at the crest of the hill and charged down toward the president. The sight of King Hjalmarr Zopfarn going into battle was not to be forgotten by any who saw it. The king was dressed in the King's Armor made of the finest silver-plated steel and inlaid with hundreds of diamonds. The Crown of Seven Points was on his head, and he truly looked like a Dwarven king from stories of old!

Even battle-hardened Taver Wrigger stopped fighting to admire the appearance of Hjalmarr Zopfarn. Vonn, seeing the Dwarven king for the first time, was amazed at the dignity and grace of his arrival. Vonn always took pride in such things, but he knew he was nothing but an imposter compared to the display by King Hjalmarr. Only Jules, among the Mounties, was not smitten, and she let out a loud battle cry and charged. This shook everyone out of the lull, and the battle started in earnest again.

Back and forth went the bloody battle all that long day. Neither side could gain any significant advantage as hundreds on each side were killed or hurt. President Wrigger would lead a successful attack, only to have it thrown back by King Hjalmarr. Never did the two come near each other, and their side had the advantage wherever they went. As dusk settled, the Mounties called off the attack and made camp at the base of Mossy Hill. The Dwarves retreated to the summit, and all rested for another day of battle tomorrow. The Magicians, under Magi Vonn, all formed up to start the evening healings that would give the Mounties their traditional advantage.

The Protector, Jim Herrick, and Cathy Williams were just bored. The intense fighting went on and on as they hung out in the middle of the large Mounty camp. Cal, the Recorder, had disappeared to pray for guidance. All three thought it might have been a mistake to come with the Mounties on this military offensive. They had no idea what might happen with the battle, although the Mounty fighters seemed very upbeat.

Late that night, Cal excitedly called Jim and Cathy to his tent.

"I have had my prayers answered," said an excited Cal Williams. "I now know what is going to happen and why we are here. We must be ready to move out at my word, and we will not be coming back once we leave. Have all your stuff packed and ready to go within five minutes of my saying. Events are about to unfold that will change much in the world, but I will not say more till the time is right."

Despite intense questioning, Cal would tell them nothing more, but both of them could tell he was excited and anxious about the future.

Late that night, one more thing occurred that would lead to the events of the following day. The rapidly retreating Mounty army led by Bagatur Rincon was driven into the camp of Traver Wrigger and Vonn from the back! The Dwarves had finally driven General Rincon out of the positions across Smith Creek and, led by General Stonehead and the Huckendublers, began a rout of that army. President Wrigger had not kept in contact with General Rincon in his haste to defeat the Dwarven military in front of him. Once President Wrigger realized it was the king of the Dwarves that he was fighting, he made the military mistake of not watching his rear.

With Bagatur Rincon being completely routed, Dwarven troops, including the destructive Huckendublers, now surrounded him. General Rinson was beaten badly by the Huckendublers, and he had lost control of his army, and the retreat turned into a rout. The panic of General Bagatur Rinson had filtered down to his troops, and the Dwarves had taken full advantage. General Rinson only had about two thousand of his forces still with him in fighting form. Many had died, but just as many had deserted under his leadership. His disgrace was plain to all the Mounties. The mood of the Mounties could not have been lower that long night.

The Dwarves of Knolt and King Hjalmarr did not know that the rout had taken place either. Finally, late that night, a scout for the king made contact with General Stonehead. The general was surprised and thrilled to hear that they had accidentally surrounded the Mounties. He immediately mounted up and rode the relatively short distance around the encamped Mounties and up the hill into the Dwarves' camp.

The stunned king and his advisors were amazed at the Huckendublers and the leadership of General Stonehead. Knolt advised Hjalmarr to be patient in the morning and to keep a lookout for signs of surrender. Knolt knew that the Mounties lost this battle, and he and the king had a very long meeting that night discussing what might come next. Hjalmarr prepared to contact both his sons in the morning and to organize messengers so they could react quickly to whatever might happen.

Chapter 23

SURRENDER

In the early morning of the third day on Mossy Hill, King Hjalmarr Zopfarn received reports from both of his sons. Prince Ronjit in the south reported heavy fighting but very little progress on his push south. The Mounty armies had dug in about a half-mile from the bridge, and Ronjit hesitated at using too much manpower to take the bridge. It would be high risk, with significant losses, and might not work. If it did not work, the counterattack from the Mounties would be difficult to contain. The king quickly responded to hold the current line until the battle at Mossy Hill was decided. Hjalmarr wondered if there would be another day of heavy fighting. The Mounties were in deep trouble, and Knolt was expecting surrender from the Mounties. Hjalmarr found that hard to believe from Traver Wrigger.

Prince Ragnar reported very little. No troops had attacked from the north, and his scouts were ready to enter the forest to discover the whereabouts of the Druid. King Hjalmarr showed this to Knolt, who laughed heartily at the message and told Hjalmarr to have Ragnar find out how the poor little Druid was doing. The king was puzzled by the apparent sarcasm in the old Dwarf's voice and decided to do as Knolt suggested. Knolt was too busy chuckling to care what Hjalmarr decided. Not for the first, or last, time did the king question the old Wizard's sanity.

Hjalmarr and Knolt decided to reroute General Stonehead and

his Huckendubler troops to the east near Smith Creek and the Beardly River to protect the king's position on the left. There was no need to have the Mounties surrounded by the Huckendublers. General Stonehead immediately made his way back to the troops that had so routed Bagatur Rinson, and they headed back to where they had been when the war started.

President Wrigger, Vonn, and Bagatur Rinson held a very somber meeting in the Mounties' camp. The long faces were those of defeated soldiers.

"How do you propose we surrender and ask for terms?" asked Rinson.

"You hang a white flag on a stick and walk up the damn hill!" replied the irritated president. "How would you propose, Speaker?"

"Well, I meant, who will go meet with them and discuss terms? What are the procedures, how do we go home?" whined the man who had panicked and put them in this situation, Bagatur Rinson.

President Wrigger was caught between anger over losing and the joy that the blame would fall mainly on his political enemy. Such was Mounty politics!

Vonn watched this unfold, and his dislike for Rinson was making it somewhat better, but Vonn knew what must come next. "I will, of course, be glad to go negotiate a settlement," said Vonn. "You and the president must tell me what general terms are OK and what is not negotiable. I think the Dwarves will be ready to end this for a reasonable concession."

Even though Vonn addressed Bagatur Rinson, Traver Wrigger now took command. "Thank you, Vonn. Your service in this and many other things are a credit to your office. We, of course, will acknowledge the general borders of Ngarzzorr. This will allow the Dwarves the same rights as any other people when visiting our Republic. No longer will Dwarves be banned from trading in the Republic. We would like the long war between the Mounties and Dwarves to end with this treaty. Also, we will withdraw our troops to a reasonable border in the south, preferrabley the Mowkers

River and we must have a defined border in the east, north of the river. I am very flexible on that. Beyond that, see what they want, and we will see what we can do. The deal breaker will be any mention of Elves as that is our situation and problem."

Vonn listened to this and was surprised at the generosity of the president and the lack of protest by Speaker Rinson. "I will go and carry that white flag up the hill and see if I can arrange to hold some meetings to resolve this."

Soon after that meeting, many Mounty troops were very upset at seeing the Magi and his assistant walking through camp holding a white flag on a stick. The always brave Mounties were ready to fight to the death if it came to that. Cathy Williams saw Vonn and ran to tell the other two. Jim was shocked, and Cal was not surprised at all and simply said, "So it begins." And he walked back into his nearby tent, where he had been isolated for many hours.

Vonn and Jules walked very slowly through the camp and out into the no-man's-land between the two armies. This was always the most frightening time as no one knew if the Dwarves would accept surrender. In the Dwarf camp, many soldiers ran to tell their commanders, and it wasn't long before Hjalmarr heard about the white flag. The king immediately yelled, "Hold all positions! No more fighting!" And to a nearby runner, "Get me Knolt."

Knolt arrived on the scene, and both he and Hjalmarr looked down at the white flag, and the king asked the obvious first question, "Do you think it's a trick?"

For the second time that day, the old Dwarf laughed heartily at Hjalmarr. "That is the Magi. I can tell by the robe. I will meet with him. He has a second with him, so find Simpson Hucken to be mine."

Vonn watched the movements of the Dwarves and whispered to Jules, "They are going to talk. I see the king talking to a smallish Dwarf who seems to be getting ready to head this way. He is definitely not a warrior. I expect a cleric who is close to the king."

Knolt was told that Simpson was twenty minutes away, so he decided not to wait. He walked slowly down the hill, made his way past the defenses, and walked out to where Vonn was waiting. His beard changed colors several times during the walk, and Vonn was slightly entertained by it despite his nervousness. Knolt walked up, and before Vonn could say anything, Knolt started talking. "Welcome, honored Magi. I do not know you, but I have met with your kind before. Zigfurn was his name."

Vonn was taken aback for a second, and then his studying of history paid off. "Is it possible that you are Knolt?"

"How do you know my name, Magi?" replied Knolt with a touch of anger.

"My apologies, Knolt. I am Vonn, the fourteenth Magi since Zigfurn the Great. This is my assistant, Jules. We both study our history books, and you are mentioned many times before the great wars. Your colored beard is mentioned often, along with your great skills at many things. I am honored to meet you."

The always-vain Knolt was impressed (whether at them knowing him or him being mentioned, we don't know), and his beard colors flared brilliant blue. "Thank you, Magi. Now I understand. I am indeed Knolt the Wizard. I will soon be joined by my second, Simpson Hucken. May I suggest a tent be set up at this very spot for us to negotiate? I much prefer to do these things in some comfort. I also suggest that both armies pull back to give us some working room."

"Excellent ideas, both," replied Vonn. "Shall we say both armies pull back another one thousand feet, and we can be served by our seconds and two other nonmilitary personnel to provide comfort and food?"

Knolt smiled, and his beard turned soft silver in approval. "I will return in three hours. That should give both sides time to pull back and for me to consult with my king. We will provide the tent and set it up after our troops are withdrawn."

Simpson had joined Hjalmarr by the time Knolt returned, and

both were frothing at the mouth to find out what had happened. The king spoke first. "Who are they? Are they surrendering? What do they want?"

Simpson was almost as bad. Neither of them was acting professional, and Knolt took them to task as he often does. "What are you two fools doing? I went down there and met with representatives of the surrendering force. We agreed to pull back troops and set up a tent. I did not ask stupid questions to embarrass them. I agreed to meet civilly with them, and their representative was professional enough to realize that we need to do this properly. If you two fools want stupid answers to your stupid questions, then send someone stupid to negotiate! If you want me, then we will talk seriously and in comfort."

Soon the Dwarf and Mounty armies were pulled back, ordered to stand down, and the large white tent was set up with everything needed for writing a treaty, in comfort, to resolve the long conflict.

In the Mounty camp, Vonn had a quick word with Traver, and it was organized very quickly.

Cal Williams ducked his head into Vonn's tent, and the two had a short conversation that no one overheard. Cal returned to his tent without a word, and Jim and Cathy wondered what that was all about.

Knolt brought a list of demands from the king to the first meeting. Chief among the demands were: recognition of Ngarzzorr, surrender of lands they had won, and travel and trade terms. These were similar to the president's ideas. Other demands caught the Mounties off guard, including all the land north of the Mowkers River to Darson City and rights to return to Luul Almas and some land on either side of the river Jarven to the ancient mine. The Mounties had almost forgotten about the old caves that the Dwarves lived in before the war. Unbelievably, the Mounties did not even know the Dwarves desired a return to Luul Almas.

The other surprise was the Dwarves' idea to make Beardly an

independent city controlling the lands from the Rocky Point road eastward to Smith Creek. Although this was presented as a Dwarven idea, it was really Knolt acting on his own. He knew that his friends, the Dondlings and Javit Black, would control the whole area. The black-skinned humans would once again be a power among the lands of Western Wyndliege. Knolt felt that this would be important to his legacy.

Vonn and Knolt immediately took a strong liking to each other. They were both very vain individuals who enjoyed complimenting each other. They both liked fine food and drink, and they both were in no hurry to speed the process of a complicated peace treaty while they could enjoy food and drink.

While they were going slowly forward on the long-term treaty, the Mounties under General Caapo finally crossed Smith Creek just south of the forest, then ran into the remaining Huckendublers under General Stonehead. The Mounty general had heard nothing about the surrender of his president, and he finally decided to move. General Stonehead had heard about the ongoing peace negotiations and was surprised to find a huge Mounty army attacking his meager troops. General Stonehead retreated, trying to avoid a trap offensive by the Mounties. The Dwarves, with their superior communications, knew of the movements of General Caapo before President Wrigger, General Bagatur, and Vonn knew. Simpson Hucken interrupted a fine lunch of crab and shrimp salad to tell Knolt and Vonn of the troop movements.

Vonn sent Jules to find the president and have him do something about General Caapo. The ever-angry Traver Wrigger jumped on a horse, and with ten of his guard, rode from Mossy Hill. Simpson Hucken hurried on horseback to catch the president and his group and help them get through several Dwarven checkpoints to the line where General Stonehead had reported he would engage the Mounties. President Wrigger and Simpson were too late. The battle had already happened.

General Stonehead of the Dwarves had arranged to send one

of his troops with a note to General Caapo. The message told of the ongoing peace negotiations. General Caapo did not believe the note and had the young Dwarf soldier assassinated.

With the young soldier's bloody head stuck on a pole leading the charge, the Mounties attacked with several thousand Mounty troops. General Stonehead had used the small ridge between Smith Creek and the Beardly River as the line he would not allow the Mounties to cross. Almost ten thousand Mounty troops attacked the four Huckendubler platoons and about two thousand defending Dwarven soldiers. The battle was a disaster from the beginning. The bloody head infuriated the well trained Huckendublers. The angry Dwarves met the main assault of the Mounties with a cold fury. General Caapo used the very best troops he had in the initial wave. When it broke against the strong, infuriated Huckendubler line, the offensive slowed and then rapidly reversed and turned into another rout. General Caapo's weakness as a leader doomed the Mounties. Very few troops were willing to die in battle for the general.

For the second time in this war, the Huckendublers blasted the troops of General Caapo. Trying to hold together his rapidly disintegrating lines, the general and his guard got caught in the front line, centered against a now-charging Huckendubler line. The cowardly general and his guards were overrun, and he and his guards and magicians were all struck down by the charging Huckendubler platoon. No mercy was shown as the Huckendublers that engaged the general were from the same platoon as the luckless messenger that had been assassinated. General Ormarr Caapo fell beside his fellow Seven River area leaders. He was beheaded by the awful headdress swords, and his body was ignobly stuck on the strange headgear for several minutes before being discarded.

The rout was stopped only when General Stonehead could bugle out a signal to stop the counteroffensive. The disciplined Dwarves stopped the counterattack, but the Mounties broke into all-out retreat, and many did not ever return to the army of the Republic again.

President Wrigger and his small guard arrived on the scene about two hours after the stopping of the counterattack. General Stonehead was very impressed when he got word that the Mounty president had ridden hard to forestall his idiot general. The angered president met with the Dwarven general and was amazed at the damage done by the Huckendublers. Traver Wrigger had heard about the strange headdress-wearing warriors and the damage they could do. This was the first time he had seen it with his own eyes.

Over three thousand Mounties had needlessly lost their lives in a battle that should have never taken place. Traver was shocked by the treatment of the Dwarf soldier who was assassinated as a messenger by General Caapo. Traver Wrigger and all the presidents of the Republic had, during the long years of war with the Dwarves, treated messengers with respect and safe return. The president was greatly saddened but now knew that he must end this war once and for all.

General Stonehead and President Wrigger were surveying the battlefield. The general's direct, honest answers to the president's questions and comments made a good impression on the often-hard-to-get-along-with president. President Traver Wrigger found in General Stonehead the kind of military man the president liked. Much like Willey Swordsinger and Donaghy Kinched of his army, Wyot Stonehead of the Dwarves was the hardheaded warrior President Wrigger admired. No nonsense, good discipline, and loyal troops were what made General Stonehead and the Huckendublers so effective, not the fancy headdress and quality armor. Those things just helped. Traver Wrigger now knew the secret of the Huckendublers was the quality of the fighters and their leader.

President Wrigger thanked General Stonehead for his courtesy and went to meet with the remaining Mounty troops to organize them to fall back to Crossroads. As he expected, he found low morale and heavy desertion rates at what remained of the once-huge armies of Cadon Arsestrong and Ormarr Caapo. Both leaders were now dead, and the troops once commanded were devastated by losses and failures. It would be many years before the Mounties north of the Gray Front and from the Seven Rivers would return to fight in the Republic's army. The Mounties' armies were greatly reduced. Traver Wrigger knew he would need several years to recover from the losses on this accursed offensive. Little did he know how little time he had before he would face an even greater foe than the Dwarves.

Chapter 24

TREATY

P resident Wrigger made his way to the Mounty troops of General Caapo and made it clear that they were to retreat. The president ordered the demoralized troops to go home as the war was over. The disgusted president began the long, slow ride back to Mossy Hill. The Dwarves, through Simpson Hucken, had heard about all that had transpired and were careful to allow the defeated president to return safely to his camp until the treaty could be completed. Many Dwarven troops came out to honor the president of the Mounty Republic as he rode by as the Dwarves knew his reputation as a great fighter that deserved respect.

To the south, Prince Ronjit called for a cease-fire, and all battles ceased. General Donaghy Kinched met with the prince, and the Mounty leader heard the story of the northern battles and knew peace would be coming soon. The Mounty general and Prince Ronjit of the Dwarves had great respect for each other's battle tactics, and the former combatants got along surprisingly well. General Kinched prepared her troops for an orderly retreat of the Mounties when the time came. General Kinched had performed very well for the Mounties by holding the Lower River Bridge. She and Old Willey Swordsinger had performed honorably and well against the younger of Hjalmarr Zopfarn's two sons. Their place in Mounty society was safe.

In the north, Prince Ragnar had done nothing in the battle. Now, he was ordered by his father to get the Druid Dwarf from the northern forest. Grumbling about these orders, the prince entered the woods with a sizable marching force. To the great surprise of the Dwarves, they were met by a sizable Human force coming toward them on horseback. Prince Ragnar knew immediately who these Humans were. He called for a stop, then strode forward to meet with the leader.

The prince had heard about the black-skinned Humans in this area, and he had seen many of them in Beardly. However, he had never seen a contingent this large of these Humans in one place, fully armed. The prince rapidly sized up the tremendous fighting power of this group and was impressed *and* a bit frightened. These were larger, more organized, and seemed more intelligent than any Humans he had ever met. This group seemed important, and the prince wanted to know why he had that feeling.

Javit Black was leading a group of his warriors toward Beardly to find out how the war was going. He had already found Greentea and had discussed her part in the war. He was always glad to be on the side of the king of the Twigbots. The powers of Greentea as king were a bit unsettling to the Dondling leader. Now, he had come up on a patrol of Dwarves entering the forest. Javit called out first to the Dwarven group, "We come in peace to all races."

The prince answered back, "If a group your size comes in peace, then why are you so heavily armed?"

The Dondlings were immediately on guard behind their leader. Javit, however, relaxed. "Ah, young Prince, what brings you so far from the beautiful falls of Whiterock? Trust me; we do not fight the Dwarves of Clan Zopfarn." Javit had recognized Ragnar from a visit he had made to Whiterock decades ago to talk with the king.

The Dwarves were taken aback that their prince was known to this Human. Even Ragnar was surprised. "Who are you, and where do you come from? My limited knowledge names you Dondlings, and we are aware of your presence in this part of Wyndliege. Please identify you who name me a prince of Whiterock."

"I am Javit Black, leader of the Dondlings. I met with your father in Whiterock many years ago. I now travel to find information on how the war goes between you Dwarves and the Mounties along the Beardly River. It is a time of war, and to go with insufficient arms would be foolish."

Prince Ragnar accepted this answer and replied, "Perhaps the war goes the way you wish, or perhaps it does not. We could discuss tidings of war over a short break."

This whole exchange had taken place along a heavily forested part of the path. Off to one side, Greentea Gravelt and two of her Twigbot leaders had overheard the ending of the exchange in person as they had felt the disturbance of the meeting of the forces and tree-traveled to that area. Greentea had finally mastered the Druid trick of tree travel. She could move from tree to tree as long as she could place a clear picture of what the tree looked like. She would wrap her arms around one tree while thinking of another tree, and she would magically be transported to the tree she was thinking about. She found that she had an excellent memory when it came to remembering what trees looked like. She also had learned to listen through trees to what was going on in this forest. She was sitting with Strif and Proop when they heard the meeting of the Dondlings and Dwarves. They decided to interrupt.

Just as the prince called for the break, Greentea spoke up. "Perhaps we should all sit down and find out what is going on with the war."

Both Javit and the prince spun around to where the Druid Dwarf and the two strange-looking creatures were standing. The Dwarves were shocked at the appearance of Strif and Proop. Never had any of them experienced such a creature before. The prince rapidly recovered. "Perhaps we could sit along the edge of the road and have a short talk. We came to find you, Greentea, upon orders of the king."

Greentea replied, "I think I could do a bit better than that." As she said this, the trees seemed to open up a bit from the edge of the road, and a small meadow was suddenly there to set up a nice camp. Both the Dondlings and the Dwarves were caught rubbing their eyes, trying to figure out where the pleasant meadow had come from.

Javit found this very funny and began laughing at the looks of surprise on many of the faces around him.

Somehow, Greentea and her two strange creatures had a very delightful luncheon set up with soft green chairs to sit on for the prince, Javit, and Greentea. Strif and Proop stood nearby as they always did. Greentea shared her story of the troops of the Mounties invading her forest. The prince was amazed at what the young Druid had done. Never before had he heard of such things, and his respect for the powers of Greentea Gravelt rose considerably. Prince Ragnar told what he knew of the battles to the south and the seeming complete Dwarven victory. Now, Javit and Greentea were the ones amazed. Javit was very excited at the prospect of ending the long wars between the Mounties and Dwarves. The prince asked the one question that was bothering him. "Why are the Dondlings moving out of the forest in a military fashion?"

Javit was slow to answer. "We have had a sign that things are about to happen in the outside world and that we are to go out and take our rightful place."

Greentea asked, "What does that mean?"

"We are not sure. It is not the sign we were told long ago to await. But things are moving, and we do not want to be caught on the outside looking in this time."

Now, both the Dwarves were more confused than before. The prince tried again. "You talk in riddles. Where are you going?"

"I really don't know. I think we go with the king."

"Huh?" replied the prince.

"I think he means me," said Greentea.

"Oh," said the confused prince. "How could you be a king? You are a female Dwarf."

"The Twigbots call me their king."

Now, the strangeness for the prince overflowed as Proop broke the silence of the Twigbots. Speaking in his odd common language accent, he stated, "It is time for the Dondlings to rise again. The sign you await is about, and you are all to go with the king. Find Knolt as he has more answers than before."

Hearing the strange creature speak was too much for the Dwarves. Many of them began to pack up to leave this strange place as soon as possible. Prince Ragnar stared at the creature, and there seemed to be some form of communication flowing between the prince and the strange Twigbot. Even Greentea was confused by this. Suddenly, the prince sprang to action.

"Get the horses saddled up! We make for Mossy Hill immediately! Find horses for all. We ride hard and fast to King Hjalmarr!"

"To the king!" shouted all the Dwarves in response to this.

Greentea and Javit would, years later, wonder what the Twigbots had communicated to Prince Ragnar. It was like a fever had come over him to get to Mossy Hill as fast as possible. He would push all of them to get there, and they would, just in time. Never would he talk about it.

Knolt and Vonn finally finished the treaty and had spent several days deciding how to make the signing ceremony appropriate. Both the old Dwarf and the Magi enjoyed the other's company and wanted to make this a special event. With the weather continuing to be rainy and somewhat dreary, an outside ceremony would not happen unless the weather broke. Finally, the wind changed, and both Knolt and Vonn knew that tomorrow would be the day, so they spread the word.

The signing would take place after a luncheon near the treaty tent. The location at the bottom of the hill made for easy viewing for most of the Dwarven fighting force. One area had been cleared of Dwarves, and many of the Mounties were able to climb the hill in that area and observe the historic signing. Shortly before the luncheon started, the mounted Dwarves of Prince Ragnar, along with Greentea and the Dondlings, rode over the top of Mossy Hill. There was much excitement at having the crown prince return to his father's side in time for the signing. Knolt even trudged up the hill to greet Greentea and Javit. It was easy to provide additional room for the three late arrivals at the luncheon.

The luncheon was attended by President Traver Wrigger of the Mounty Republic, King Hjalmarr Zopfarn of the Dwarves, Magi Vonn, Wizard Knolt, Druid Dwarf Greentea Gravelt, Dondling leader, Javit Black, Speaker of the Republic, Bagatur Rinson, Crown Prince Ragnar Zopfarn, and several other leaders, clerics, and Magicians. It was an impressive who's who of important and powerful leaders in Western Wyndliege.

The importance of the event about to take place weighed heavily on many in attendance. King Hjalmarr was excited and thrilled that his people could finally be recognized and even return to their ancestral home, Luul Almas, in small numbers. President Wrigger knew that he would go down in history as the president that lost this war, but the peace could bring unprecedented prosperity to his people. Trade with the Dwarves could be very good for the people of the Republic. Vonn and Knolt were much more concerned with the quality of the food and service. Javit Black and Greentea sat together, and both wondered about the wisdom of being here at this time. They both felt slightly out of place. Bagatur Rinson was distraught over the loss of the war and was despairing about his future. Most of the rest were just there to enjoy the company and fare.

After the lunch was cleared, a large table with beautiful lace coverings was carried out into a clearing at the foot of the hillside. Many Dwarves cheered loudly at the sight of the signing table. The principal players in the signing had ducked into the tent, and now they walked out. First, Knolt and Vonn walked out of the treaty tent, side by side, each carrying a copy of the document. It looked to be about twenty or so pages long and was covered with a green hardback binder. Next, Jules and Simpson Hucken came out carrying quill and ink. As the negotiators reached the table and set down their burdens, they organized the luncheon guests along the path the signers would take.

After a few minutes, President Traver Wrigger walked out of the treaty tent in his full battle armor, carrying his magnificent battle sword, "Chopper." He looked every bit the perfect Mounty fighter. The sight of him caused a huge cheer to come up from the Mounties stationed on the hill. Even a few Dwarves joined in as he was a truly remarkable sight to behold. The president stopped next to the two documents and placed Chopper on the table just above the document on the left, and like everyone else, he turned to the tent flap to await the king's entrance.

King Hjalmarr Zopfarn was assisted by his oldest son in donning his magnificent diamond-covered armor. When he was finally dressed, Ragnar stepped aside and opened the tent, and the regal king strode out into the afternoon sunshine. Once again, the sight of the king's armor stunned everyone for a few seconds. Surprisingly, Javit Black recovered first and began to clap his hands in appreciation. Soon, the others caught up, and to deafening cheers and applause, the king strode to the table. The president and king shook hands and turned to the documents.

Before the signing could take place, Vonn and Knolt loudly began to read the treaty to all in attendance. The Magi and the old Dwarf Wizard magically magnified their voices and took turns reading the text of the treaty. All in attendance could now hear for the first time the completed document. Both the king and the president had gone over it and approved it prior to the lunch.

Many gasps were heard as parts of the treaty were read. Many cheers came from the Dwarves as they learned what they had gained. Javit and the Dondlings were stunned to hear that they had been given a large piece of land and control of the critical city of Beardly. For a millennium, the Dondlings would remain friends with the Dwarves from this wise move by Knolt. Their support would help the Dwarves survive the trials ahead. The Mounties heard the name Luul Almas for the first time in many of their lives and were amazed at the Dwarven reaction to those portions of the treaty. The old cleric Hludowig was moved to tears at the thought of returning to his childhood home.

As the reading ended, a commotion in the back occurred, and

walking from the Mounty camp were three Humans coming to see the signing: the Recorder, the Protector, and, of course, Cathy Williams.

Cal had heard all about the signing luncheon and had turned down an invitation from Vonn to attend. As soon as the signing ceremony started, he went and found his traveling companions and told them to come with him. They arrived at the ceremony just as the reading ended. While the Mounties mostly ignored their appearance, Knolt wondered who the Humans were coming from the Mounty camp. He was standing next to Vonn as they arrived, and he quietly asked who they were.

Vonn replied in a whisper, "They claim to be a Recorder and a Protector."

Knolt was momentarily shocked to silence. The two leaders were busy signing papers following the instructions of Jules and Simpson. No one noticed Knolt walk over to Javit and whispered to him, then both of them immediately made their way over to the three Humans.

Knolt took command and asked in a rather loud voice, "Who are you Humans?"

Cal Williams answered immediately, "I am Calvin Williams, Monk of the Stone Abbey, recently named Recorder."

Jim hesitated a bit. "I am Jim Herrick, chosen Protector." Jim's voice gained loudness as he spoke, and King Hjalmarr heard this last part as he had just finished signing.

Hjalmarr immediately headed in that direction. Unlike the short-lived Mounties, the Dwarves had been alive for centuries had seen the appearance of the Recorder and the Protector before. Vonn knew about them from books. Knolt and Hjalmarr Zopfarn had lived through a time when a Recorder and a Protector walked in Western Wyndliege. They both understood the significance of this appearance. Javit Black could only stare in disbelief. He was speechless.

King Hjalmarr walked up, and staring intently at the duo in front of him, loudly demanded, "Prove yourselves, you who claim the titles Protector and Recorder." His voice was bitter as he replayed in his mind the memories of the last time he saw a Recorder Monk and the Protector from the Herrick family.

Cal responded, "I do not have to prove myself to you or anybody else. I am what I am."

Knolt and the king looked at each other with a peculiar look. Vonn walked over, then spoke to Knolt. "He has proven himself to me. Traver and I have tested him many times over. They are what they say they are."

King Hjalmarr had more experience with a Recorder than anyone there except, of course, Knolt. His father's death and his subsequent retreat from Luul Almas had seen the accompaniment of a Recorder and a Protector. They had followed his mother, and it was the Recorder and Protector who had witnessed her heroic death to save her people. They had brought the bitter news back to Hjalmarr. Suddenly, it was too hot for the king. He quickly removed the upper half of his spectacular armor and asked for his tunic. Ragnar quickly ran and replaced the heavy armor with the Kingly Tunic as Vonn made formal introductions.

On the hillside, the party for the Dwarves had begun in earnest. The mead was flowing, and the good times were starting to happen. The Mounties had retreated down the hill, and many started preparations to leave and go home.

President Wrigger, Bagatur Rinson, Greentea, Jules, and Simpson stayed by the signing table as all this was going on. Knolt had realized that Greentea could not be left out and called for her to come over the twenty or so feet to where they were standing. All those left behind began to drift over as Greentea walked over to be introduced to the Recorder and Protector. The effect of the name Greentea on the Recorder was profound. As Knolt guessed, a real Recorder would be shocked by the very mention of her name. Knolt knew that the mystery of the Recorder was that they never knew what name would affect them, but when they heard it, they would know it was important.

Upon watching the reaction of the name Greentea, Knolt knew, without a doubt, that here was a real Recorder. But why here, why now?

Bagatur Rinson had watched this peace process reach its conclusion, and he was very bitter. His political career was over. His command had been defeated and routed in the recent battles. His constituents would not forgive that. The voting Mounties always voted out humiliated generals who had suffered a terrible defeat. He knew he would be blamed for the Mounties' loss in the war, for many of the concessions, and the shame of his performance in the battle. Suddenly, he was taken with the idea of how to salvage something of his pride and maybe, just maybe, change the fortunes of what was going on this day. No one else was paying attention as the disgraced general reached over and picked up the jewel-encrusted sword of the Dwarf king. Hiding it under the long coat he was wearing, he silently walked up behind the crowd around the king, Knolt, and Vonn. Greentea stepped forward upon being introduced to Cathy Williams to get a better look at the young lady. This gave Bagatur the opening he needed. Standing directly behind Hjalmarr Zopfarn, he silently removed the sword from his coat and swiftly and mercilessly slid the king's own sword directly through his cloth tunic, through his heart . . . and out the other side. Before anyone could react, King Hjalmarr Zopfarn fell dead at the feet of the Recorder, Cal Williams, and Protector, Jim Herrick.

Every one of the strong and famous standing there that day was slow to react. First to respond was President Traver Wrigger. He grabbed Bagatur around the neck, and many of those who were there that day would later say they could never forget the sound of Bagatur Rinson's neck being broken by the great, powerful arms and hands of the president. The crack sounded out just as the uproar began.

Ragnar and Greentea were both immediately on their knees, crying and screaming beside their fallen lord. Knolt and Vonn immediately began powerful magic. Vonn fell into the healing magic he knew better than anyone alive. Or so he thought, as, beside him, Knolt launched into his own healing magic spell. Both powerful Wizards knew it was futile, but both kept trying. Together, they pulled on the magic of the land and weakened it tremendously. Both the Dwarf Wizard and the Magi used their strongest magic. Both actually collapsed from the effort. Heart wounds, in particular, and Dwarves, in general, were not susceptible to healing magic. King Hjalmarr Zopfarn was truly dead!

The celebration of the Dwarves would rapidly turn to great sorrow. Prince Ragnar understood that this was not the evil of the Mounties but the evil of one deranged Mounty general. Through his grief, the young prince, now turned king-to-be of Clan Zopfarn Dwarves, clearly saw his duty.

President Traver Wrigger was so angry that Jules and a recovering Vonn had to keep him from killing himself. The president had seen the foolishness of these wars and had worked hard and gave up much to obtain peace. Now, his great political enemy had taken one last shot at stealing his attempt at a lasting peace. President Wrigger kneeled over the dead king's head and asked Ragnar to behead him to make this an eye-for-an-eye tragedy. Knolt and Ragnar, though grieving and tearing their beards, refused to make this event more sorrowful than it already was.

Vonn sent Jules to gather all the Mounties to begin an immediate evacuation to the south. Soon, all the Mounties were in fast retreat from the area, going straight south to cross the bridge and be back in Mounty territory. Within a couple of hours, the Mounties were gone. Their retreat was made in record time as the president and Magi drove the Mounty troops southward at a tremendous pace.

Knolt and Simpson Hucken were chosen to tell the now-partying Dwarves that victory had come with the ultimate price. They would also be planning a ceremony to crown Ragnar. The shock went through the Dwarves' camp like wildfire through dry grass. The stunned and angry Dwarves were incredible. All that long night, the Dwarves were shocked beyond belief. All who heard it would never forget the crying and yelling and grieving of the Dwarves.

To the credit of those soldier Dwarves, they never once seriously considered attacking the retreating Mounties. The president of the Mounties had killed the murderer with his own hands. The Magi and Knolt had done everything they could to save their lord. Finally, Javit Black and his Dondlings had gone amongst the grieving Dwarves and told of the efforts of the president and his willingness to be sacrificed. Even the angriest Dwarves would not kill a man who wanted to be killed. Assisting a suicide was in Dwarven society to be the lowest thing a Dwarf could do.

The Dwarves had quickly moved King Hjalmarr's body into the treaty tent, and that left the Protector, Recorder, and Cathy standing outside the tent right where the great tragedy had occurred. Jim finally asked the question that both he and Cathy were thinking. "You knew this was going to happen, didn't you?" he directed at the silent Recorder.

"Yes, I prayed the name of Hjalmarr Zopfarn, and I was given a vision of him falling at my feet with a sword through his heart," answered the suddenly timid Monk. "Then later, I prayed about the upcoming treaty, and I saw the vision again. Then I knew what would happen. I then prayed about what would happen if we were to leave and not attend the signing. I thought this might save the king. That vision was too terrible to imagine. I will not speak of what I saw, but to say the Speaker would have killed the king, and it would have been worse. Also, it is my job to record the history and not interfere with what happens."

"I cannot believe my brother knew that the king of the Dwarves was going to be murdered and did not do anything about it!" said a suddenly agitated Cathy. "Why didn't you tell someone? Are you on the side of the Mounties?"

Jim also fired questions at the besieged Monk. "Why not tell Vonn or the president to ban the damn idiot Speaker? Why didn't you at least tell me? I could have protected the king. I am the

Protector!"

"Calm down, both of you," said the quiet but obviously unhappy Recorder. "Do not forget, Protector, I am the leader of this job, and your job is to protect me, not anyone else. As for you, sister, do not forget that I am the one who sees what can happen if I do not let history play out. You are here to cook for us on the open road, not question what I do or why I do it. I do not interfere with history. I am charged to be there and record it."

Just as Cal finished this statement, two Monks riding mules had ended their long trip across the plains north of the Mowkers River and arrived at the campsite. Not an hour after the king's death, the Monks had come to take the Recorder's work back to the Stone Abbey. Cal seemed not at all surprised they were there, and he simply said, "Follow me."

The three travelers and the two just-arrived Monks went back to the small tents they occupied in the Mounties' camp. The Mounties were quickly packing up their tents and heading out to the south. As they began to realize what had taken place, they were all hurrying to get out of there, rushing to get away from the upset and very angry Dwarves. Cal went into his tent and, within five minutes, came out with a large number of pages carefully wrapped in an oilskin pouch. Jim and Cathy were amazed. Cal had written it down before it had happened.

Cal spoke. "It is all there, a recording of all that happened in the Battle of Beardly, and the death of the great Dwarf king, Hjalmarr Zopfarn. This is the first chapter of my recording of history."

One of the Monks spoke. "Thank you, Recorder. We will return when commanded by the head. May your prayers be fruitful!" With that, the two Monks tied the package onto the back of one of the mules, and they immediately headed back.

Amazed, young Cathy spoke first. "How did you write it all down? We were in our tents and never knew what was happening."

Equally amazed but catching on, Jim stared silently at the young Monk in a new light.

"Well, I knew nothing until I started writing. Right after I had the vision about the king's death, I knew it was time to write. Once I put ink into the pen, it all started to flow out. Even though I had seen none of the battles, I could write about them as if I led every battle charge. After I finished writing the scene where Bagatur stabbed the king, nothing more came. Now, I don't even know what comes next. I think we should stay here until I can pray."

"You mean you could write about every battle of the recently completed war . . . even though you weren't there?" asked Cal's poor overwhelmed sister. "How could you know if you are correct about that which you wrote?"

Jim now spoke up. "Cathy, I think you and I have now seen, first-hand, the power of the Recorder. We are taught in training not to question the ways of the Recorder. I understand now. We will wait for your prayers to guide us, Recorder." With a slight bow, the large man drifted off to his tent. He had a lot to think about.

Cathy was not convinced, and Cal could see it on her face. "Aw, sis, I'm sorry I can't explain how it happens. Sometimes, it doesn't even seem like me doing the writing. I was chosen, so I must do. It is our way." With that, he opened his tent and disappeared inside.

CPSIA information can be obtained
at www.ICGtesting.com
Printed in the USA
BVHW071931260721
612929BV00006B/206